AUGGIE'S REVENGE

ALEX KUDERA

First Edition
ISBN: 978-1-940761-24-4

for
xyz
&
bc

Part I

"The intelligent poor man of course is a much finer observer than the intelligent rich man. The poor man has to look carefully around him every time he takes a step, he wisely mistrusts every word he hears from others; for him the simplest acts involve obstacles and problems. His senses are sharp, he is a man of feeling, he has experienced painful things, his soul has been burned and scarred."
—Knut Hamsun, *Hunger*

"Heidegger's parlamblings on 'Nothing' and 'Not' and 'the Nothing that Nothings' were the last supposedly respectable gasp of classical philosophy."
—John Gardner, *Mickelsson's Ghosts*

Chapter 1
Searching in the Supermarket

First there was Auggie. Jonny November I'd meet soon enough. His trailer is where we hatched the plan. Melony was already in my life, but I'd learn much more about her as we embarked upon the kill. If you'd asked me a year before if I anticipated a life of sex, murder, and sleeping in vegetable patches, I would have replied "no," but all of it led me here. To these cramped quarters, with three hours of sunlight like a beam from the heavens. My friends' visits long ago ceased, but I still hear their voices. Auggie and Melony and Jonny November. Their words inspire me to write it all down. And so I sink into this past. With Auggie, where it all began.

Before I met him, I was a moody but functional philosopher. In grad school, I contemplated the nature of power, and for most of the last decade, I felt it pressing down upon me—against my face, like a cold rubber soul of a shoe just in from puddle hopping. Firm and wet, but causing no burns or puncture wounds. In clear terms, I was an adjunct, a hired man, a brain paid poorly by the contract, but at least it was for a speaking role. I was on the books, eligible for social security, and far removed from the realm of shift work and supervisors breathing down my back. Until Auggie crept into my consciousness like a tropical insect that crawls in through the ear, and into the brain, where it hatches eggs and murders the man.

It began as fall progressed and the cold set in. It was late October, and in the late-night public places, where Auggie would go to meet college girls half his age. It was hours past bedtime, yours or mine, but I was there too. The point cannot be denied. I was moping around the supermarket, searching for a late-night snack, oscillating wildly between megalomania and omniphobia, but in particular, I feared death.

Soon we became city dwellers who knew each other. As friendly acquaintances, we would chat at the supermarket or in the park, on public transit or in between. As the holidays approached these meetings would occur when everyone was off with family. We were the ones who'd slipped through the cracks, had avoided the domestic mooring of marriage, and had time and tendencies to drift alone through public spaces on Labor Day or Thanksgiving weekend. And so I endured another fifteen-week semester of teaching general-education classics to job-hungry students—ethics for engineers, and that sort of thing. The undergrads were people of this world, not the more abstract one that I myself had become increasingly skeptical of.

December came, and late in the month, between Chanukah and Christmas, I bundled up and headed out into freezing temperatures for open-all-night shopping. I was searching for a savory snack when I saw Auggie in the aisle for crackers and cookies. He was leaning, unsteadily, against a brick wall of Graham cracker boxes, talking to a tan girl his junior by a score. I smiled condescendingly, pitying this mere mortal who had to prove his manhood again and again. He had to seek out his conquests on a daily basis because he received no regular compensation. My pay wasn't much, but I received it at the end of each month, or in a lump sum for a summer session, and for that reason I could hold my head high, high above Auggie at any rate. Because I knew for a fact Auggie lived week-to-week with little in reserve. Each month, I even had a little left over. I could even save.

But for now I silenced my ego, my feet, my fluttering hands and everything else, all so I could eavesdrop. With Auggie, whether he was speaking to you or not, it often felt like eavesdropping. On the phone, the barrage of calls that came later, he would talk and talk, offering a labyrinth of conversation, which seem less directed at me than it was fully exploratory of his own condition. Talking for his ears as much as my own. This is how I came to know him. In whispers about abuse and other agonies. The stepfather. A prison bid. Probation. The older girlfriend who led him to crime. All of it jumbled together, in and out. A man of forty-four. A life.

But back to supermarket reality.

"So yeah, next summer, I'm headed out to the coast where I'll check out this business opportunity."

"Yeah?" The tan girl nodded and glowed. The promise of warm weather, soft dollars, and Auggie's youthful optimism were contagious. Auggie, for his part, was perfect at eye contact, occasional soft, shy glances at the girl, nothing below the shoulders, nothing noticeable anyway.

"What I do is I take a business, take it apart from top to bottom, get into the books, troubleshoot, tweak the numbers, massage a deal here and there…"

I drifted away from Auggie's spiel and more closely examined his *prey du jour*.

No more than twenty-two and quite possibly cute, even according to the standards of the boys in her peer group, she was not merely young flesh to dazzle the minds of middle-aged aisle drifters. Insomniacs grateful for the bright lights of supermarkets with early a.m. visiting hours. In fact, she was quite the specimen. I zoomed in on her ripe mounds like a famished chicken hawk, just as any critical if lazy male mind would.

A pale, yellow sweater covered the two points of local resistance, a generous v-neck unafraid to reveal ample square inches of tan flesh. Firm, not overly broad shoulders, and a sunny, confident disposition—the optimism and focus of a girl raised on milk and orange juice and fortified by two parents dwelling in one home. Hetero tendencies, no doubt. The parents, I mean. I could not help congratulating myself on these keen observations.

Allow me to apologize for my crasser self. Now, on the inside, I can see that I've always been stupidly full of myself, and in particular, I've thought too much of my critical powers. I suspect it was a conceited nature that drove me into philosophy, the idiotic idea that someone would pay salary for my cerebrations.

Alas, it was the same narcissism with just a hint of boredom that drove me out of that thinking field as well.

But back to conversation.

"Yeah, just drop ten digits, and I'll ring ya up, and we'll check out the scene." Auggie's cell magically appeared, and the girl gave a phone number before she disappeared. With the digits secured, Auggie wheeled around, and nearly smacked into a sales display wall of vanilla crème cookies in his efforts to avoid me, the taller man. When he looked up, he recognized my skeptical frown, smiled broadly, and shouted out, "Howdy, Prof! Caught me in the act! Seminar in the frozen food section?"

Auggie was a true middleman, a backpack full of blank exclusive-brokerage contracts, and without a college education. Degreeless as he was, he seemed to enjoy speaking with a genuine professor, if one as tangential to the university as I. His expressed zeal toward my occupation appealed to me, and this was undoubtedly a reason that we'd fallen into friendship.

The disciple of earthly delights led me around several corners and alleys until we were together chilled by a frozen sea of carrots and peas. We stared at each other, Auggie smiling, happy to see me. Frankly, I felt sour, tired, and surrounded by succotash. I was discomfited by the warmth we shared. It was too much, too common and non-professorial. Around Auggie, my eleven seasons of higher education seemed all the more worthless; before I knew him, and learned how meager his winnings truly were, I assumed he made far more than me, wheeling and dealing in brokerage contracts and limited partnerships as it were. I assumed this middleman earned monthly my entire semester's take. It was only later that I understood that Auggie had about three grand to his name. He was truly close to broke.

"What's up, Prof?"

"Your spirits." I noticed that Auggie was in one of his better moods.

"Yeah, I can still get the digits. No prob." Auggie waxed eloquently about his verbal acumen, his prolixity with the babes. He seemed almost aglow, a forty-four-year-old man in solid physical shape. As a slight Epicurean myself, I enjoyed Auggie's crass materialism, his myopic focus on the flesh, and although I would ordinarily, particularly in a room full of undergraduates, preach the life of the mind—as if a brain could survive disconnected from a body—around Auggie, I more freely played with my full hand. Shuffled and dealt, as it were.

"Whatcha got goin' on?"

"It seems I've hooked a twenty-year-old."

"Ya bang her? Any backdoor action?"

I was taken aback by Auggie's crass words comingled with my new girlfriend. I felt strange thinking of the twenty-three-year-old in those terms, but that's truly what she was. Or what she had become since we'd begun exchanging e-mail three months ago. Wild torrents of grammatically incorrect passion, like nothing I'd ever so openly professed to the world. Soon, a first meeting. After that, a date?

I wasn't certain until we were touching tongues on her couch three weeks later. Before the first kiss, she aired her last suspicions. She wanted to know one last time that I hadn't slept with an extensive array of students, that she wasn't merely another young conquest, that I wasn't a cad.

I ignored my odd failed phone call, sent with longing, or the one one-night stand I'd fallen into with a former student—a flower-power, free-love type—six days after she finished college. Instead, I replied, "No, not at all." My main reservations, or so I disclosed at the time, were the fact that she was twenty-three, I knew she had her whole life ahead of her, and that I didn't want to get hurt.

Was she twenty-three or twenty you ask? Why yes, the former, truly, and I felt guilty for robbing the cradle, yet, for whatever reason, with Auggie, I wanted our age difference to appear even more extreme, and I don't need to know what this says about my character. Or lack of it. Regardless, he was the sole person with whom I'd gotten close to broaching the subject of a girlfriend, and the age in question for such, and he knew that I was thirty-nine.

Well, you can imagine she found me vulnerable and thus desirable when my last reservation was disclosed, and so, at once, to alleviate my pain, after she said, "You're so sweet," we made out on the couch. Frenching. Fondling. Petting. The new, improved first base. By contemporary scoring standards, I was leaning toward second, in danger of getting picked off. Even daydreaming that I could steal third base when she pulled out the blindfold. I got scared! But after tying it on and tying me down, she tickled, pinched, examined, and explored while I imagined myself as a philosopher who shared secrets with a second-base umpire and shortstop.

After that night of being tied down and tickled, I knew I was involved. This elevated my confidence to the point where I'd primp and pose in front of my full-length mirror. It hung on the wall in my bedroom next to my bookshelf. I'd offer the glass a wink and a smile, upon occasion, a bow or box step, but never a belly dance. To be candid, I knew my looks were above average at best, and that my khakis and sweaters were unexceptional, most outfits procured from bargain racks or as online specials. But the man I saw in that mirror was stylish and handsome—no doubt, somewhat delusional as well.

Was I flying to close to the flame with the unpredictable younger set? I knew it would be exhilarating and exasperating all at once. At times, I feared I wouldn't manage my affairs well or even survive at all.

* * *

Back to Auggie, it is still unclear as to how or why his phone calls began. I remember the first message, "Professor, it's Auggie, you know the guy with the dog, the really short, really neurotic Jewish guy." I would have recognized the voice even without the name or explanation, a raspy quick-paced word producer. It seemed odd that he would refer to himself as "the Jewish guy," particularly if communicating to a fellow Heb, a half-breed albeit, but a *landsman* nevertheless. It took me a couple weeks before responding to that call, and at the time, I certainly didn't realize it would lead to regular calls, too many calls, and for a while, I screened my calls, for fear it would be Auggie intent on entrapping me in a late-night conversation cum therapy session. After a long day of my own problems, I was often too tired to listen. There was too much give and take, rambling bullshit, and requests that Auggie repeat himself because his words came out in such hurried bursts. He spoke so quickly he'd skip over syllables and articles, and I, the articulate, if long-winded "professor," could not comprehend. These climactic moments of Auggie's speech patterns were like a spoken version of instant messenger, a linguistic efficiency all his own.

So the phone would ring, the machine would pick up, and Auggie would give a quick version of the days events—three phone numbers from girls under twenty-five; a deal termed "done"; an asshole who aborted a brokerage contract; or a combination of all of the above. If I questioned whether or not he was working hard enough for his dollar, he'd tell me he did something positive for his future each day.

But although I knew Auggie from these phone calls, that had stretched on for over a year, I had known Auggie, or at least known of him for much longer than that. I'd seen him in the center city parks and bookstores. Walking his dog, Schlomie, and wielding his anti-Semitic humor. It was hard to call it Jewish self-loathing when in his prolonged giggling, his jokes seemed so self-pleasing. When not attacking his own, he expressed his animosity toward the *schvartzes*. Always some story about an ignorant black person whose antagonism, or at least perceived antagonism, was somehow the bane of Auggie's experience. Auggie's imagined blacks were always either simpleminded or belligerent or both; that was the extent of their human complexity. He'd tell me Schlomie would prick up his ears when a "negro" approached. This was Auggie's favored term, and Schlomie could sniff fear and rage from sixty yards away. Auggie didn't take the dog to therapy, but the psychologist described Auggie's racism as the acutely base-level, instinctual kind. Auggie claimed he had a right to his racism, because of all he'd suffered in his life.

In the more recent phone calls, he referred to Southern California as *schvartze*-free. He insisted he'd read this in guide books about the coastal towns. Southern California was the dream, the place he could pick up and go to, begin anew, start all over again. In Philly's parks and bookstores, Auggie seemed superficial, a character yes, but a secondary character in the drama of my life. But the phone calls rounded his character, gave him shape and texture. Over time, I felt I knew Auggie's cravings and needs, as well as his hatreds and phobias, better than my own.

* * *

Yes, it started with venting over the phone. Badmouthing. Rage. Neuroses. Insanity. Directed at Auggie's mother. The stepfather. The older girlfriend, the witch. Even the therapist he had paid to listen for so many years. I would sit prone on my couch, phone close to my ear. Dog-eared copies of self-help and guides to writing screenplays were spread-eagled over either thigh. My notes were scribbled all over the place. I scrawled movie ideas in the margins of *The Feel Great Handbook*, and jotted down my physical symptoms—real or imagined—in *Lew Hunter's 434, A How To Write a Hollywood Screenplay*. I doubted very much that in Auggie's ranting I would find the cure, but he could take my mind off things. I could become entranced, or at least ensnared, in Auggie's labyrinth of twenty-something girls and financial ambition. Yes, it took my mind away from Hollywood yearning and psychological need.

His constant flux of negativity and optimism was overwhelming. Auggie was shockingly upbeat and high on life the one moment, in pained neuroses and memory the next. Sometimes, complaints about the stepfather would trump the ecstasy of a new deal, a coffee contract that could make him a millionaire. He dreamed of selling hemp-based coffee as a novelty item; stoners near and far would eagerly sip such *haut café* according to the dollar signs flashing in his pupils. He would suddenly change topics, right after one of my brief interjections—an "Is that so?" or "Good for you, Auggie"—a few words to let him know I was listening. The topic would change to the older woman, the theme of the savior as conniving seductress, once more the adult come to help him only to make his life worse.

He would tell the story as if she were thirty-four and he only fifteen or sixteen. As if it were like what one hears regularly on the news, tales of thirty-five-year-old female teachers seducing their high-school sophomores. The new feminism of social engineering. Take the male young and teach him hands-on how to treat a lady, how to behave like a gentleman. Perhaps it would only be a matter of time before this version of pedophilia would be acknowledged as just and legal. Indeed, I cannot say for certain that these women should face severe jail terms for their acts; in several instances, the loving couple married after the leading lady completed her bid. A few are known to have children. But Auggie was twenty-three when he met his seductress. And she was thirty-one. They were consenting adults, and their years were not so far apart.

But allow me to introduce how Auggie would tell it.

Chapter 2
Auggie's First Adult Crime (No Time)

She came on to me at the club. They call 'em "cougars" now, but back then, they didn't have a name for it. Let's just say that chicks dug it even more than the guys. The young stuff. I was minding my own business. Yeah, I was a drop out. So what? I'd left school a few semesters before we met. I hadn't really dropped out; it was just that I hadn't enrolled in three consecutive semesters. I was always so bored at Urban State. It was like nothing was happening. So that first night, we fucked on the rug. I liked that. She knew what to do. She did everything. I was seduced. She let me bang her whenever I wanted. Stick it wherever I wanted. You can't do better than that. It ain't a score if it's not backdoor.

So I told her all my shit. About my mother and my stepfather. She listened. She was sympathetic. Somehow she got me believing in all these plans we concocted. We were going to embezzle the death benefits. She believed what I believed, that the money was mine. My stepfather didn't deserve it, but the courts could never be trusted to set the record straight, and pay me my inheritance. Besides, by law, he was in the right. Money goes to the spouse— no matter how fucked up the spouse is, no matter how much he fucked over the children. Which was only me. Anything criminal he did was a separate legal matter.

But she was the first adult in my life to take my side. She convinced me what we planned was okay. Moral even. Like I had a moral duty to myself, like selling the house out from under him was my karmic due. My duty.

So I did it. And for a while we were living on easy street. I leased a cream-colored Cadillac, and we drove all over the country. To the party places, anyway. Stayed in fancy hotels. Sped down to New Orleans, and all the way over to Vegas. She made me feel happy. She taught me to enjoy my life. Made me feel like a normal, decent person. Not just like my stepfather's whipping boy, or my mother's pain in the side.

She got me interested in going to school again. Had me studying for the MCATs. See, that was my dream. It was part of the plan. I was going to become a doctor. I was going to use the money for good purposes. To pay for medical school. When the Feds showed up, that's how they found us. I had the Princeton Review MCAT book open, and I was studying for the test on the black leather couch. With the dough, we'd bought furniture—real fancy, okay, pleather, not leather—but soon after we sold the house, we got good at not overspending. Keeping it in the bank to pay for the nicer things. For the test, I was really good at the analytical section, but I had to brush up on biology and organic chemistry. I had passed my science classes four years previously at Urban State, but I needed to review the material. The Feds laughed when they saw me with the book. Just a nice Jewish boy studying to go to medical school.

"So this became a federal case?" (With Auggie's tendency to produce tangential information, at times my queries steered him back on track.)

Yeah, it was crazy. A twenty-three-year-old Jewish kid with no priors involved in a federal investigation. At the center of it, really. I was the suspect. When they checked to see if the Caddy was stolen, they only looked into my priors. I would naturally say "we" and "our" when describing the plans, but they never took much interest in my girl. Or woman, I should say. We weren't married, and it was all in my name. Plus, I was no longer a minor, so I could be held as an adult. "Personal responsibility" was how the judge put it as he handed me my sentence. But it was just like my mother and stepdad; she was the one in charge, guiding me along.

"Did you go to jail?"

Nah. The Feds sympathized with me. They understood and said they were just doing their job. I got five years probation.

"So a criminal record, but no jail time?"

Exactly. That's why I'm in small business. A middleman. Figure it would be hard to get a regular job so I've been hustling on my own.

* * *

Another conversation turned into my own fact-finding mission. I had no boots on the ground, so I needed to interrogate the source. I needed to find out what happened, why he almost went to jail, and how he avoided it.

"But what did you actually *do*? What was the crime?" In Auggie's disjointed ranting, I would find myself lacking basic facts.

"We tried to get money out of my stepdad's account."

"How'd you do that?"

"How'd we try? Forged checks."

"So forgery?"

"One count of that I had removed. The bank robbery charge is what stuck."

"You robbed a bank?"

"I was young and vulnerable. She had huge knockers and a spectacular ass. She told me she had the tits done by a professional. I was twenty-three, and she was thirty-one."

"So she got you to drop out of school?"

"I dropped out six months before I met her. I usually blame my Mom and Stepdad for that one, but she can take some credit, too."

"But you told me she got you studying for the MCATs and enrolled in Organic Chemistry."

"Enrolled is a strong word, Prof. Once or twice a week, I'd sit in on lecture. But I had no dough for college. My stepdad got Mom's money. That was the problem. After she locked me in the closet, he fucked me in the ass and stole my inheritance. The second part legal and legit in the state of Pennsylvania."

"Did you take a job?"

"I could work, but only if I could get work. This was 1989. The economy was collapsing into the ocean. What was I gonna do? Work behind a counter at Mickey D's like Leroy, from 53rd and Negro?" I ignored Auggie's demographic slang and his use of such an archaic pejorative. It was clever, the first time he turned a phrase, but by now, I felt a slight embarrassment every time I heard his racist words. It was easy to attribute to his childhood abuse, Auggie's need to place himself above the black man.

"But you could rob a bank." I was catching on.

"Exactly."

"I see."

"She disappeared as soon as she could. Sure, she stood by me, held my hand at the trial, and cried at the sentencing. But she was never charged with a damn thing. It may or may not have been her idea completely, but she was older and she liked it. It thrilled her."

"Turned on by your brazen criminality?"

"I was in shape back then, Prof. I could perform."

Auggie raised his fists and eyebrows over his head. He made a muscle-man face. It was an comic Incredible Hulk he-man grimace, yet enough to remind me of my own fading promise. My fallen arches and aged knees, and around the middle, a slowly inflating spare tire. Thank god, little was visible with my clothing on.

After a pregnant pause, another "I see" was the best I could do.

"But don't think for a moment I can't still perform." Auggie winked.

This was another area that I'd have to evaluate another time.

"Back to the robbery. Was there a lot of planning?"

"Yeah, lots of plans. Big plans. We'd escape in a fighter jet across the Pacific. An amazing theft after the fact. She'd lean over, planting her rack in my back, and I would plan away. It wasn't hard to get to aircraft."

"Any realistic plans?"

"That's the thing, Prof. She had me dreaming big. I could see myself flying away off the top of the bank in a stolen fighter jet."

"How did she get you thinking you could rip off the American Air Force?"

"Full throat stardom. Amazing head. She'd get the whole thing in her mouth. The tip would slip down her throat, and the balls would bounce off her tonsils. She'd brush her hair aside, so I could watch. A woman who made pole work look easy. I couldn't see it at the time, but I was wrapped around her finger."

"You had to realize you were responsible for your actions? Or at least know that a court of law would see it this way."

"Responsible? Who the fuck was responsible for making me the way I am? My stepdad ramming me in the ass? My mom who locked me in the closet? The state who sent me to live in a cage with abused and abandoned black kids intent on taking their suffering out on me? The social engineers who gathered under one roof all the single-to-no-parent neglect and delinquency? Is it my fault they stuck me in juvenile detention with *schvartzes* whose only punching bag became pale molested me?"

I didn't know, no, I did not. Who was responsible for how Auggie turned out?

Where was personal responsibility in a world where Auggie had been screwed from the start? So to speak.

Do we blame his mother? His stepfather? The state that allowed such a predator to roam free? On the streets and able to seduce a nut job like Auggie's mom? It was the state who had nothing more than a jail for kids as a way to "save" the child. I had to ask what was on my mind.

"How come your stepfather never went to jail for all of this?"

"It's the laws and the courts. The judge stated that the spouse would inherit. But even if there were a disagreement or room for interpretation here, what money does a kid have for pursuing litigation?"

"I don't know."

"Zilch. And how would a kid know he could do this anyway?"

"I don't know."

"That's right, Prof. You don't know squat. Never forget that."

"I see."

"But don't sweat it. I was stuck with legal services for the poor. I got snoring lawyers and yawning judges. Folks who called it in years ago and were playing out the string with a hand extended on pay day. This was in the early 1980s. Bad recession. Everyone had problems. No one cared. No one ever cared. That was my life. That's what I know. That no one would ever care, so I better look out for number one, but no one ever taught me how to do that well."

I had to admit I was out of my league when evaluating Auggie's life. Sure I was short of money at the end of most months, but I'd no experience with the trauma he'd known. The closest I came to it was interacting with the occasional disturbed student.

And there was always that unanswerable question lurking behind it all. How do things like this happen? Not only here, but especially here. How and why and when will it ever end?

* * *

Auggie's disjointed ramblings, discursions and tangents are too much. I cannot stand it anymore, that voice, that voice that still visits me, even in here, some days the only foreign sound to penetrate these bare walls. On some days, the voice lingers, vibrating in my brain far past lights off. But Auggie was not the only man who led me to crime. Allow me to introduce our most valuable player and our leader in crime, so to speak. Jonny November. His voice comes to me, too, and much more often than Auggie's or Melony's. He was Auggie's other role model in youth, and his role cannot be underestimated in leading me to this current confinement and its bleak routines.

Jonny was a mentor who took Auggie under his wing and helped him survive. When Auggie was a teenager, they lived in apartments facing each other over a narrow piss and rain-soaked alleyway. This was up by the university, just a few blocks from admissions. In aged brown and red brick four- to six-story buildings, the rotting units came with water-stained ceilings, broken fixtures, leaking toilets, and creaky hardwood floors. These are now almost exclusively pan-Asian grad-student ghettos, but back then they housed many working Philadelphians meekly subsisting and enduring meager lives. Jonny was a man missing moral scruples and half a leg. He was a stump at the knee, but in some matters, he saw clearly, without doubt or pangs of conscience. We couldn't have plotted to kill Auggie's stepfather without him.

Life Lessons from Jonny November 1

Here's how to run the scam. You locate a Rite-Aid or CVS or Walgreen's to do your work. Avoid Fat Sammy's big box empire. Those fuckers are litigious and frugal. You'll wind up getting the poor clerk shit-canned or worse, and you'll end up doing time for stealing a chocolate bar.

So here's what you do. You get a partner, a girl, you know, the opposite sex. The scam works best if the person isn't your age or race, isn't dressed like you, and can't be associated with you in any way.

OK. You have your partner.

You go to the bank in another town or another part of town and get yourself a hundred dollar bill. On the bill, you write, "Happy Birthday, Grandma." When you enter the retail chain, you buy something cheap but not the cheapest. Buy a few items; try to spend around seven or thirteen dollars. Seven because it's a lucky number and thirteen because it's unlucky, but we're unlucky too, right? And that's why we do what we gotta do.

So anyway, at the counter you pay with the birthday hunchie, grab your stuff, collect your twenties and change, smile "bye bye," and leave the store.

Your partner enters the store a few minutes later. Remember, if you're an older guy dressed like cheese blintzes, she needs to be younger wearing lamb vindaloo. You know what I mean. So she picks out a couple items, goes to the register, and evens up with a ten. When she gets her change, she says, "I'm sorry, but I paid with the wrong money. I just gave you the hundred dollar bill I was going to give Grandma for her birthday."

The hunchie you paid with should be right on top or in a worst case scenario, under the change drawer with the return receipts and personal checks. The clerk is a good person and underpaid enough that she isn't paying close attention. Even if she thinks it's weird, it's so unexpected, it's disorienting. A retail prole isn't paid enough to figure it out. She sees the bill and says, "Happy Birthday, Grandma," and hands it back to your partner. Your partner returns the change she received and pays for her stuff with other money from her purse. Only in America.

Have a nice day.

Chapter 3
Be Patient, Rover

Past 7 p.m. I sat alone in my office, a windowless place I shared with twelve others. I was perusing aphorisms and contemplating the good. In other words, I was spacing out with a book in my lap. I often stayed late because I liked the solitary moment even if I was surrounded by sallow textbooks and metal desks and shelves. If I required nature, I could walk among the tall pines and oaks that Philadelphia generously offered its residents. Many lacked jobs and health insurance, but as true democrats we could all share equally in the city's green and shade. Manufacturing's decline in the City of Brotherly Unemployment meant that jobs had disappeared, but people were also gone. There was little work for the destitute and plenty of low-rent gigs for the rest of us. But since my childhood the population had decreased by over half a million, and this meant it was easier to get outside and alone with the squirrels and trees. In post-industrialized Philly, the state of nature, its bushes and ambushes flourished. We'd become a city of highway robbers and beautiful parks and streets.

I had the fragments of Heraclitus splayed across my thighs, but I was lost in this kind of thinking, staring at the books, above the desk I shared with three or four others. My thoughts turned to Cyrus Duffleman, plump and exhausted knowledge cog who one day rose from his shared swivel chair, left the office, and never returned. Did he disappear or was he disappeared? No one knew what happened to him although rumors were ripe and sensational. They ranged from his escape to a lectureship at a small Baptist college outside Odessa, Texas to a crime spree that culminated in his assassination of Leytan S. Peche, a chair-grubbing full professor who was found washed up on the shore in the Gulf of Mexico, exact cause of death unknown.

On the topic of murder, others said that he drove straight to DC to defenestrate a stocky, bald man he called his "publisher" despite the fact that searching on google and amazon revealed no titles attributed to any Duffleman at all. Around the office, I would hear him muttering about some "retard" former student, a "back row baseball cap," sticking his dirty thumbs into the Duffler's novel. I never knew what to make of it and guessed his book was out-of-print, unpublished, or unread. Unless it was entirely imagined by its author.

Still others said Duffy had finally met the love of his life, a three-hundred-pound black nurse—a tranny post-op, no less— who smiled sweetly at the exhausted instructor and let him quit teaching and lay about reading on the couch all afternoons because (s)he so loved him and her own work. And on the topic of retreat from public affairs, a final working theory was that his sexual urges, fantasies, and nightmares had gotten out of control and the resulting priapism so constant and nagging that, understandably, he could no longer leave his apartment for fear of imposing his pronounced view on the masses.

Interrupting my reverie, the phone rang.

"Baby, I told you not to call me."

"I'm lonely."

"Baby, I need to keep my job."

"They aren't going to fire you for answering the phone."

"You know what I mean."

"Can you be here in thirty minutes?"

"Yes, ma'am."

So, yes, although it was the freaking most fantastic thing that had happened to me in years, it also scared me shitless. She wanted to be seen in public like we were a normal couple, even on campus and in the philosophy department, but I wanted to keep my job. Twenty years ago, perhaps, that would have played out okay, an all-male department minding their own student concerns and liaisons. Nothing bad could happen unless you happened in on someone else's turf, as in someone else's young philosopher. But then there was departmental evolution over the decades. There'd been liberations and reversals. Shared power and female majorities. Dialogue with the Other, from homosexists to future citizens of an inevitable gynecocracy. The boundaries had shifted. The times had changed. Straight men were suspect at best and sleaze at worst, even if they voted left of center and ate their cheesesteaks with free-range beef on whole wheat loaves.

Philosophy, like most of the humanities, had been overrun with women. Bulbous or emaciated, hairy and barren, pinkish but paling over the years from staying locked in offices and library stacks. It would gross out even the worst among us to touch one of these overbearing blobs or frail anorexics, and yet they petitioned their universities to provide locks on the women's bathroom doors on their offices' floors. Female careerists would no longer settle for adjunct work, dieting, typing their husbands' monographs, and correcting his terrible spelling. So they rebelled, showed what they could do, and well, it was quite a bit more than what most men had proven capable of. They stole the show, divorced lazy-shits-for-spouses, and that's another reason I adapted so easily to the departmental dredges. I couldn't compete with these Kristevan-cows-come-lately. They were intent upon peer-reviewed publication and frustrated by a dearth of quality men among that most oxymoronic of castes, the bourgeois intelligentsia. That their career ambition had perhaps sidelined such would-be penises in power was beside the point. Indeed, it was possible this latter appendage was not even their desire, that, with good reason, it was the young women they wanted as much as we did.

Anyway, as you know already, I got the girl. Some days, some nights, she would even call like she needed me. That made me feel good. Respectable, perhaps, and even of value as a human being, as I was in a relationship with an actual *other*.

So I rose from my desk and burst into action. I sped around the corner and into the bathroom, where I saw a fat puddle of water on the floor seeping toward the entrance. There were ten dark toes in the water, and my eyes scanned upward to find a figure of sinewy muscles and glistening ebony. A butt-naked black man held a razor to his lathered cheeks, and with a delicate touch, he was shaving over the sink. He turned toward me for the full frontal shot.

"My bad."

We stared at each other until my eyes withdrew because I couldn't help but check his package. It was as long and dark as they come—a scepter of might even when dangling in a flaccid state. I knew I could use a bath to improve upon my strong manly scent and its meeting with Melony, but I found myself resisting an impulse to shed my exterior layers and splash and frolic about with this fellow. Two spent gents awash in the camaraderie of the public sinks by the fifth-floor stalls.

I wiped a strand of saliva from my chin, and turned to leave. As I did so, I heard a final, "Say, could you spare some change?"

I shielded my eyes, dove in my pocket, and tossed some coins and a token at his sink. I then ran to my office, grabbed my belongings, and left the building by the back stairs. I leaped over another man fully clothed and fast asleep on the stairwell two flights down.

The homeless were all over Collegetown, but this was the first time I'd seen one in his birthday suit, five floors above the fray, where the untenured class was shelved a person per four square feet in storage spaces—rather, offices—of painted cinder block. "Water flows through a rock," said Heraclitus two or three thousand years ago, but the homeless were immutable. Poverty would persist no matter what other troubles befell the planet. It would outlast us all.

Just like Auggie, Melony hated the homeless. She called them "yucky" and said they were rude and stunk. They had some nerve not working all day while she was at the Wawa thirty-five hours per week and enduring twenty credits a term of college education taught by know-it-all liberals who took the homeless' side. She resented their free-loafing status no matter how cold the hard concrete got late at night. She also hated unions, green vegetables, and half the kids in her major. But she could stand to be with me, and I came to love her rants against everything in existence even if the only ones

I knew to be true were directed at me. "You walk too slow," "You're such a wimp," and "You need better clothes" were the common complaints. The evil world had us both scared and selfish and clinging to what little we had, which turned out to be little more than each other and subsistence-living in tiny apartments.

Wary of my slow pace and not wanting to leave Melony waiting, I strode as quickly as I could toward her environs. I passed the pink and green neon signs of retail environments, selling every manner of plastic and cloth to the contemporary consuming college student.

Of course, five blocks later, my strides strong and my heart pounding, she "tapped" me on the cell to say she had to cancel.

"Please, baby, I need to see you."

"You're too pent up."

"Please."

"Be patient, Rover. I suppose I could meet you later at the bar."

The bar was *our* bar, where we'd sit in the back and drink sugary specials with little umbrellas.

"Okay," I replied before she hung up.

To kill the time and knowing of nowhere else to turn, I entered the all-night supermarket. It was full of the pricey, gourmet items you'd expect near Ivy Green's campus. The affluent students were well represented in the aisles.

Among the exotic condiments—olives and pickles, kosher or Kalamata—I ran into Auggie. He was in action once again, collecting the digits from an unseasonably half-clad coed. She laughed but left, backpedaling away from his gift of gab to chance upon a younger suitor. No doubt she sought a taller man, a mate under thirty and endowed with hair.

Once she disappeared from our view, Auggie turned to me and smiled. "See how I do it? I can teach ya all ya need to know, Professor."

"Well, if you must know, I have another date with the twenty-year-old."

"It ain't a score if it's not backdoor. Any sodomy I should know about?"

Ugh. How he could throw me and in the process introduce me to a new world, one where the realities and expectations were all askew. For meager me, the twenty-three-year-old was transgressive enough, but for Auggie she would only be the end for the means. Or something like that. So to speak.

"No, well, er, I wish," was my first attempt. "I mean I've only known her for a month." A lie, yes, but I didn't want Auggie to know she'd been my student three semesters ago. "We've only been out a few times."

So we walked the aisles, meandered in this way, around the sugar cereals and gourmet olives and kosher dills and frozen meats and leafy greens and overpriced fruits until conversation had run its course. When I realized I was on the verge of being late for Melony, I apologized and departed. Do you think I should have invited Auggie along? Was this what normal friends did? Well, of course, I didn't need a third wheel in the picture, but Auggie never imbibed and rarely spent money unless it led directly to sex legally exchanged for a movie or dinner.

I left Auggie, ran late to the bar, and was extra disappointed to find no girlfriend waiting for me there.

* * *

On the first day of class, the students wrote about their summer experiences, whether they stayed home with Mom or went to work at the Jersey Shore. Melony wrote about her internship in Cleveland at the Rock and Roll Hall of Fame. Her high-school hero had been Joan Jett, of the Blackhearts, and how that ever led her to me is unfathomable.

But teaching so many classes, brief comments, check marks, and smiley faces in green ink were mostly what I wrote on these pages. For no reason I can easily explain, before I could even connect a face with a name, I was inspired to note on Melony's letter my musical tastes. I told her that David Bowie singing "My Death" on *David Live* was, in fact, my favorite live song of all time. On a whim, I added a few lines: "My death waits there between your thighs/ Your cool fingers will close my eyes/ Let's think of that and the passing time." Yes, I quoted explicit lyrics on her paper, and even used slashes for line stops.

I didn't think much of it, because I'd written personal anecdotes on student papers many times before, but when I ran into her at the Wawa, where, as it turned out, she worked a graveyard shift, as she rung me up—the usual six-inch hoagie, salad, chips, and peanut chews—she asked me if I was going home to sulk, sip wine, and contemplate my "demise" as she called it. Needless to say, although this routine was not uncommon for my Saturday nights, I was taken aback. She must have seen my shocked or sad facial expression because she quickly added, "Oh, sorry. That was an allusion to what you wrote on my paper, about listening to Bowie. You said, 'My Death' was your favorite song." That put a different slant on matters entirely.

This encounter led to exchanged e-mails a week after I'd searched for her information at the university website. Then the quarter ended, and the e-mails grew extensive, and she hated her mother, and I hated grading papers, and her mother's boyfriend was boring, and so were the papers, and didn't I ever ask a girl out or did I just send long e-mails forever, and it took me until three days later, but by the following Saturday, we were seated across from each other in a chain restaurant, and I was watching her shake a bottle of barbecue sauce and pour maroon goop all over crisp iceberg lettuce.

* * *

After my second shared moment with the Jack of Daniels over ice, I gave in and called.

"I have to cancel."

"But I'm already here, baby."

"Sorry, baby."

"I'm already drunk and lonely."

"Sorry. I'm just too busy. I hate it when you pressure me."

"I'm sorry, baby." Was I entirely without self-esteem? I supposed so.

"I'll call you later."

When!? I mean, "Okay."

I went back to the bar and downed three more. Drowning my sorrow and anything remotely connected to my ego, I left the bar after midnight but before last call. Walking like an imbalanced man, the way I always imagined inebriated characters walked in commercial novels, I made unsteady progress until in an unlit slither of Collegetown sidewalk, a gruff voice said, "Give it up."

I saw two men, one gun, and my fate in the hands of these three.

There was nothing like two strangers and a deadly weapon to return an abstract dreamer to his sobering darkness. Quick as a drunken philosopher, I turned my pants pockets inside out and screamed: "You see all I got!? I'm broke as you motherfucker. Fuckin' frisk me all over. My girlfriend no-showed, and I'm horny!"

The two faces turned to each other.

"White boy crazy."

"He a crazy motherfucker."

"His shit ain't right."

"Should shoot his shit to end his misery."

"Put a white boy down."

"A mercy kill."

"Take a life, get life."

"Sentence 'n shit."

"No way I go back."

"Nah."

"Put white boy out of his misery and go to jail for that shit?"

"Hell, no."

"That ain't the way."

"Word."

They ran off and disappeared into the darkness of our fair city. I stood for a moment. Shaking. Nerves? Adrenalin? It was as if my fear acted on delay and arrived five minutes late to the scene of the crime. But just like that, it abated. I was fine. Or at least I could walk.

I resumed my journey, and as I strode further into dark night, I questioned whether the highwaymen were real or not. The increased perspiration under my arms seemed to be the thing-in-itself, but could these robbers have been my hallucination?

* * *

I was reminded of the time that I saw a large brown bear on the Appalachian Trail. A few summers past, I had gotten the insane idea that I would escape city living for a few days of Edenic bliss. It was a back-to-nature jaunt to refresh and rejuvenate an urban intellectual. This was several years before I'd met Auggie, and I still saw myself as an almost normal gent. Yes, I was working on contracts, without the routines of a full-time job, but I was more or less part of the usual in lower-middle-class living. A vacation was what regular people did, so I felt obliged to take one.

I rented a compact Mazda 3 at an obscene rate that with tax and insurance totaled over ninety dollars a day. It only took me an hour to get out of the city and onto I-95. Indeed, I was stuck in Chinatown traffic for thirty minutes with no idea of how I arrived there.

After escaping Center City East, I drove six hours and arrived at a verdant land of trees and hills. Northwestern Virginia was beautiful and provided all that Philadelphia lacked. On my own, I breathed fresh air and navigated Skyline Drive and stopped at overlooks and points with a view. After a fresh, farm-fed lunch, I filled up my water bottle. At the next "scenic view," I saw signs for the Appalachian Trail, which apparently ran parallel to much of the road and only a hundred yards below. I decided to go for it.

So descend I did, and about twenty minutes into my walking tour of the natural world, at fifty yards ahead, I saw the bear. It was big, brown, and scavenging for berries in the bushes. Terrified, I hurried off so quickly, that to this day, I am somewhat uncertain if I panicked over reality or hallucination. I do remember being so certain of my vision, that when I chanced upon a family with children heading in my direction, I told the mother exactly what I then knew that I had seen. It wasn't until the parking lot that doubt set in.

How would a Kant or Kierkegaard handle this question? No doubt with their eyesight diminished, corrupted by decades of reading, they would have both been too blind to ever see a wild beast looming fifty yards ahead. Yet the thought led to larger questions, of course, of how we could know anything at all to be true.

* * *

Fresh night drizzle awakened me from my somnambulist dreaming, and I realized I'd like nothing more than a midnight snack to take my mind off Melony's rejection and the two men with the gun. Truth be told, rejection made me horny and mad, but once my libidinous humors abated, I found myself with hunger pangs so severe that I could stab a mutt and feast upon the yelping cur.

At the deli, I first selected steaming hot New England clam chowder and a six-inch long Italian hoagie. Turning around, I spied a rack of tortillas, chips, and pretzels; I grabbed the largest bag of Cheetos available. These were the cheesy kind that made love to the tongue on cold, winter evenings, when, alone on the sofa, I enjoyed "borrowed" cable television, absorbing the absurd biases and vulgar patriotism of Fox News. That Melony was a Cheetos lover, who had gotten me hooked, was for the present, a reality I wanted to ignore. Yet spying the photo on the package, I couldn't help but conjure images of her salty, orange-flaked fingers and tongue.

From there, I chanced upon prepared salads. They were fresh and sealed, and little compartments kept ingredients separate within each plastic bowl. The single-serving dressing came separately as well; I chose Caesar over vinaigrette and grabbed a plastic fork.

At the cashier, I lifted two sampler packages of peanut chews. At three bite-sized for twenty-five cents, they were a bargain compared to the chocolate aisle's sixty-nine-cent, full-size bar offering six of the same, but I preferred to steal these delicacies as proof of my free will. I'd let them rest in my book bag's side pocket, and if anyone at the counter noticed, I could say, "Oh, goodness. I forgot."

The fifty-cent cost made it too preposterous to be taken seriously as crime, at least not for a white man dressed as I was. Inside trading, tax fraud, and cronyism were my domain, but philosophy had led me away from the Caucasian male's worn path. Yes, you can see that Auggie was negatively impacting my race-consciousness, and his stories about Jonny were adversely effecting my consuming decisions. I didn't have to steal peanut chews to survive.

The New England clam chowder was packaged separately, so I clutched it close to my chest while dangling the grocery bag with everything else. I pushed the glass door open with my back and walked briskly down the street. I didn't mind the rain so much, but hoped the droplets wouldn't pass through the plastic bag's opening and dampen my comfort snacks. My thoughts increasingly turned to food and how I would indulge once inside my apartment. I felt rich and free, able to snag from the convenience store most anything I craved.

Interrupting my food and freedom, out of the corner of my eye, I spied forms on church steps thirty yards ahead. As I approached closer, I heard sounds. Voices. Was it a homeless man yapping to himself? At a closer point, I heard he was speaking to someone else.

I saw a mass lying atop the steps, half protected and half exposed. It was a large form, maybe two heads staying dry under the church's awning, but legs and feet getting soaked. They were huddled together underneath several blankets. Moving closer, my vision improved, and I saw another person in a worn sleeping bag lying on the lion's share of dry porch.

I drew my plastic bags closer to my person and prepared to veer to the right to create as wide a birth as possible from the lost and rained upon. I clutched my late-night dining closer to my chest, ignoring any possibility that such a sudden move would cause the soup to leak. On another night, I would have sacrificed the bag's entire contents.

Almost upon them, I couldn't help but turn my head ninety degrees to stare at my fair city's indigence, clutching my bag even tighter as I did so. But at least, these two were not robbing and pillaging. They were minding their business, trying to stay dry. Perhaps they stayed awake to stand guard against more corrupt or crooked sidewalk sleepers.

In the moment, I got a close look and saw, yes, there were three of them—two men were seated on the top steps while a woman stood fully covered by the stone ceiling and wall protecting the church's front porch. The object I mistook for bodies getting wet was in fact a mattress, at least full-sized, with a metal frame on wheels no less.

Despite my myopic concerns over my stomach and Melony, I winced when I saw our city's citizens lacking shelter. Thank god it was past January and spring would arrive soon. With it, however, a famous Indian snowstorm or two, and I realized I should be grateful it was raining, particularly at night, and not snowing upon us all. Even as this last thought occurred to me, I heard, "It's too late for the train station" from one of the men. The homeless were evicted from the train station every night at 10 p.m., a cruel fate I'd experienced more than once, when the police came through and banged their night sticks against every green-grate table occupied by anyone who appeared indigent. Almost any seated solitary man could be mistaken for such.

I'd experience anger at the city, its police, and the homeless themselves, sure, but also an intense tingling of intermingled guilt and pleasure that in fact, I had a warm apartment that I could return to, and even a taxi ride home was not out of reach. I was no Diogenes, the ancient philosopher, living like a dog on the streets of Athens. My two-room studio was a king's palace compared to what awaited the less housed in the city's shelters. So many men and mites shared the same cramped quarters I shuddered whenever I imagined it. Even living like Melony, as one of two coeds in an efficiency apartment, was more than I could handle.

My mind returned from the prison house of the train station or the antechamber of Melony's apartment, or vice versa, and I came to in the middle of my walk. I was standing still and getting rained on and staring at three homeless and their half-wet bed. Not wanting to offend anyone, I nodded at the man who established the most eye contact. It was the middle man, a charcoal-navy colored man, whose shining white teeth and eyes acted against the dark night and ebony steps as a glowing epicenter, like that of a Rembrandt portrait. He returned my nod but stared at the bag.

"Can you spare any of that nutritious food?"

The moment of truth.

I turned to shove off and nod, "No, sorry," while averting my eyes, but I felt his stare remain glued to my packages.

Rejection or no, my few soft comforts led to a surge of guilty conscience, and I was soon intent upon feeding these lost souls.

But did the poor peasants merit some peanut chews? You've got to be kidding. The soup? Off limits. The salad? No way. And so that was that, and I dove into the bag and produced the six-inch hoagie and the large bag of Cheetos.

"Cheetos?" I asked with some doubt in my voice, if not a hint of despair that I'd lost an evening with Melony's orange-flecked tongue.

"Man, what the fuck am I gonna do with junk food? I said *nutritious*."

I stepped back, alarmed.

"*Psych*. Boy, I'm only playin' with you," and I could see the human warmth of his grin. "Whatever you got, man. We're grateful."

"Oh." I moved back toward him and extended my free hand to give him the hoagie and Cheetos.

With alacrity, the man hopped off the church steps, smiled at me, and grabbed the snacks.

"You're a good man," he said. "God bless your soul."

He kept smiling at me, then. It was late-night assurance of the decency of my soul, and I wasn't disappointed to receive such alms for the poor of spirit.

I lingered only for a moment to watch the three dig in, and then onward, I continued home. The soup, salad, and peanut chews would be enough for me.

At a brisk pace, I marched away from poverty, and once around a corner, where they could not see me, I ran. It was too much, the guilt slapping me like a cold fish across the cheek. I felt sick and twisted. We had so many showering at public sinks and engaging in highway robbery and going without and sleeping on the street in the cold and rain. But I felt grateful because I had enough. *Fuck it.* What I meant to say is I was fucking ecstatic that I had *more* than all of these poor lost souls. As meager as my own wages were, I took pleasure in my relatively higher net worth.

Up the steps to my second floor rear apartment, I bounded in ecstasy, taking them two and three at a time, whereupon once inside my cozy abode, I collapsed on the couch and rethought the moment once more. These were poor, starving homeless people, and I gave them junk food and half a hoagie, not nearly enough for all three of them. Then and there, in my warm residence with running water, I wished I were the kind of man who could give away the hot, scrumptious New England clam chowder no matter how much his own stomach growled for sustenance. "You cheap piece of garbage," I muttered to myself.

Just as quickly, considering further, what if these were winos or drug addicts—abusing heroin or crack or worse—failing to enroll in the city's services, so their addictions could be fed? They were choosing to avoid the puritanism of the shelters in favor of the wanton life of the streets. After all, they weren't starving. I saw no distended stomachs or signs of thirst. They didn't look desperate for three squares and a cot. For all I knew, even the mattress was a prop, similar to the dust-coated cheeks of beggar children sitting on Mama's lap in Parisian metro stops. By feeding them, I fed only their addictions. I was encouraging laziness and depravity. They were part of the public blight.

Shifting again, I imagined that all these lazy and depraved souls were lost due to no volition of their own; rather, it was impoverished parents, neglectors and abusers, who had informed the formative years of their lives. They were as bad off as Auggie, and there was no just world that could ever correct their unfortunate origins and lead them to healthy, prosperous lives—not to imply those of us who had avoided such horrors were much better off. How fucked was this world we were living in? Could anyone ever avenge the lost and wounded and abused and forsaken? The properly bred people administered universities and corporations and stuck their hands out, demanding copious quantities of cash and gold from the beaten and weak as they established higher tuitions, new classes of assets, additional fees, and alternative minimum taxes. And the world spun round and round, the patter of this steady rain never ceased, and it seemed impossible to stop.

I devoured the salad before I had time to mix ingredients and add dressing. After that, I sucked the soup straight from its paper container. It was lukewarm but tasty. Last, I turned on the television and sat back with my peanut chews.

That was when news broke of the football "tragedy" and the seemingly just as tragic cover up. *Nightline* was discussing the case—a big school with an even bigger football program. A scandal, only five hours from Philadelphia. The reporter stated that a former coordinator of special teams, a larger than life kind of old-school jock, had been violating the sanctity and borders of children, a dozen allegedly, and there were investigations into new cases popping up each week. He was retired now, and throughout his fifty years had contributed thousands of hours to charity. So far, there were nine kids prepared to testify against the monster, but questions remained. Were there others? If so, how many? Were there girls? Was he pimping little boys to donors to the prestigious athletic programs?

Of course, I thought of Auggie's situation, and how the adults in power and on the prowl got away with it one way or another in this land of football and freedom, home of overpriced education, end zones, and offshore tax havens. An oligarchy disguised as democracy, and you could read all about this at any corner Internet café. At the commercial break, a hot model and former megastar told us to buy a German car to support resurgent Detroit, so I rose from the couch—satiated, bloated, and not half-numb. Finding the remote, I changed the channel, and reduced the sound. On a public station, I saw two polar bears on Mammal Planet sniffing crotches, and by the middle of my second package, fifth chew, they were fornicating like animals on late-night cable TV.

Life Lessons from Jonny November 2

It's like I always tell Auggie. America is one big Ponzi scheme. The whole thing is a pyramid. Who owns the stock? The original shareholders. Plantation owners, your Washingtons and Jeffersons and Jacksons and Adams. Well, yeah, their descendants, and later, your Edisons and Fords. Their great grandkids and so forth. See, you have the new rich, the competitive fuckers. They're either smart and industrious or brilliant at playing it slick and crooked in a capitalist world. The worst thing about it is that so many were spoiled children. Single-child policy over there or traditional rich and spoiled here, it was all their parents' slaving or inheriting. All the love and educational software and financial support, even after graduate school, are what enabled these newbies to succeed. A self-made man ain't shit in the United States, and in fact, for the most part, he doesn't exist. All that libertarian bull and conservative baloney about individual responsibility doesn't slice the cold cuts in the twenty-first century. Even in the past, it rarely did. Show me a self-made man, and I'll show you his made-up stories and falsified records.

So where does that leave you and me?

It means we work. The guys in charge got the legal hard guys—yeah, the cops—on their side, and they throw you in jail or tell you you're nuts if you refuse to shovel their shit. You think protesting ain't a crime? Go to those lefty websites and think again. So it's attention to detail in whatever we try. The world is against us. The rich shits in charge are either oblivious to our suffering, or they just don't give a damn. They might think it's funny. To them, we're labor, tuition revenue, spare parts, free jokes. That's it.

Or, it's even worse. They think they're serving us. Protecting us and our interests. That kind of jerk off is the most ignorant of all.

Okay. So you want to know what kind of work?

I'm sure as hell not going to recommend that you slave away behind a counter for minimum wage. That's bullshit. No one should settle for that crap.

No. You gotta work the system as best you can. Disability payments? Section 8 housing? Food stamps or the card or whatever else they got these days? If it's free, you take it. Most of the good-paying gigs are under-the-table anyway.

Chapter 4
Man was born free,
but Auggie fought back.

Man is born free, but everywhere remains in chains. Auggie was intent on breaking out of the old rusted manacles of his childhood. They were stronger than the meanest steel, or so his therapist had suggested they would be, and in his moments of despair, regret, and humiliation, Auggie would lament his formative years. "I'll never see the world as a bright, hopeful place. I'll never trust people fully."

It began when his father disappeared. Around Auggie's age today with a full head of hair, smart suits, and a hop to his step like he knew where he was headed and felt good about it. Auggie told me he'd hardly met the man, and would describe him in these glowing terms like some oasis in the dessert that could have not only saved his camels, but perhaps the entire wandering tribe. His mother had told him that his father died young, of leukemia, but Auggie had such deep resentment of his mother that he doubted the veracity of her report. His mother, after all, had married his stepfather, his sworn enemy, an evil man. She tacitly consented to the sexual abuse and contributed her own share of parental malignancy. And that was the basic predicament of Auggie's childhood—an absent *ubermenchen* and a present sadistic mooch.

After his father's death or disappearance, he grew up in his grandmother's home, until his mother remarried and they moved into the stepfather's place in center city. The stepfather had a small two bedroom house in the winding labyrinth of alleyways East of Broad, around 11th and Waverly. It was in what today would be distinctly the "gayborhood," but back then was less homogenous, a finer 1970s blend of culture and sexuality. Not all was as out in the open as today, but nevertheless, the area was textured and authentic.

Auggie would cite this fact as the first indication of malicious intent. He would question how the stepfather gravitated to this location and came to describe him as a "fucked up closet fag hiding his stench under an ocean of cologne." This was before prices were so exorbitant, when a regular person could afford center city. The stepfather was no ordinary man, of course, according to Auggie, and even as far as earnings, he seemed somewhat extraordinary. For he appeared to live on almost nothing at all; in fact, his mother was most often without work herself. Auggie said that the three of them lived off his father's insurance. So his absent father was also the provider, and this furthered Auggie's claim that his Mom had his real Dad "knocked off by some Kmart Goombahs." For Auggie, these were guys too stupid for the real mafia and too lazy to work the counter for minimum wage.

The stepfather was lazy; he did nothing around the apartment once Auggie and his mother moved in. Auggie was given constant chores. He set tables, scrubbed toilets, and watched his mother slave away under this mean man's iron fist— washing clothes and mopping floors and cooking meals and making beds. It was torture for Auggie to think about what deeds this false master made her perform in the bedroom. But when he described what he imagined to me, he seemed to take delight in expressions like "dirty Schuylkill water sports" and "a three-salami hoagie with oil and vinegar on top."

After a year of bondage, Auggie had had enough. So he rebelled. Oh, how he wished he had poisoned the master's food and ended the relationship entirely. But he was nine. Precocious yes, but only nine. But he was old enough to conspire at least a little, and so he plotted. Yes, you could call this his first plot.

His grandmother grew up in a West Philadelphia in transition. Its colonial vacation-home years long gone, it currently consisted of whites—it was important to Auggie that the neighborhood's Jews and Irish were considered as such—moving out, while

"Negroes" moved in. This is how Auggie would always refer to African Americans; to him, they were always either Negroes or *schvartzes*. In his imagination, what they stood for could only be represented in these words. His therapist referred to his racism as something primal, even instinctual, and not a learned condition he was socialized into.

In all honesty, I am ashamed to say I would encourage his racism in our conversations, his constant need to stigmatize an Other. A category or group he could laugh at and make fun of. As Auggie would chortle and belly whoop, I was laughing too, even as I would cringe and tell Auggie that these terms were outdated, inappropriate, and wrong. Like a schoolmarm, I'd insist that he was a grown man who shouldn't talk that way, never mind, that African Americans all over the country were far more successful, "well behaved," and "adjusted" than Auggie or myself. But then, I would smile, add my own impulsive giggling, and my lesson would be betrayed.

But Auggie held close to his heart the concept of the African American as a universal, a simple, inferior being. As a young child, He had seen all of his grandmother's white West Philly neighbors flee to the suburbs, and as a child, he heard her constant Yiddish epithets hurled out at her new neighbors. *Schvartze. Meshugenah. Schmuck.* "*Kish M'in Toukhes!*" she'd scream from the crosswalk as a driver zoomed past them and through a red light. But perhaps seeing all of the white people disappear, leaving his grandmother stranded in her small brick home, contributed to his hostile world view.

After Grandma, he moved back in with Mom, and after the abusive stepdad, he was trapped in a group home on two separate occasions. His stays occurred between the ages of ten and fifteen. He told me he was the only white kid among dozens of black boys with behavior problems. Outnumbered and isolated, the other boys picked on him constantly. He was in fights each day, often with boys much larger and always with boys much darker. He'd get thrown against a wall or onto the linoleum floor, kicked and punched, and all he could do was bite and kick and scratch and survive. So his group life was no better than what Mom and her husband gave him on the outside.

His persecutors were fatherless boys, and he told me his being Jewish made the situation even worse, although I had trouble imagining Judaism as something young African Americans would know about at all. Unless they themselves were Jewish.

Auggie hated "Jews" himself, and used this term in a derogatory fashion to describe some rich distant category off in affluent suburbs ignoring the plight of those trapped in metrosexual ghettos and surrounded by black pedestrian traffic. But he said his young companions had learned their anti-Semitism from churches where ministers taught them Jews were cheap connivers who did not believe in Jesus Christ. Trapped in the group home, he bore the brunt of it. I never asked Auggie how often such marginalized boys could have attended church, as they were victims of such poor to absent parenting themselves.

* * *

Thinking about Auggie's stepfather and the murder, my crime, would at times bring me back to my own father. He was nothing like Auggie's dad although he wasn't perfect either. He was divorced twice and had children from two women who were not the same two he married. At times, he held jobs, even good jobs, and at times, he held drugs—yes, even good ones—and at times, he held both. He went to work stoned out of his gourd through most of the seventies, somehow avoiding the recessions of that decade. Although he was divorced, swinging, into disco, and more, he was involved in my childhood and never smacked me.

He fought it loudly and vigorously when I declared that I would pursue a life of the mind. This was at nineteen when I told him I'd filled out a form stating that I was a philosophy major. The further I fell into the depths of graduate studies—Marx, Nietzsche, Foucault, the French, the usual progression—the more hopeless he saw it all and the more distant we became from each other. I knew he was disappointed and certain that I was doomed, and I wouldn't learn that he was right until my early thirties. That's when I could see how unqualified I was, as any job left in philosophy went to someone with significant publications and fantastic interpersonal skills. Preferably a woman or minority candidate, so the university could compensate for its over-representation of tenured white men in STEM fields, administration, and everywhere else if you went back far enough. So I was not merely theoretically screwed if I wanted to teach at the college level, but I'm not sure why I stayed in grad school, and then with adjunct work. For no reason I could easily understand, I never tried to gain entry into corporate America, or some other sunnier world of opportunity and pay.

But even as I engaged in more and more schooling, year after year of higher education, I knew there'd be no position for me, no good one anyway, waiting for me at the end of an academic rainbow that had faded a long time ago. I fell out of the loop slowly at the end, spent a year on a first chapter of my dissertation and then two more on the other three. It wasn't coming together, not as far as my committee thought anyway, and they'd return my typed pages with neat scribble, little questions in the margins, that sort of thing. I became aware that at the pace I was writing, or thinking, or reading, or whatever it was exactly I was supposedly not doing well enough, that I'd never finish and that even if I did, I'd never win a position in my field. The jobs were scarce, the competition brutal, and the outlook bleak.

As the semesters slipped away, it felt as if my committee ignored me, and I saw them losing interest in the entire project. At times, I was almost certain I'd see a snarl or even a yawn when they saw I was knocking on the door. I'd pass them in the hall, see them speaking with those younger, cheerier doctoral candidates. Some of these were males, at times with exotic minority status, but more often young women, occasionally voluptuous or even anorexic in an erotic way. No doubt their cleavage, dimples, lipstick, and smarts would carry the day and win the tenured appointments if there happened to be any in the future.

That my committee was apathetic toward me, and possibly even held me in contempt, a hanger-on who should have finished or fled a few years ago, made it easier to dislike them and finally file the papers to drop out of the program. But as soon as I completed the paperwork and handed it to the departmental secretary, there was a reversal. Sudden interest in my predicament meant that for six months, they pushed me on, something about "finishing up what you set out to do" and "retention rates" and "your diligence and respect for the institution." Somehow or other, they got me walking down the aisle to receive a doctoral degree. I felt ignored once more almost as soon as the ceremony was over. It was all so awkward. I put in only a half-hearted effort at a tenure track search and quickly lost interest in the problems I'd been writing about, or not writing about, the past few years. I've barely spoken a word to my committee since then.

I drifted into teaching at the lowest rungs, first philosophy exclusively and then through a tip from a friend, I wound up in a general education "Intellectual History" program, a major requirement at Urban State, the university I taught at up until my life on the lamb. It was watered down Western Civilization for the above-average masses who told me they had no time for reading outside of their major. It became my life's work, my duty as it were, to teach these sections again and again. I grew to enjoy it, the routines of reading the same books each semester, the delight in familiarity with a few difficult, if essential, texts, and the occasional class discussion or joke in between all the lecturing and listening to students who rarely had anything original to say.

That's how I first met Melony.

Life Lessons from Jonny November 3

You got all that?

Good.

Write this down, too.

You see the quarter, pick up the quarter. Don't let me catch you walking past twelve cents glimmering on the asphalt. Got it?

There's no shame in saving coins from the sewer. I knew a guy in the stir who did three bills a day snagging change from the sidewalk and gutters. As in *three c-notes*, brother. No lie. (And no, I don't know why he killed his uncle. I do know why he did time in the hole, but I swore I'd never tell anyone on the outside.)

But for us mere mortals, of average eyesight and work ethic, you'll clear two to four American dollars a day.

That's your coffee money, right? No, wrong, 'cause you're gonna drink coffee for free. Only in the U. S. of A, my friend. And I'm not talking about empties left in the garbage with two teaspoons of saliva and sugar sludge caked to the bottom of the cup. No. You'll just walk in at rush hour. Act polite and like you belong where you are. Gracefully go to the counter area where they leave the drinks. And wait.

Don't get greedy. I know a guy who lost all feeling in his pinky and ring finger when he swooped in for an overpriced "executive" drink and on impulse, the tattooed slut churning out fancy lattes slammed his hand with an espresso machine handle. He was not the same thief again.

So what you do is nice and calm, you wait for the moment when there are two tall-sized coffees on the counter, and grab one and go. But not straight out the door. You go to the station for half 'n half and brown sugar, and you add your ingredients.

You loiter. You smile. If anyone asks you whether you paid, you say, "I believe I did." You haven't lied, see?

In a worst-case scenario, you'll have to pay from your loose-coin fund. That's a minor setback, but no biggie. You even take a few slurps before you leave Captain Starbucks. Don't belch; that's disgusting and also draws too much attention to you and your pinched caffeine.

Another guy I know always stays and chats up the chicks at the tables. But they're all lesbo or reading for exams or looking for young ass. Who can blame them for wanting to avoid old man leaky dick? For Willy Wilted, small talk's a waste of time. You can always pay for it if you gotta have it, but if you can go for a single month without, the urge will go away. Trust me. I know. I won my freedom this way.

Getting rid of your urges—for sex, dope, TV, booze, etc.—is critical to your accrual of wealth. That's the only way a regular guy can achieve success and freedom.

Always, I mean always, stay focused on priorities. Your survival is number one. That's survival without working for the man. No nine-to-fiver, graveyard shift, or any of that donkey crap. As far as I'm concerned, you go around the wheel but one time, my friend, and you don't want to waste your life working yourself to death. That's for suckers, not for you.

You deserve better than that.

And don't give me that bull about working hard to get ahead and the American Dream and all that baloney and horse manure. There's no America and never was one. If America was America, if individual responsibility ever existed, it'd be called Hispaniola, Columbia, or Dead Indiana—or better yet, some clever chump writing marketing copy for England or Spain would have found a way to make "indigenous peoples" sound like a country with room to dream in.

Chapter 5
Jacketless in New York City

I loathed being stood up and drinking alone, so to win back Melony, to regain her attention, I knew I had to act boldly. Barbecue sauce over iceberg lettuce was no longer enough for a dinner date, not even if it was followed by romantic liaisons on her roommate's couch. She was the hot, young chick. She wanted to be entertained. Required it. Deserved it? I knew I was a bore and couldn't imagine what cretins and slobs the young men of Melony's generation might be for me to be fortunate enough to have stolen one of their prized desserts. But I'd been stood up at the bar, so who knew what my status was? Even if the blindfold only led to negotiations with middle infielders, I wanted to make sure I hadn't argued with the umpire to the point where I'd gotten myself thrown out of the game.

So when she proposed a trip to see a show in Manhattan, I couldn't refuse. In fact, I was honored that she would be willing to be seen with me in public in such a famous city, and for such an extended period of time. Which made it all the more bizarre that she was certain I was the one intent on wearing a disguise for our weekend jaunt to the city.

We met Friday afternoon in the train station, once more intent upon the cheaper fare—a local to Trenton and then a run, skip, and hop to NJ Transit and an hour later, New York City's Penn Station. All we could find were aisle seats, and so we sat across from each other, chitchatting about this and that—school and work and Auggie—as fellow Friday-nighters wagged their butts down the aisle.

I had begun talking more about Auggie with Melony. I even let it slip out that he was a bit of a player, a two or three-timer who would not need more than a second to acquiesce to a *ménage à trois*, or even a four-scoop sundae with a cherry on top. So his childhood abuse and the pity and understanding we should all show for him became a common topic in our conversations. I suppose I should have noticed at some point that Melony showed a certain sympathy for his plight. With the girls, Auggie got a lot of mileage out of the whole abused orphan angle, and I must confess that Melony and I spent an inordinate amount of time discussing him. He became our subject of last resort, what we could always fall back upon if all else failed to stimulate. Auggie was to us as a favorite television show or sports team was to other couples. Imagine Jenny and Jonathan discussing in an animated fashion all the touchdowns and quarterback sackings of their beloved team leader, and substitute Auggie for the football star, and you have an idea of what we were like.

"Oh, Michael, it's so sad."

"He gets his revenge by seducing girls he meets in the supermarket."

"He's not supposed to like girls just because his stepdad was mean to him."

"An odd twist, yes, to 'do unto others,' but he isn't violent unless they ask to be spanked."

Melony turned sharply to me, so I quickly qualified: "Rear end, palm only, explicit permission or written request."

"Yeah," with a sigh, "A lot of girls find that erotic."

I remembered the blindfold, tickles, and pinches, as I saw a glimmer of mischief in Melony's eye.

Fond talk of Auggie, then, was much of what we shared, and I should not see it as entirely negative. Everyone needs hobbies and passions and enthusiastic discussion, right?

We were due to see *The Bird Cage* on Broadway, an early evening show that would begin a couple hours after we checked into our hotel. I'd found one only a few blocks from Penn Station, a discount deal from an online travel broker.

Outside Penn Station, the wind whipped our cheeks and brought us closer. We pressed together against the frigid evening weather. Melony claimed she knew "the city" well, and when I gave her the hotel address, she didn't disappoint. Within minutes we entered a tall brick building whose lobby was lit by glowing lamps.

A door man smiled and held open a glass door. Another fellow asked if we needed help with our book bag and briefcase. I said, "No, thank you," but withdrew my wallet and handed him a fiver. I wanted to appear professional and at ease—like a man accustomed to tipping well and escorting young hotties to hotel rooms. In line at the front desk, when it was my turn to sign for the room, Melony withdrew to a lavender cloth couch.

The prim queer at the counter had that look of grim superiority on his face—the one that says random, anonymous ass-fucking is a moral shelf above a hetero-clit-kiss with your daughter's generation. Nevertheless, he accepted my Visa card and its thousand-dollar limit, the only credit line available to me. He then sighed and gave me two key cards and informed me that they would open a door to a room on the twenty-ninth floor. I asked about free continental breakfast, and he gave a polite "no."

No worries, as I was glad to be in from the cold, and in with Melony, on our magical adventure in New York City. We took the elevator to the twenty-ninth floor and found a perfectly clean room. It had leather furnishings and was properly prepared for those far above our station. For the night, we would be earth tones. Off white, beige, and tanned pine furniture with cushioned chairs and a soft loveseat of sand and roan. That the whole building was swaying and the wind screamed at the windows seemed not to concern Melony. She popped off her shoes and jumped on the bed and lay there prone like a fresh-fruit greeting plate I should pounce upon.

But as a proper gentleman, I wanted to confirm that we were only thirty minutes from the start time of our show, so I took a chair, removed my print-outs of the agenda, and held tight when I felt the floor move.

"I never dreamed the room would be this nice."

I'd never dreamed I'd be in any such room with a young lady sixteen years my junior, yet here I was. At present, though I was experiencing fear; it was of height, wind, and swaying buildings. True, this latter anxiety was not quite as dynamic as our twenty-first century fear of burning buildings, exploding upper levels, floors on fire, and innocent workers and residents trapped and swan-diving down when the heat grew too extreme.

But back to present circumstances, knowing that life was short and terrorists could maim and kill in an instant, should I rise up and pounce? Could this be the custom among the young and informed? A quickie or at least heavy petting before the performance began?

Socrates offered only questions, but I needed answers, so I returned to my computer print-out and time piece to confirm that we were twenty-seven minutes away from show time.

Glancing up, all I could muster was, "Do you know how to get there?"

"Oh, it's easy. We're close to Broadway."

So that was that. We left our things, took our coats, and headed out.

Again, we froze and the wind smacked us in the face. We were both unprepared for extreme weather, but at least I had a wool hat. Melony wore a down jacket that ended at her waist, not a coat to protect the legs as well. A scarf was wrapped around her neck, but she was missing hat and gloves.

I was certain that her ears, which were turning visibly red, would freeze and fall off at any moment. But below freezing temperatures aided and abetted the romantic nature of our quest for Broadway, and we wound up arm in arm, hands in each other's pockets as we ventured off.

It was only a matter of time before we came to Broadway and turned onto its diagonal that crisscrossed the major grid. A blaze of light greeted us and thousands of other pedestrians braving the cold. The lighting came from neon explosions from high above, reds and greens reminding us of the winter season and the greatest theater on earth. Passersby appeared well kept and well groomed. They wore seasonal outfits, long wool coats, some in leather, no few in fur, and thus all were protected from the elements.

On this Friday night in downtown Manhattan, you would have no idea that we were said to be in one of the worst recessions of our lives—that manufacturing had stalled and the rate of worker participation had plummeted to an all-time low. Indeed, Americans hadn't failed to work in such large numbers since they'd begun to keep track of such statistics. As cold as it was, I could only imagine that people with jobs were the ones trudging ahead and behind us with tickets to musicals they could easily afford. In downtown Manhattan, no recession at all was visible.

No matter. I had the girl. Hand in hand, striding and snuggling down Broadway.

And so ignoring the working man, who in fact, was smiling to us at the door, we waltzed right in, found our seats, and sat back and waited for the performance.

A man masked in rouge over ample foundation came on stage and orated in a profound, voluminous way. He said we would enjoy ourselves, that this musical would cause us to forget our freezing asses and all of our worries and concerns. That both the national debt and our personal pain would disappear during the three-hour performance, and even at intermission we'd be jolly and gay. He promised results but wouldn't commit to a money-back guarantee.

The show was great fun; we both laughed and smiled and enjoyed ourselves. I'm not sure anyone would have guessed we were so far apart in age. I still had my hair, and by tucking in the right tee, I was able to conceal my unfortunate spare tire. And she did her best to look and act mature. As we waited for the show to begin, I let my mind drift. I imagined Poe in Virginia with his twelve-year-old. Kafka in Berlin with his niece. E. I. Lonoff at peace and at rest in the bosoms of his Anne Frank. Woody Allen in Paris with his x-girlfriend's daughter. I saw myself as following in a long tradition of artist-lovers embracing destiny. I turned to Melony and saw a wide smile of anticipation. I was making her happy. For a moment, I felt an inner tingle, an almost heavenly joy. I'd chased away the persistent background morbidity that nothing gold could stay.

The show was a great success—bright lights and bright colors and gobs of foundation caked onto the most enthusiastic of fags, the kind that uplift the spirits of even the most covetous and bitter of worn down, middle aged, heteronormative audiences. Singing and dancing and tra la la doodily da; for a few hours the octogenarian in front of me with his septuagenarian side piece turned back the clock thirty or forty years.

After the show, we popped back out onto the street. It was freezing cold. If you sneezed, tiny icicles would hang from your nose. Later I would learn that this was the coldest day of New York City winter in the past ten years. I guided Melony back to the hotel room a half mile away. As we strode past the late-night shops of the Penn Station vicinity, we saw ten-cent postcards and three-for-five-dollar, I-heart-NY tee-shirts for any frugal frozen tourist who passed by. It was an ugly, sad neon Manhattan not as frequently filmed in the movies, and I clutched her left paw snug in my coat.

Inside the lobby, we hurried onto the hotel elevator, and upstairs, inside the room, we could hear the wind howling. If I weren't prone to paranoid imagination, I'd have been certain the building was swaying in the breeze. We took our coats off and threw them on the bed. I gnawed on the pastrami on rye I'd picked up back in the train station. With polite insistence, she asked me to brush my teeth twice.

"Dentist-approved paste, if you have it, honey."

I almost snapped back, "Who doesn't pack fluoride-fortified gel with a stripe?" But I stayed silent, and as an obedient and horny old goat, I obliged.

Seven minutes later, I had her on the bed. Gnawing her neck bone, my mitts on her hips, I whispered in her ear, "You're the real money fuck meat. The best I've had."

After she slapped me, I apologized. I told her I wasn't up with my naughty talk. I didn't know what I should say and barely knew how it was done. She smiled at all that honesty and humility, and proceeded to lead the way.

Back to business, it got to the point where she had me pinned on the bed. I didn't protest; rather, I moaned like a school girl.

"Where is it?" she whispered.

How humiliating! She saw nothing!

I put her hand on it.

"No, not that, silly. I mean your jacket."

"Jacket?"

I remembered throwing it on the bed earlier but couldn't find it anywhere.

"Do you need it right now? Shall I adjust the thermostat?"

"Well, I thought we would. . ." and she whispered the rest in my ear. Exactly what I had hoped for!

So I twisted and contorted and had her pinned beneath me and was desperately trying to find the key to her clasp lock.

"No! Not until you put on a condom."

And I understood. A *jacket* as in protection. Right.

But wrong! I was without.

And so the mood was shattered. The rest of the night became my efforts at sleep and inability to do so with a twenty-three-year-old lying next to me. So then there were restless forays toward the goal and her fighting me back. She was half-asleep, and I'd have my unit tucked an inch under her undies, when she'd fight me off and roll over.

I couldn't sleep. I was lying there, in a king-size bed with my fantasy, but I wasn't carrying, and so I was left to my aimless, drifting half-thoughts and awake dreams. What was passing through my mind? That she'd let me slide it in bareback and make American babies? I had to admit this thought had crossed my mind. I was getting on in years, and was increasingly unsure of what else I could do with my time. It seemed like a good way to get a lively one, a worker, to stick around. Knock her up. The old-fashioned way. Ostensibly by accident but who knows how the subconscious operates?

I rallied again and stormed the keep. Half asleep, Melony mumbled, "Michael, no *glove*, no love." She was quoting the scene in *The World According to Garp*, where Garp has the blonde girl behind the bush and is ready to cross the Rubicon. I was over twice the age of that adolescent Garp and lost in a worse predicament. And yet, I was also grateful that Melony had favorite movies made during my childhood, before she was born.

Thus, I spent a sleepless night. Melony, however, slept like a baby and was wide awake in the morning. I needed an hour in the bathroom with the door locked—a shower, a shave, and a tardy, wet shit that fought me every inch of the way, the kind that splashed brown stuff on the inner underside of the toilet seat. I cleaned up as best I could, and Melony looked at me like I was insane when I popped out and said I was ready.

"What were you doing in there?"

Once more, the mood was shattered.

We gathered our meager belongings and walked out into frozen New York City. Sleep or no, it was Manhattan, and exciting for that reason. Saturday late morning and the crowds were out. Milling about. Cosmopolitan glocals having their way with a day of leisure in the greatest city on earth. We headed to Central Park, where a contemporary art exhibit had just been installed.

In the biting cold, with thousands outside, we went to see the outdoor exhibit. It looked like someone had placed steel red rectangles throughout the park. But it was too cold to loiter. So we found a café and sat. Coffee, eggs, and toast for me. For Melony, coffee with ample cream and sugar.

I drank coffee and ate food. I felt warm. Despite my fatigue, or because of it, I talked too much.

"It's like Auggie is saying, America is just one big Ponzi scheme. The whole thing is. Period. We're on the outside. The last folks in who get left holding the bag. Your whole generation is taking on student loans because they were told to by parents and teachers. But there's no paid work out there unless you become an engineer or nurse. That's the whole thing, nurses and engineers. Well, coders and accountants, too. But that's it. The rest of us go into debt, so we can starve in dignity. College educated and can't afford heat and hot water. Nomad gigs and freelancing for the chosen few in our fields. Bullshit for the rest. Then they criminalize debt. Mark my words. There'll be debtor's prison for people who default by the end of the twenty-first century. My father would say that to me twenty years ago, and now I can see it's true."

Melony stopped pouring sugar packets into her coffee—at seven, I lost count—and looked up and into my eyes. It was enough to make me stiffen.

"Don't you want me to be happy?"

"I want you to learn the truth about America."

"Maybe we should stop seeing each other."

Whoa. A ton of bricks. I got dumped for failing to bring protection? Or for being depressing?

I felt miserable. A failure once more.

At once, I resolved to win her back. I'd plead, beg, and borrow a line or two from Auggie.

But after twenty minutes of argument that went nowhere, we boarded a train and returned to Philly in silence. At her door, I received a romantic kiss, but that may have been only to prevent a scene.

"Let Me Explain"
by Melony Sorbet 1

I dumped him. So what? You know I had to. I have my whole life ahead of me. It's not like I was ready to settle down or quit playing the field. And even if it's a worthless piece of paper, I promised myself I'd get my degree. But it's not exactly what you think. Let me explain.

Old isn't as weird as I thought it would be. He's just like any guy. A little irresponsible, you know, unprepared. And you have to tug the leash a lot. Play with the tension in the rope. Keep him on his toes, so it doesn't get boring. Otherwise, they stop paying attention. Michael's a philosopher, which means complete space cadet. But if Rover's a good dog, I'll reel him back him and let him snack on my fishy. That was sweet, the whole Broadway show thing. More guys should do stuff like that. For the ones my age, a date is like "I'll play video games while you blow me and wash my clothes." A date is heating up appetizers while they scream at football on TV. Coin-up assholes and frozen-wing morons. At least Michael knows how to select a decent hotel room. Maybe if I take him back and he's a good boy, I'll let him write my essays. I like those old-man forehead furrows he gets when he's concentrating. Okay, I admit it. Being with an old guy makes me giggle. He's a dork, but he's sweet.

Chapter 6
Shit Shoe

Soon after that late winter frozen date, Philly began to thaw. But getting dumped had ruined my rhythms despite this hint of spring in the air. I grew agitated and unsatisfied with my onanistic routines. I had trouble falling asleep.

A couple weeks after my dismissal, I was late for class. Rushing to the room, I stepped in a big smear of soft brown stuff. Philadelphia's finest doggy poop, sticky and stinking. I failed to scrape all of it off against a broken bit of concrete sidewalk, and pressed on. I needed to get in before the ten-minute mark; that'd be the moment the first responders—as in, the first to leave—would depart. The awkward looks exchanged between a late professor and departing students were too embarrassing. I'd avoid this if I could slide behind the lectern by the nine-minute mark.

At the side door of Smith Hall, I snuck in. I held the door open, so it wouldn't slam in the face of the young one trailing just behind me. I established slight eye contact and was returned a disturbed glare. Was she upset that I was leering? That she was late? That inside, it smelled like shit? Or that I did? I had no time to contemplate all the other possibilities or the philosophical implications of each one. As she passed, I noted her firm ass and even strides. Stick to philosophy, Vittinger.

Fifteen minutes later, I had dog shit on my shoe and Diogenes on my mind. I snapped open my briefcase, removed my books, note pads, writing utensils, and tip jar. The latter I placed front and center on the desk, and after scurrying about looking for chalk, I interrupted my philosophical treatise on abstaining from earthly pleasure to dig in the garbage at the front of the classroom. Well, not interrupting as much as lecturing to a trash can filled with late morning snacks for the young and enrolled.

The students sat silent, no doubt stunned by the audacity of their instructor.

Eureka! Half a slice of morning pizza on top of crumpled printing paper. At commuter schools, with students bustling around with thirty hours a week of work and twenty credits of school, there was almost always food left behind by the consuming scholar, young, ambitious, and on the go.

No girl and no prospects, so what did I have to lose? I did something I'd never do, and as a reckless showman, I took a huge bite, chewed, and resumed lecturing with my mouth wide open. My mind wandered to the teachable moment at hand; rather, the moment was slathered over my tongue, stuck between teeth, and sliding down my esophagus.

"Wasted food is everywhere, and it's up to us to conserve. The philosophical position is simple if you attack it from an interdisciplinary perspective. Eat from the garbage when you can, but only if you're certain you munch under sanitary conditions. I make sure I never eat from a can if I think the homeless could have urinated in it, so for the most part, I enforce an indoor-cans-only rule.

"But speaking of food, what I really want to discuss today is the ethics of parents gobbling up children. You've probably read in the news about the story in Germany about the father who masticated upon his little boy. Right?

"Well, there's been a whole history of such munching in Western thought. Greek mythology is ripe with such images. The father of time, Cronus, castrated his own dad," I paused to grab my package and wince, "to grab power, and so he ate his kids to prevent the same from happening to him. Picture him popping them in and slurping them down, one gulp at a time— Demeter, Hera, Hades, Hestia, and Poseidon. So to prevent him from sucking down Zeus, as an evening snack, his wife Rhea hid her newbie and swaddled a stone she in turn gave to her husband. There are competing theories as to how Zeus got his siblings back from Dad's tummy—everything from a powerful emetic to using a knife to slice open his stomach.

"Moving on, let's return to today's paragraph from Heidegger." The new improved liberal education as capitalist practice ensured we never assigned more than two hundred per class. Not pages or paragraphs. Words, silly. The idea was to parse them thoroughly over a fifty-minute period and call that teaching kids to read and think critically.

Ten minutes later I arrived at my main points.

"He was a careerist. So the point is not that Heidegger was a Nazi, but that he was an ambitious careerist who would say or do anything for power and financial gain. At the time, Hitler looked like the winning hand and Heidegger was willing to play poker. Or at least keep his trap shut."

For emphasis, I opened wide and then proceeded to gnaw what remained of my slice. Chew, gulp, and resume.

"So what I'm saying is we have to abolish careers and ambition, tenure, money, all of it. Then, we'll have people professing their *ideas*, not writing books to substantiate the claims of capitalist superiors above them in the hierarchy. The myopic oligarchs in their field.

"Once college professor becomes a universally subsistence-wage profession with no possibility of promotion, we'll see who really wants it enough to become one. The moneygrubbers will run scared from the temple they helped corrupt, and the true educators will remain. That's when we'll hear from the best minds, those among us not driven by money or status, but by a genuine thirst for knowledge. The shysters in charge of today's university can work in finance and insurance and real estate. They call it F.I.R.E for a reason."

I cleared my throat, proud of my delivery. I wasn't certain that I believed a word of it, but I indulged in the hubris of radical thought. A pause for silence. Let them take it in. My eyes closed to humanity.

When I opened them again, I noticed looks of discomfort. Students in the front row appeared ready to retch. A diplomatic type in the second row nodded politely and with a hand motioned toward the floor. I looked down and saw evidence of my *sturm und drang*, the *braun* streaks I'd left while pacing the front of the room. So caught up was I in my critique of Heidegger's careerism that I forgot all about what the pooch brought in. Or I should say what I'd smeared all over the floor.

Everyone in the room could see and smell what I'd be leaving behind.

* * *

On my way out the door, I considered what was happening to me. It wasn't good. After months of listening to Auggie's harangues and laments, there were consequences upon this good listener.

Auggie was complicated, and I admit this is all despite his better self that flaunted his optimism. That was Auggie's other *spiel*, most often delivered in brief performances for supermarket coeds. His land of possibility concerning exclusive brokerage contracts, individual responsibility, getting ahead, indeed, getting rich and, in sum, what we know as the American Dream.

But despite all of the young women and his wheeling and dealing, and even a Melony of my own that I seemed to have won and lost, his negative side won the day. The abuse theme was lodged in my brain in a way that meant considering it was unavoidable.

Auggie's stolen childhood was a sofa-sized cockroach stuck in the hidden corridors of my frontal lobe!

* * *

From there, it was only a matter of time before it seeped into my conversations with the young and uninformed. In other words, it was ruining my teaching!

In the classroom, Auggie's abuse infiltrated, and soon took over, with the most awful and inappropriate consequences. The theme of abuse dominated every discussion, regardless of the philosopher or political philosophy discussed. Perhaps with a Sade or Sacher-Masoch, or even a Nietzsche or Camus, such a preoccupation would seem relevant, essential even, but the abuse would pop up everywhere.

Take for instance our lovely, if deluded, believer in reason, Immanuel Kant. Rather than merely laugh in the face of his "thought," *à la* Nietzsche, or destroy his mythology of perpetual peace, or focus entirely on his own predilection toward power as a member of the tenured class, I would focus almost entirely on his pacing in the Danish Gardens, his physical abuse of the public space at each point where his foot smashed down on the brick. His perpetual pacing was a switch against the bare behind of the garden's blend of man-made grey and natural green. I'd pound my boot on the dirty linoleum at the front of the classroom. Soon, my *aristeia* would elevate to smashing my briefcase against the black chalkboard and screaming about Kant's idiocy, his myopia, and his abuse of the entire human condition. If not abuse, at least a gargantuan, stark misreading. Toward a perpetual peace, my ass. In fact, Kant himself had his *Wiener schnitzel* firmly up the ass of the Kaiser and all of Germany, seeking to plug holes, so to speak, in the fabric and linens of our shared weaknesses and fascisms.

There I was in front of them all, tormenting with the constant harangue of the abuse of philosophy, and how every single metaphysical soul, with his prickly wand was probing and prodding us into submission. Okay, so maybe I didn't even know what the hell I was talking about. But it got to the point where my constant ramming in the class's ass caused students to mysteriously disappear. They'd stop showing up, and I'd never receive an electronic note concerning their status, never mind the obligatory handwritten one about a grandmother with a malignancy or a great aunt on her death bed. One student ran screaming from the classroom in the middle of my enflamed excoriation of Hegel—"Fuck this shit! Fuck you, Professor!" Another slid out of her chair, her body in a cascade of spasms until she came to rest silent on the dirty linoleum floor. Only thirty minutes later, with her prone form strapped to a gurney and carted away, did we learn that she'd had a seizure but that she would live.

Auggie's abuse stories had infected my entire syllabus, and now I was killing them off! But it was not just my teachings or my classroom. I saw that the capitalist model of higher education was the cause of it all. College was a ruthless and sinister stepfather, lying and beating and molesting our young.

It was not only the monstrous coordinators of the university legal team stealing innocence from the unprotected. The literal molestations at Rural State were just a drop in the bucket, the tip of the iceberg. The students, professors, administrators, and everyone else involved were there for all the wrong reasons, having been sold a bill of goods and untruths about what college would lead to. Money. Career. Affluence. Status. They were stuck with a hand out. It was a pseudointellectual smash and grab, and everyone craved education to get in on the action. As marginal as I was in my middling years, I was guilty too.

Life Lessons from Jonny November 4

Last winter, around holiday season, I began driving in a rented Ford Ecoline. An innocuous white van with properly inflated tires. This was South Jersey, a nice suburb, and the rain was pouring down. I vowed to be choosy, pick my spots, and stay as dry as possible. It was a weekday morning after the commuter rush. This was the perfect time. The housewives—if there were any left in America—were still asleep or in a morning daze or drinking coffee in the kitchen, which if you notice is always toward the back of the house. Why is that? It's because most folks in America are so broke, living off plastic, that food is their valuables. Forget money in the mattress or under the floorboards. There's no cash in the house.

So I'm cruising in the rain, admiring the perfect windshield wipers on the almost new rental van and looking for action. Shifting to a lower gear, I crawl into a neighborhood of stand-alone homes and see all kinds of unique builds. Brick and stone exteriors; Victorians and Cape Cods . No multi-units or rentals that I can see. Most of the houses are grey and brown and beige. Rainy day colors. As far as I can tell, it's a quiet bedroom community.

I'm looking for the perfect score. Christmas boxes left on the porch. The best time to check is late afternoon. That's before folks come home from work but after most deliveries. Late afternoon also has its risks—kids returning from school, folks with irregular schedules, shit like that. Pardon the French. Late at night is good too, of course, and if folks are out of town, it's a perfect chance to make an easy score. But I like to throw on my uniform and drive my route during the day. That way, I can pretend I'm a regular delivery guy picking up packages that were left for me. I can smile at the neighbor if he sees me. The old lady swinging on the porch can check out my ass if that's her thing.

It's theft in broad daylight; to me, that's the American way. The best is the "double steal"; that's when you bang the housewife and steal the boxes at the same time. It's called "stealing home" if you bang her back door. A triple play is when you shag her daughter first. Unless the daughter is under eighteen. Then, it's called fifteen to twenty for corrupting a minor. Don't go there, my friend; that's all I got to say about that.

So cruising under twenty miles per hour, I come across a porch flush with boxes. I double-park on the street, don my brown hat, grab my clipboard, and march to the porch. The coast is clear; this will be easy. But as I turn around with the second box, the door opens.

"Hey, mister, what are you doing?"

I turn and see it's not the wife. It's the teenager. Still in her pink pajamas.

"Shouldn't you be in school little girl?"

She gives me a slight smile and a baby sneeze.

"I'm home sick."

Yeah, right, and now you're gonna flirt with Mister Softee until his criminal charges rise to the level of statutory rape, breaking and entering, failure to ignore a teenaged slut, and worse.

"Look, little lady, I'm with Express Delivery," and I tip my hat, "so I hope you can get some rest and feel better soon."

The slight smile turns to a slight frown.

"Express, my ass," she whispers to me.

At this point, I have half a mind to slap her. Who needs a mouthy chick's interference when there's a job to do, right? But, hey, I don't need to get pinched, either, so I paste on my best polite smile, add a "have a nice day," and head down the steps.

"Hey, mister," she calls to me as I'm on the pavement, walking toward the van. Despite years of training, I can't help but turn and look.

And sure enough, it's pale flesh and pink nipple. She flashes me. This little girl is headed to stardom, a future lap-dancing queen or night walker for sure.

I turn away, accelerate, toss the package in the van's side door, and escape to the driver's side quick. Keys in the ignition and I'm out of there. I don't breathe again until I'm at the stop sign at the end of her winding road. From experience, I know that girls like that aren't the ones who memorize license plates and turn in criminals.

Chapter 7
Heroes and Stumps

"Don't believe a word Jonny says about the puddles of wet pink he slurped up as a younger guy. His heroic days of cavern excavation and nibbling around the avocado. Have you ever seen Jonny with a woman? Have you ever heard him have a conversation with a chick? Stale or fresh? Old or new? Do you think it was any different for him two decades ago? He's probably told you that he used to be a lady's man before the motorcycle accident, as if half a leg missing wasn't the perfect pity ploy that would have him surrounded by females. Did he try to tell you that he catches women staring at his ass, his bony behind that nobody'd even retail on the discount rack? Jonny and women. Tell me another one. Yeah, right."

I slumped into my couch and listened to Auggie go on and on about Jonny November's celibacy and scams. It was helping me take my mind off Melony. She hadn't replied to my calls, and I was beginning to believe she never would.

"Yeah, here's another one. Last Christmas Day, he went out in his truck and searched for gifts on porches. He found more than a few. HDTVs. Stereos. Pounds of cheese and salami assortments from Hickory Farms and such. He likes to lift. He's a grifter. A regular Jonny-con-game."

Auggie's voice broke up into a high-pitched cackle. His words became inaudible. I rested my cell phone against my shoulder, but could still hear Auggie's noise. Losing interest in deciphering Auggie's message, I turned my attention back to the television and raised the volume. The local news was on. This was my soothing routine, like Kant's walk through Königsberg. For Kant, daily exercise; for Vittinger, murders and fire.

Now at 11:13 p.m. in South Jersey, I saw the end of a fire report in Pennsauken and a clip from Haddonfield.

"Now we turn to another kind of horror that makes you wonder what the world is coming to. This evening a man in a white van in Haddonfield was seen removing boxes from a front porch. Friends, this is no regular delivery man. Authorities says that delivered boxes have gone missing from porches since Christmas, and this particular Scrooge matches a composite sketch on file. Let's zoom in now and take a closer look at his features."

I heard the scold of the anchorman as the screen produced the close-up. It was the usual in middle aged and mostly bald. What hair remained was marginalized to the sides and turning grey. But then I recognized the face, and I squinted to be sure.

"That's right, folks," the anchor continued. "This gentleman is ruining our local consumer spirit, so if you have any information, please do phone it in."

I did, but not to the proper authorities. Cell phone back at my ear, "Auggie? You still there, Auggie?" He was. "I just saw Jonny November on the late-night news. He's been touched. On security video. Stealing electronics and toys off porches in Haddonfield."

I felt a surge of pride that I knew *touched* like a real man of the margins toughened by the informal economy and alleyway survival.

"Jonny can't get 'touched' since he's already got a rap sheet. They've had his details in the system since before you started grad school."

I winced when I realized my usage was off.

"Jonny's in his trailer, dozing in front of the TV. You got the wrong grifter. Couldn't be him."

"Well, I saw a guy, and it's caught on tape and being shown on the news. Live on local news."

"Holy shit."

"Auggie, I think you should stop calling Jonny so much. You've got a record and you know how these investigations work. You could wind up in jail as an accomplice."

"Nah. They can't nab me. All I got is information. I have no way of knowing if the crimes are real. I'm here, and he's there. How could I know what he's up to? They'd have to nab me for stealing a CIA spy drone before they could cut me into this caper."

So that was that. I wandered back to my own reality, less involved in stealing from porches than in disseminating information. Could anyone consider me a criminal for the ideas I spread among the masses of Urban State students? Could I be implicated if someone were to take my knowledge and act in a criminal manner?

That the philosophical life could lead one in any manner of directions is beyond doubt. By sheer number of college classes taught throughout the years, it was mathematically impossible that at least one student was not in jail, and it was anyone's guess as to what ideology, discourse, or dogma drove him there.

"Be careful, Auggie."

"Care? What do I care about care? Do you think my mother and stepfather gave a damn about me? Did they care at all? Life is short, that's what Jonny always tells me."

I don't know why, but I was in the mood to feed his fire: "Yeah, life is short. Who gives a fuck!?"

"Now you're talking, Professor."

"If I'm still teaching on the academic margins in ten years, I'll kill myself."

"Easy does it, Prof. Say you wanna check in on Jonny with me this weekend?"

"Melony has me booked on Saturday, but Sunday I'm free."

Why was I lying about plans with Melony, when I hadn't seen her in almost two weeks? Even with her job and school, it seemed likely the dumping was permanent, at least to her. What was wrong with me?

"Well, it ain't like Jonny November is attending church. We'll head to Camden in the afternoon."

"How do we get there?" Of course, there had to be a reason Auggie needed me for this venture, and I imagined the worst.

"It's easy. We'll drive."

"That's fine," I said, recognizing that he needed me for my automobile.

I hung up on Auggie and tuned back into television. *Nightline* was showing a torso with four stumps and a head wrestling on his high school team. In the televised highlights, he pinned a guy who had both arms and legs clearly intact, so I turned up the volume and heard about the heroics of this amazing young man, overcoming his physical disabilities to pursue his dreams. Cut to commercials and back and there he was on the defensive line, in the scrum, playing football with the varsity. The kid had no arms and no legs, just stumps less than a foot in length. He crawled through mud between the left guard's legs to tackle a running back behind the line of scrimmage. He was a hero, and I was watching from the sidelines.

I felt meaningless and soft, like a big cry baby with no accomplishments whatsoever. New York City had been a failure. Great theater, freezing cold, no protection, and as far as I knew we weren't even dating anymore. I wished I could do something heroic like Stumps on TV. And then, I fell asleep.

Life Lessons from Jonny November 5

Life is short. This much, I know. I also knew one guy who lived his long quiet life in the house he was raised in. He never married, never even moved out. It was big beautiful brownstone in Collegetown, the kind of place clearing an easy half million these days.

He taught school for a living. Put in his forty years and took retirement at sixty-two. So what was his life? He read books. Graded papers. Took walks. He strolled. He admired items in storefront windows but was parsimonious in his purchases. He never indulged. That was his life. That summer, his first in retirement, promised to be the beginning of a leisurely life.

But then, his neighbor, whom he knew well from their adjoining rose gardens, noticed she hadn't heard from him or seen him in a week. This was unusual because he was always around. "A homebody," as they say.

She noticed his cat started popping up around the backyard, even on her porch. Purring, maybe moaning. This was weird because the cat was an indoor pet.

So she got the big idea. She broke into the place to see what was what. For a civilian, it was surprisingly easy work. With a screwdriver and knife, she went to work on a first-floor window frame and was inside in twenty minutes. She scoped out the entire first floor, but she couldn't find him anywhere. She walked up the hardwood stairs, and, again, she couldn't find any traces of the man. The queen-sized bed was made, nice and neat, and she wasn't sure of what to make of this detail. She had her own problems, her own busy life, and it was tempting to lie down on the clean sheets and take a rest. But this lady was on a mission, so she returned to searching the house.

So onto the third floor, and again, no sign of life. Walking back downstairs, she had an idea to check the rear shed, between the kitchen and the backyard.

Sure enough, he was in the shed. Collapsed and lying on his side, an open bag of kitty litter was on the floor near his right hand. This was his life's last act, changing the cat's litter. What's worse was that his face was lying in the old litter, and the shed stunk of the stuff. She called the police and fire department right away. When they got there, they told the neighbor that the man still had a faint pulse. He was alive. So she watched them work with care and bring in a stretcher. As gently as possible, they got him out of the house and into the ambulance. As they were lifting him, she saw that the entire left side of his face was stained with cat shit, and bits of piss-stained kitty litter were stuck to his cheek. He was warm enough, possibly conscious, too, so the medical guys knew that he knew he'd spent his last days dying in cat shit. He was pronounced dead in a hospital two days later. They say it was a stroke.

That's it. A life. Death in the shit.

Chapter 8
In Camden with Jonny November

I woke late in the morning, lonely and sad. A quart of coffee did little to lift my spirits. It'd been two weeks since I'd heard from Melony, and the only positive thing I could think of was that we were far removed from freezing temperatures, and winter seemed to be on the run at last. The cold had finally waved the white flag. I was thankful for the promise of warmer weather and knew that in no time we'd be regularly past sixty degrees.

I walked half a mile to my most recent parking space where I found Auggie plopped on the hood and drumming the beat to "Start Me Up" by The Rolling Stones. I drove a 1989 four-speed manual Tercel, its original green greying and pockmarked with rust, but I winced each time his palms slammed down on the car. We exchanged pleasantries and hopped inside. For several minutes, I twisted the key in the ignition and pumped the gas, before turning to Auggie to tell him that my car wouldn't start.

"Jeez, what the fuck?"

Auggie cursed the fifteen-year-old machine. I flipped the hood, so I could pretend I knew something about cars, something other than the fact there was almost no way I'd be able to afford to get this one fixed.

When Auggie saw it was hopeless, he calmed down. "No worries, Michael. We'll take the trolley and walk to the high-speed line."

Thirty minutes later, on the underground platform that led to New Jersey, I told Auggie about Stumps.

"You expect me to believe that?"

"Auggie, I saw the footage, on the television. *Nightline*."

"Professor, you're the one telling me not to believe everything I see in the media."

"But this is a personal interest story, not news about the war on terror."

"You think they don't create those feel-good, positive stories only for one reason?"

"And just what would that reason be?"

"It's to humiliate us. Make us feel like even larger loads of crap because we haven't accomplished anything."

For humiliated man, he'd come to the right place. Alas. It was hopeless. Yet Auggie had a valid point. Had I seen what I'd seen? If so, why had I seen it? Because big media instructed that this would be viewed? Could I have fallen asleep before *Nightline* and dreamed the impossible? Maybe Auggie was right. Stumps was a corporate media gift meant to make me feel worse about my failure chasing tail and lack of academic advancement.

The high-speed line arrived, and I waited for others to board, so I could know that I had not merely imagined the train's arrival. Then, I recognized that I could be hallucinating not only the train but also these fellow travelers, and I had no idea of how or why I should or should not trust what I saw. So then, with the raw data, the empirical evidence, in such doubt, all my not-so-clever ideas seemed to be worth no more than a pile of horse poop.

"Professor, get on the train. Quick! The doors are gonna close."

Just like that, once more, Auggie saved me from my intellectual self. He grabbed and shoved me between the closing doors, and into the car of a moving train. I was even failing boarding the train, a big fat F grade that could result in flunking out of life itself. I took a deep breath, and vowed to overcome all this futility. After all, I was an educator. One who could make a difference.

* * *

After the high-speed line crossed the Delaware River, Auggie and I shuffled off at the first stop, and we were soon immersed in such extensive poverty that it made me feel slightly successful as a self-supporting studio-apartment dweller. In Camden, the poor were set against a *mélange* of renewal and decay. On the main shopping thoroughfare, unoccupied first floors were common, and too many storefronts had crazing in the window displays if the glass was still intact. A waterfront aquarium catered to children of breeding affluence just minutes from this shabby downtown full of dollar stores for dead souls and broken folks, the pillaged and plucked of urban America. All the signs and symptoms were here, from lack of work and liquor stores to shopping-cart drifters and garbage-can sifters. Almost all the people were shaded tan and brown and maroon and black, but skanky skinny white girls in hot pink miniskirts and pumps stood out from the dollar-store crowds. They were "working girls," no doubt, but it was hard to see who had cash to pay for services, either *à la carte* or *prix fixe*.

Folks moved slowly, many seemingly dying ahead of time, but still lugging their belongings over their shoulder or pushing them forward as if it were some Sisyphean mountain they were endlessly climbing and not merely urban America's obstacle course of broken glass and mangled concrete. It was Nietzsche who said that the greatest civilizations sprung from the greatest mixing of races, but I had doubt he meant precisely this caste of middling hues mingling in the dollar-store checkout lines. Then I came to the more familiar doubt that I could know exactly what Nietzsche meant about much of anything at all.

In the distance, we saw the Delaware River, brownish blue, cleaner than the Schuylkill perhaps, but in no condition to swim in. My mind wandered to an image of George Washington and his defense of a young country founded on philosophical principles—Rousseau, Locke, and Paine and all the rest of that idealistic crap that did nothing to alleviate the suffering souls of contemporary Camden, New Jersey. I imagined the thousands of poor "American" soldiers, sockless and freezing their asses off in New-World winter, while King George was getting his wiener waxed by English handmaidens. Across the ocean, their own fearless American George, home for the holiday, had a slave girl by the hindquarters in a plantation outhouse in old Virginia.

I imagined that just as it had been done to Auggie, both Georges were, when occasion presented itself, doing it to little revolutionary boys while teenagers a few years older were fighting for freedom, half-frozen and sleeping in tents sixty miles up from Camden, now historic Washington Crossing. Tired of chicken, then order the duck. Cluck. Visions like these made me wonder how I ever got snagged in the trap of teaching this mind-fuck crap. Academic philosophy had no purpose, no relationship to cold, miserable reality. There was that fascist jackass Heidegger, scribbling his gobbledygook, and all of his imitators, and millions outside the stone keep, begging for table scraps from a dehumanizing, frostbitten world. Enough!

We wound our way down the grey, blue rusted steps to the ground level. Auggie led me through the crowd of the shopping district and down an alleyway and across the street and around a corner until we were only a few hundred yards from the entrance to Jonny's trailer park. I didn't know such places existed in northern cities, but as we walked through the maze of aged, dilapidated, water-stained trailers, it became evident that our poor could live in conditions best associated with displaced Katrina survivors and southern rednecks or "trailer trash." I had never known that there were trailer parks in Camden. Now I knew.

Jonny November answered the door on the second knock. He was taller and thinner than I'd thought he would be. He ushered us in, and with his cane he directed us to sit on a puce corduroy sofa that looked like it'd fought in battle before the Vietnam War. The cans of V8 he served were warm, but the Oreos with banana-flavored "stuf" were rare. From his perch on a maroon leather love seat, he told us you could only purchase them in Japan but refused to divulge how the cookies had arrived at his trailer. He let his can of V8 rest at the end of his thigh where the right leg disappeared. It appeared to be perfectly balanced, as if Jonny had practiced this maneuver many times before.

We sat and sipped and said almost nothing. Finally, Auggie broke the ice.

"Say, Jonny, where's your can?"

Jonny got up, went back to the kitchen, and returned with an old coffee can. When he handed it to Auggie, I could see it was rusty at the rim.

"What's this for?"

"That's the can I use."

Auggie looked perplexed. He stared at the can.

Was he uncomfortable due to the lack of indoor plumbing or the fact that the can was shared?

"I had to shut off the water after they raised the property taxes. My disability's no good. Certified by three different therapists and with the leg here," and Jonny raised his missing piece high, "and I haven't worked in nine years and two bucks over a K note is all they let me spend each month."

"Say, Jonny, how come you get twelve hundred a month, another guy gets double that, and some other fellow only gets half? Ain't somethin' wrong with that?"

"That's America. I get over a grand because my disabilities are physical and some of it happened at work. Maybe your mental health was ruined by work, but we don't acknowledge mental health in this country. Michael can tell you that much."

Was he was looking for leadership from me because I taught college classes? I wasn't sure. I was drawing a blank until I remembered my midnight television.

"Late last night, after I hung up with Auggie, I saw this young guy without arms and legs playing high school football. All he had were stumps, and he's playing in the game."

"Sorry, Jonny, but Michael can't help yapping about this big success."

Jonny interjected, "See, superheroes like that make it harder for all of us. I can't even keep water running to take a proper shit, and studies show two per day is normal. Not only am I screwed by the state, but there are hundreds of thousands on the waiting list for disability benefits. I'm lucky I get what I get. There's folks who worked their whole lives, had some bad luck, and Uncle Sam's minions tell them to take a dump in the alleyway or behind a tree in the park."

Jonny was making sense, so I added, "I have all my arms and legs, and I don't feel like I've accomplished anything at all." I resisted blurting out about losing Melony or smearing poop all over classroom linoleum.

Auggie looked agitated. "It just fucks me up even more when I see him waltzing around in his luxury style, and we're suffering without heat and running water. Just what the fuck is wrong with this country!"

"See who?"

"My stepfather."

"Whoa." Jonny November glanced at me, but I wasn't sure I knew why.

"He was swishing by, walking with that man, the guy he's afraid to call his lover. I don't know if he recognized me or not, but he ignored me."

We all knew about the stepdad. A molestor. A rapist. Sodomizer. Auggie's "homophobic asshole" who fucked him over and got the inheritance when Auggie's mom got cancer. That's why Auggie had resolved to rob the bank—to get the dough back from his evil stepdad. He thought the money belonged to him.

"Oh, how I'd like to get even with him."

And then it came. *It was my idea.* As soon as it came out, it felt weird, out of character, inviting and terrifying all at once. These mixed feelings comingled with sarcasm and regret, but once expressed the thought took a life of its own.

"We could kill him."

Auggie and Jonny both looked at me as if I was out of my mind. Maybe I was, but it didn't feel that way.

"He deserves it," I explained. "There's no justice. No fairness. No law to protect the innocent. Let's kill your stepdad, Auggie. I got nothing and want to do something that matters before I leave this shithole."

They looked at me aghast, so I clarified, "This life, not this trailer. Jeez."

"You're crazy, Professor. Don't you think I never thought of that?"

Jonny looked like he was meditating.

"You know, I've been reading about police layoffs. I've heard cities are bankrupt and violence is down anyway. Stop and frisk ain't just to cop a feel. It's no pickle tickle. It works."

"What's your point?" asked Auggie.

"I didn't mean it like that, Auggie. I'm just saying that maybe Michael has a good idea here. That guy fucked you pretty good—the ass, the mouth, the wallet. . ."

"Dammit, Jonny. I don't need a recap."

"I'm just saying, Michael is right. If it were a just world, your stepdad would be dead by now for all the evil he did to you and you'd have his money. And I'm getting tired housewife tits and ripping off televisions. I want more."

"I got a record. If the cops find out I'm in on it, I'm screwed."

"Me too, Auggie, but at least for you there'd still be mitigating circumstances. Michael and I would face more severe penalties. But fuck it. I wish I could feel like I'm making a difference. I want action!"

"No way we can pull off this kind of caper and get away with it," exclaimed Auggie. "End of story!"

But Auggie had a sly smile on his face. That smile told me the story wasn't over.

* * *

Back on my couch that night, I returned to *Nightline*. The episode took me far away to Siberia. An ordinary Russian, who had been a mere traffic cop, was laid off and soon after had a vision that his was the word of God. Now he was living on top of a mountain with thousands of followers. The television babe sent to interview him was the smart hottie *par excellence*. She appeared packaged from the material world—perfectly made up and dressed in suitable fashion. For a moment, I caught myself wondering if this new emperor—he called himself Vissarion—had been granted the gift of foundation for his rosy cheeks, the same way major media would cake it on for President Fern, the new guy, or the next one. They panned out to the view from Vissarion's mountain-top home, and the hills and forests looked green and peaceful. Once more, *Nightline* allowed me to see all I lacked.

I had arms and legs, and I wasn't even close to becoming a new messiah. I didn't even have a full-time job. Just a few courses a week to make me feel as if I was part of society.

The idea of killing Auggie's stepfather was positively insane. All killing was insane unless it was in immediate self-defense or state-sanctioned, right? But could it be any worse than walking into class with dog shit on my shoe? And eating cold leftovers from the classroom garbage receptacle? All in the name of radical approaches to the classroom, but indeed mainly for my own passive-aggressive efforts at freaking out the contemporary college undergrads? Was it jealousy or merely cheap thrills in the name of higher learning?

These kids hadn't yet fucked up their lives, and they presumably hadn't had someone fuck it up for them the way Auggie had had it done to him. That took me back to murder as social justice. By aiming to murder Auggie's stepfather, it wasn't like we were plotting revolution. There'd be no women and children murdered by the millions or dead Tutsis or Jews smeared across the grass or piled in a ditch.

No, this was simply killing a dirt bag who deserved it. I was never one for any Leopold and Loeb misinterpretation of Nietzsche's superman, but this murder would be just revenge.

Life Lessons from Jonny November 6

You want a car? OK, I understand. We all wanna ride.

Consider your options:

You could break your back working your whole life and pay for one with hard-earned dough left over from mortgages, food, kids, phones, wives, and utilities.

Or, you could steal the car and risk ten years for grand theft.

Or, you rent the car, pay by credit card, and never pay a cent.

You see they can throw you in jail for stealing the car but unpaid credit cards still aren't a jail crime in most states. It's like my Dad used to say, "The bank ain't your friend. The bank's just the one who lets you pretend you own the house until they decide the party's over and evict your ass. You get left with a bankruptcy."

Don't give me that bull about life being wasted if a guy's nothing by age thirty. The truth is, that's just the end of the first debt burden for most guys—loans for college, grad school, bad deals on random shit, crap a hot chick talked them into. Or maybe just jumbo, subprime mortgages. Another reason to secure an automobile in proper fashion.

So for most guys, thirty is when it all begins, or maybe thirty-five. When you finally get a chance to show what you can do. It's the same for guys in the slam. I know veteran criminals who are successful leaders in their field—chimney sweepers, master locksmiths, credit-card fraud millionaires—and these guys were nothing by age thirty. In fact, at that ripe young age, some of them had barely escaped their origins—working class or worse, stupid ghetto thinking about crime. They were still stuck in that mindset of the hard guy—you know, violence is the only answer, and I'll shoot this guy after he gives up the cash because I don't like his look. A blade or a piece, stuck in the belt, is going to get the job done. They hadn't even gotten to the point where they saw that the master thieves earned their take by outthinking, not outmuscling, the other guy—the suits in charge, the straights, bedroom-community dwellers, etc. These guys began their real education at age thirty. It wasn't until fifty that they made their first big score without getting pinched. I kid you not.

So you got time. You'll be okay.

A buddy of mine likes to say that life ain't over at age forty; in fact, that's when it begins.

Chapter 9
Uncle Sam's Blood Money

But the thought of murder, like most others, drifted away, and I resumed my daily grind. Taking attendance and grading papers. Designing lessons. Lecture or discussion. In class, expounding upon the poverty of philosophy, or at the very least the philosophy of *my* poverty. Making a jackass of myself in front of undergrads so certain they wouldn't wind up like the sloppy joker in front of the room.

One afternoon while strolling to the street corner after classes, in the middle of my muddled thoughts on philosophy, Auggie, humanity, murder, et al., I spied a thick wad of bills. I was in a crowded area, but everyone was headed in their own direction, a myopic herd of pedestrians avoiding each other's eye contact. The money was miraculously unguarded, under the sunlight and in open view. So I approached, making sure not to alter my rate of progress, and stamped my foot down on the found cash. I reached in my pocket for my pen and tiny notebook so that to passersby, it could appear as if I was examining some directions or scribbling an idle or important thought or two—one of those lightning bolts that came as a rare surprise and would be lost forever if I didn't write it down. Then, after a few minutes, I stooped down, as gracefully as a man in decline can, grabbed the cash, slid it between notebook and palm and suavely pocketed it all.

A few blocks later, I found a coffee shop. Knowing my pocket was full, I ordered a large with lots of goodies—cream and mocha and cherry and more. My constant regulars—milk and two sugars—were far too proletarian for my philosopher-king tastes.

Seated outside, at the grate tables, I took out my notebook and collected my thoughts on the found cash. Yes, this before counting it, because I wanted to assert that I was so cool, and yet, I also didn't want to draw attention too soon. I found myself jotting down notes about *karma*, a concept I thoroughly disbelieved and how finally the money in my case could mean that I was cursed—say, if some drug-dealing tough guys were to hunt me down, claim ownership, and demand interest payments.

But the natural next move was to determine what to do with the dough.

Stashing it in the bank and adding it to the other nineteen-hundred dollars—enough to know I would never have enough—was briefly introduced to my brain and quickly dismissed. Forget "buy and hold" and "stay the course" and all that financial-advisor baloney. The stock-market rollercoaster was an absurd place to "save" cash. Ed Saferi, in corporate communications all across town, had already smiled and told me that the fees for my funds were higher than the dividends. Although I didn't know what this meant, it sounded bad and I still hadn't bothered to check out his advice about moving my meager amounts to a more consumer-friendly environment.

No, that was bullshit and the philosopher's fate no doubt was to remain among the people. It was not to waste away in any sort of luxury of a private retirement facility or home for the materially advantaged. No, my destiny, if I were lucky, was to find a cheap, pay-by-the-week motel near Miami and deconstruct the margaritas with a friendly Cuban cigar. Yeah, Jonny said we'd only need a cigar, and a weekly visit to the Asian parlor for all services rendered if we were fortunate enough to have functioning parts or funds for little blue pills at that late stage.

Saving dough would never do. And that was when I counted it.

I cautiously pulled the wad from my pants pocket. Sneakily, warily, I kept the bills well below the grate table. I paused. I took a deep gulp of air. I held them clasped between my hands and my lap. I neither sensed nor saw that anyone was watching me; in fact, only a few pedestrians or coffee sippers were out and about.

Then I noticed a young woman. She was riding on a coaster bicycle, an older model, and she had some dust on her cheeks. She wore a brown and beige peasant skirt and a peach spaghetti-strap top. Her hair was a swirl of orange and purple, but even without make up, she was attractive, perhaps just a notch below Melony if properly sanitized and packaged for mainstream consumption. There was a woven basket stapled to her handle bars and an orange milk crate behind her seat. Inside the milk crate, with a furry head just above the rim, sat a tiny mutt. It was a calico, a white dog with brown and black splotches. Part terrier, most likely.

The young woman, perhaps a peer of Melony's at the other school in Collegetown, rolled up to the garbage receptacle, stopped, arched her back, and stretched her arms high to reveal fluffy brown patches under her arms. The healthy hair growth of the independent mind. She then leaned over and down, and sifted for buried treasure.

She reached in and pulled out various Styrofoam packages and other containers. I saw her lift up one such package, dig beneath it, and grab half a cheeseburger. She then proceeded to take a small bite, chew, and savor the meat. Despite classroom theatrics with post-garbage pizza, I winced. She looked uncertain, so she took another bite. Swallowed. *Ugh.* Satisfied, she opened it up, removed what appeared to be the remains of a beef patty, and fed it to the dog. As small as he was, nevertheless, he gobbled the grey brown meat all in one gulp.

It is then that I took action. I pocketed my own findings and approached the woman. For the moment, it was my fate to play not only the hypocrite, but also the altruist.

"Say, miss."

She turned and regarded me with suspicion.

"I couldn't help but notice you were digging for gold there."

"Dude, I wasn't invading the nasal caves. It's your kind, middle-aged men, the almost incontinent crowd, who hunt for green squiggles and yellow worms."

Er, okay, the wrong foot I had decidedly approached upon. Some clarification seemed to be in order.

"What I meant was that I saw you there with the garbage, and I wanted to offer you this."

I extend my hand holding a ten-dollar bill.

"Dude, fuck you. This is about a sustainable world, not Uncle Sam's blood money. Why you capitalist scum, I reject your paper. Fuck off."

For good measure, she flipped me the bird.

But I was drunk on found cash, so as she moved to shove off, I dropped the tenner into the straw basket attached to the handlebars.

Five full peddle rotations later, she saw what I'd done, screamed like she'd been violated, and did a pinky-to-pointer, two-finger grab of the bill, and tossed it out of the basket. Disgust reddened her face, and her dog yelped in my direction.

I watched the ten-spot drift and turn in my direction and gently descend to the asphalt. At this point, not caring if anyone was looking, I briskly walked into the street, picked it up, and returned to my seat.

Back with my dark triple shot, extra whipped cream on top, I sorted through the bills. The retrieved ten. A fiver. Three ones in a row and then a full house—three twenties and two hundred dollar bills! Three more tens after that and a single two-dollar bill in back. Three hundred ten dollars even. The tens and hundreds were as crisp as Rice Krispies fresh from a sealed box, but all the others were as worn as I was, and a sole single looked like it had been running companion to a triathlete in a tropical storm.

I heard Auggie's voice, "Not a bad grab for ten minutes of work," was how Auggie would describe it to me no doubt.

Just like that, as if I'd conjured him, from above I heard his familiar yelp: "Hey, where d'ya get all the cash?"

I looked up and there he was. All I could think to do was raise a finger to my lips, indicating quiet, and in a low voice, "Have a seat."

I motioned to the opposite chair, and he plopped down at once.

"I found it on the street."

"How d'ya do that?"

"It was on the corner. I stepped on it. No one passing by said a thing to me. Then, I checked high above and all over for candid camera. Nothing high, nothing low."

"Sharp thinkin', Professor." Auggie nodded approvingly.

"So, I waited. Occasionally darting my eyes about to see if anyone looked as if they were looking for money. Or as if they were looking at me."

"And then what?"

"I bent down, grabbed the cash, stuck it deep in my pocket, found this place, ordered a drink, and sat down here."

"So how much d'ya get?"

"Three hundred dollars." *Why did I round down?*

"Not a bad grab for two minutes' work."

I thought to myself, here is poor Auggie, alone in the world, with little backing him up—no family and not much in the bank. And so I made my offer.

"Say, Auggie, I'd like you to have this."

I reached over with twenty dollars.

"What's this?" Auggie eyed the bill with suspicion.

"I'd like to share. I really just got lucky, and I'd like you to have some of it."

I watched Auggie stare down the twenty. When he spoke again, he said, "How about seventy?"

"I beg your pardon."

"Thanks for the deuce, Prof, but hit me up with five fingers."

"Wha...?"

"Fifty dollars. You know my deal, always short on dough. I could use a few bills."

"You want me to give you seventy dollars!? That's a quarter of the total."

"Yeah. But don't ya see the significance? It's a celebration of our friendship. Male bonding, dig?"

Dug I did not, but I felt my suspicion turn to apprehension and then to pensiveness before final acquiescence.

Auggie sat silently and waited until finally, I peeled off two more twenties and a ten and handed them over. He added them to the first bill, bent them over, and slid them into his wallet.

Unless I was hallucinating, I saw him push them snug against a few twenties resting warm and unspent.

He smiled and winked. "You're an easy mark, Professor."

I felt like I'd just been had, but hadn't a clue as to how to get the money back.

"Pardon me, sir. Would you care to have your picture drawn?"

Abruptly ending my financial considerations was a man who appeared a bit scruffy, aged around the edges, with some greying settlers in the beard.

"Ah, a portrait," said Auggie, calmly, as if he expected such a man with such an offer to show up at any point. "That's quite flattering. So how much, Leroy?"

Auggie's way with African Americans was rather distasteful. It dated back to his days at the home for abused boys—a home where he had told me many times that he was the only white kid, the only Jewish kid, and as such, subject to constant harassment and abuse.

Despite the dated pejorative, the man smiled and responded pleasantly, "Only five dollars a head."

"You got a bargain, sir. It just so happens that it's payday for the gentleman seated across from me, so we'll take two."

Without blinking an eye, he turned to me, and said, "You can swing this one, right?"

I had half a mind to reach over and rap Auggie on the ear, or even grab for his pocket, but alas, I was the reasonable, employed fellow, not some barbarian rummaging at will and eating from the garbage. So what else could I do but remove the bills once more, unfold and sort, gather two fives, and hand them to the pen-and-ink specialist hovering over us.

The man smiled, graciously accepted, and asked only that we avoid staring directly at him as he worked. He needed our faces at an angle.

He found a seat two tables down, removed his supplies from his bag, and measured us, using his fingers and pen.

I tried to strike a bit of a pose while Auggie kept yapping.

"Hey, look at that chick with the dog."

"Where?"

"She's on a bike. Over there."

I turned and sure enough, it was the crusty punk, riding back to us. This time, her yelping mutt was in the straw basket. As she approached, I saw that the orange milk crate in back now held a huge orange container of national-brand liquid laundry detergent. Food from the trash was fine for dog and lady, but generic-label detergent wasn't good enough for her clothes. As she rode by and on with her concerns for all of us in the ecosystem, pillaging and polluting throughout the world, I couldn't help but pay attention to her long, wide rainbow-colored sneaker laces tied high at her ankles. They kept her feet snug in pink canvas high tops.

She back-pedaled to apply the coaster brake and stopped once more to sort through the garbage. When she found a suitable carton, she again took two nibbles of half-eaten sandwich—in this case, fish or chicken unless the beef had turned a sickly pale color—and gave the remains to her famished cur who gulped it down in one bite.

"Filthy bitch," muttered Auggie. "Someone ought to report her to a shelter for abused animals. Doesn't she realize that both homeless homeys and Ivy Green frat boys like to piss in that garbage? Once I saw case-quarter Leroy squat at the curb, and politely clean up by dumping his dump in the receptacle. A few days later, I saw a drunken sophomore climb on top of a garbage can and show off his balance to his brothers with a no-hands squat and crap."

Auggie went on about asshole frat boys and indigent Negroes, and moved on to dirty women and clean girls—the Cosmo-reading, fancy-thong kind—a false dichotomy no doubt, and despite how rudely I was treated when I offered ten, I was disappointed to hear Auggie exclaim on such things.

I was thankful when the artist returned, bringing with him two pen-and-ink drawings.

He handed us our portraits, and when I looked at my likeness, I saw a mixture of an older Richie Rich and a younger Karl Rove. In disgust, I shoved the sketch face down on the table while trying to smile politely. The artist was already grinning, in anticipation of praise, but all I could manage was a nod and muttered thanks.

"Nice work, Leroy," chirped Auggie. "You've thinned my face, given me hair—I look like Al Pacino after a chase scene. I like what you did with my stubble," and Auggie rubbed his ample 3 p.m. facial growth. "Say, Prof, let's see yours."

I handed over the portrait. Auggie glanced at me and looked down at the picture. Then, another glance at me, and down again.

"Chin's chunky, but not bad at all," he said.

I sipped my coffee in silence.

Life Lessons from Jonny November 7

Look at me. I'm missing half a leg, roughly an eighth of my body. So I'm half Jewish, but I'm thinking the Jew isn't perfectly distributed throughout my bones and blood. The brain isn't Jewish; in fact, I never did well in school. The nose? Only so-so. My gut flab? Maybe. But my legs? The good one is long and without much hair, hardly Jewish at all. So if the part I'm missing is more Jewish than the rest, that means I'm majority gentile. *Goyim*. And what does that mean? I don't know. But it's something to think about.

Even though Auggie is all Jew, I had to teach him America. They say Jews are good at America, but Auggie's parents weren't those Jews. He needed me for support.

So I taught him what I know. I taught him how to survive. I've known Auggie since he was a tiny kid. We lived in apartments across a narrow alleyway back then. These were brown brick buildings for townies or grad students. The occasional slumming post-doc or an almost professional or two in his field. The hookers and fags lived east of the river back then.

Our windows were so close, two yards apart, that I could spy on his naked mother—fantastic tits, firm behind, no lie—so as a teenager, I'd try to get over to their place whenever I could. I think Auggie's Mom knew the deal, so she knew I owed her one. That's where the childcare came in. When his grandmother wasn't with him, I'd wind up taking care of Auggie after school. Not only did Mom neglect her son, but she was a cheapskate too. She'd pay me fifty cents an hour, sometimes less or nothing at all.

Yeah, so she was cheap and her boyfriend beat the hell out of both of them and fucked him bad, but Auggie never told me this shit when he was little. He was a young adult when he told me what happened—you know, specifics—but I always knew there was something going on. Because you see the signs. Black and blue. Moody behavior. Sulky and sad. I may look like a tough nut, but even I was shocked at the extent of what he told. Gruesome things. Disgusting things. Leather belts and locked closets. Stuff you get killed for in prison if the homeys in the yard find out what you're in for.

But back to America, and why I love it, is that even a kid like Auggie can overcome these obstacles. That's the amazing thing. It ain't like this in other countries. Over there, some places even criminalize the abused. Wives in Pakistan? Kids in India under obscure cult religions?

No chance. Nada.

But with a little mentoring, Auggie wound up okay. Did you notice that he's a self-supporting adult? I set him up so it could happen for him. I told him what's what in the land of the selfish and home of the Great Recession, long depression, aging workforce, what have you. We've all been burnt—by capitalism, racism, the white man, the Jew—yeah, you and me, right?—all of it, more or less—but we make do and subsist. And we can do okay, too. Yeah, America's one big Ponzi scheme, the rich on top and raking it in, but that doesn't mean a little guy can't survive as long as he can understand the system.

So I told Auggie there's a system, and there are rules in place. I helped the kid see the long and short of what's at stake. How to survive or subsist, not exactly beating the system but enduring from within it. Not the way the bullshit con artists selling twenty-dollar paperbacks and five-hundred-dollar exclusive seminars teach in self-help and personal-finance scams, but the real way—the combined graft and mooching required to survive in the land of plenty and its crippling, but generous, welfare state.

Chapter 10
The Hug

A couple days later, we were in the supermarket. Jonny, Auggie, and me. Jonny was going on and on about America the Ponzi scheme and beating the system while Auggie instructed on the ways of the pick-up artist.

"You see, Prof, ya gotta get the tapes."

"The tapes?"

"How to Pick Up Women."

"On DVD?"

"Well, actually, just voice recording is okay. You can buy it online and download."

"Buy it?"

"Yeah, it's only four hundred bucks."

"Four hundred!?" I must have looked aghast.

"But that's no biggie. You find another guy, and you split it with him. The tapes have everything you need to know."

Still burning from the Melony disaster, I wasn't sure I needed to find another girl.

I looked over at Jonny who'd removed the biggest bag of pretzels from the Herr's display. They were supersized nuggets. He broke open the package, palmed a huge handful, and began stuffing his face. He made another big grab before placing the open bag back on the shelf.

Chewing with his mouth open, he said, "Sounds like a scam to me, Auggie. Some sleazeball who scored once or twice back in the day—make that back in the decade—is ripping off lonely guys who can't buy a date. He's getting poor pent-up saps to drop four bills on how-to bullshit."

"Jonny, what would you know about picking up chicks? I haven't seen you with a girl in years."

"Yeah, but that's because I've got other priorities."

"Don't blame your years in the desert on your jail time."

"I meant I'm focused on this thing." Just as he said this, Jonny had just popped open a can of salsa con carne and broken a bag of tequila and lime tortilla chips, so it was hard to tell if his priorities were anything other than the food in his face.

"What thing?"

"This thing with your stepdad, Auggie. Michael's big idea. This is the plan. You want a tortilla?"

Auggie and I nod, "No," and proceed to watch Jonny slam the last handful home.

"We'll rob him, too, to make it look like a robbery gone bad."

"Great idea, Jonny. He's loaded." Auggie turned back to me as if only to shut Jonny up. "Let me let you in on a little secret. You know 'The Hug'?'"

"What hug?"

"The goodbye hug, the hug you get if you've been warm and entertaining. Chatty but no diarrhea of the mouth."

I could say that although it wasn't my lot in life to receive such alms on a regular basis, or at all, I knew the hug he spoke of. I'd witnessed it a thousand times—always seemingly the ugliest brutes and pimply savages on the receiving end of these hugs from kind, cute young women. What I was witnessing right now was Jonny November in the breakfast-meat section of frozen food, eyeing the scrapple, bacon, and sausage.

"Yes, I think I know it."

"Wha-da-ya mean, ya think you know? Either know you know or you don't know. Forget all that known unknown bullshit."

"Okay, Auggie, I admit it. I don't know the hug. But we're in a supermarket."

Jonny put down the two scrapple packages he was sniffing—Amish pork versus kosher turkey—and interjected, "When Auggie knows something, he likes to emphasize that point."

"Jonny, go back to your breakfast *treif*, unless you want to learn the secret to the hug." Auggie paused to observe three girls in shorts walk by. I was surprised when he didn't forget us and follow after.

"I can't believe I'm giving both of you the goods for free. I should be charging top dollar for this content."

"Just go ahead, wise guy. Give up the hug."

Auggie flipped Jonny the bird, but then continued.

"The key to the whole thing is hands on the hips. Most guys, when they move in to hug, they place their hands on the torso or the back. But ya gotta go lower, like so. Hey, watch this—"

With his mouth full of tootsie roll and graham cracker mush, Jonny turned toward Auggie's incoming prey. My eyes followed too.

"Hi, Elisa!" Like a trained professional in his field, Auggie moved right in for the hug. I watched as he received a generous peck on the cheek as he placed his dirty mitts on the hips, right at the waistline of this "Elisa," young enough to be his daughter, even a granddaughter in several counties and continents. She didn't flinch at all, and if I'm not mistaken, I saw her cheeks darken a shade of red. Rosy. She smiled.

As Auggie chatted up his lovely, I turned back to search for Jonny. I spotted him yards away from fruits and vegetables, but he held a green organic banana at waste level, and he was positioning it at various angles by his left pants pocket. Was he measuring his unit? When he saw me staring, he placed the banana on a shelf of canned soups and walked over to observe.

"Odds are one in five he bangs this broad, but if he winds up in a relationship, there's a chance he won't want to go through with the thing."

"The thing?"

"Our thing. The thing we have."

"You mean the plan?"

Jonny nodded. I knew what he meant even if it wasn't clear we had anything at all. The sex could distract Auggie, take his mind off his misery and thirst for revenge.

Meanwhile, Auggie had produced the magic phone and after two more minutes of conversation, he had the digits stored in his cellular device.

Chapter 11
On the Changing Station!?

A few days later, pacing through the supermarket, I peered around each bend expecting to find Auggie. But alas, he was not at home. And so I got lost in contemporary packaging. In the ice cream section, I came upon the old king, Häagen-Dazs. Peering closely at all the pints, I saw what I took to be another capitalist attack upon the American spirit. Häagen-Dazs had reduced their "pint size" to fourteen ounces. What thieves! Those corporate fuckers. Then, I saw it in a new light. They were in fact, saving fat Americans from further clogging their arteries and inflating their spare tires. Was it altruism, pure and simple, charging more to fight our national burden of high caloric intake? Was it the company's efforts, by any means necessary, to save the health of a people? Nah.

Lost in my discursion on illusion versus reality in consumer packaging, who should appear but Auggie—and with Melony!

She was smiling, and I could tell she'd been giggling.

"So I says to the *schvartze*, I'll tell ya what. I'll make a deal. If you don't want two for twenty I can get you three for fifty, and I'll throw in half a watermelon and a bucket of drumsticks. How about that? And he looks at me like I'm an angel sent down from heaven to save his wallet. And there I am, raising the price!"

Melony liked what she heard. Auggie had tapped her funny bone. It confirmed all she knew about welfare, food stamps, and *their* wasteful spending in the Wawa, where the poor child had been forced to work due to the absence of her father.

"Oh, heh," she giggled when she saw me, and sort of moved in my direction but then leaned back toward Auggie. *Hmm.*

"Anyway, I've got to get to work. Thanks, Auggie. That makes me feel a bit better." She smiled slightly and giggled at me. "I'll call you later," she says to me and expected me to believe it.

There I stood, left with Auggie. In less than a minute, conversation confirmed what I feared.

"You fucked her?"

"Yeah," He answered, sounding insulted, as if he couldn't believe I doubted him.

"How?"

"Back-end deals only, boss. Like I told ya. I practice what I preach."

"But I just introduced you. When did you arrange it? Where did you go?" *Exclusive-brokerage contracts in bed?*

"Follow me, Professor."

I was in stunned disbelief as Auggie guided me past the frozen vegetables, beyond an open door, and into an area with his and her restrooms and a water fountain.

"Right here? In the hall?"

"Nah, chief. Relax. They gotta a family room with a changing table."

"On the changing table!?" I imagined Auggie raising and lowering her pink bebe shirt and panties.

"Not exactly, Prof. We were standin' up. A girl can just throw herself down and lean on it. It helps if you have a pillow."

"Whah," was for the moment all I could manage.

"It ain't a score, if it's not backdoor. Remember what I taught ya?"

I was flabbergasted. "How could you do that?"

"She threw me a look like she wanted to. What was I supposed to do?"

"You were supposed to ignore it."

"But you know how it is."

"Auggie! I never even slept with her!"

"Jeez, Michael, you think I'm the kind of guy who feeds off his friends' sloppy leftovers? Do I look like I swim downstream from transient adjuncts? No way."

All of those walks through the supermarket, all of my listening to his complaints and laments and my plan to help him get revenge? And this is how Auggie repaid me?

I had to get out. I had to escape.

Life Lessons from Jonny November 8

You think this Malarkey business is bad? He earns six figures from state-sponsored football and the brain-trauma thrills aren't enough? So to ease the boredom, he rapes a dozen kids, give or take a few? Allegations of payments to boosters? Their donations paying for his little-boy ass and all that? I tell you that this is nothing.

Last year, they snagged a business professor at the College of Convertible Securities who was using craigslist to e-stalk and reality-rape the college's grads. Coeds only, as best I understand it. What's sick is that he would lure them in with sympathy. He'd bring up the student-loan topic and express "solidarity" for these "victims" of the "capitalist education complex." He'd get to know them a little, exchange e-mails over a couple weeks, plan a meeting, buy a decent dinner, then a few rounds of drinks. They'd meet again, more dinner, more drinks. Within a month, he'd go back to the girl's place and what would start out as consensual sex would end up as perverted insanity. The girl would wake up in the morning, no clothes on, and find sticky stuff on her chest and in her hair. She'd go to the bathroom to wash his juices off, and that's when she'd see it scrawled all over her body. He'd write her total nut, student-loan debt plus credit-card totals on her stomach in big letters: "57K had my thick tenured schlong whispering to her tonsils all night" or, "83 grand and uninsured swallowed load after load of my premium gold." This guy was a sicko. But finally, despite aliases and multiple e-mail accounts, they caught up to him. No, it wasn't with the help of Silicon Valley or the NSA. It was much easier and more legal than that. As it turned out, his choice of computers was limited to his local branch of the Free Library of Philadelphia. The cops got a warrant to trace the e-mails back to the servers. This guy was teaching Database Management, and his only disguise was dressing up as a bum, scrawling a phony name on the library sign-up sheet and using a public terminal.

What a fucker in a fucked-up world. The guy was grossing over six figures a year and looking to leave his slime and crust glued to the torsos and limbs of these girls. All they wanted was a quality education, and they wound up as his statistics. His victims. He took eleven girls before one came forward, and now they got him by the balls for a life bid. Serves his sorry ass right.

Chapter 12
Interrogations

I should have been happy enough to have her back, but I made the mistake of mentioning what Auggie told me on our first date since the break up. In the lobby of the movie theater, popcorn flying, Melony screamed in reply: "Are you crazy?"

"That's what he said." We had almost escaped to theater darkness, but now we were exposed under the pink and green neon of concession lighting. Crowds peered in our direction. They could care less about popcorn and cola at six bucks a serving. We were making a scene.

"I wouldn't do him on a changing table!"

"So he made the whole thing up?"

"Well. . ."

"Well, what?"

She gives me a sheepish grin like what Auggie said was partly true.

What had they done on the changing table? Leaned against it while he fondled and groped? A kiss? Did he get underneath her top or inside her proverbial pants?

"It's all your fault, Michael."

"My fault?"

"You don't do it the right way."

"We haven't done it yet," I replied.

"Not that 'it.'. Everything that leads up to it. You're awkward and too indirect. Then, you act faster than a fool, in the most clumsy fashion."

"Begging you to show up as planned is indirect?"

"You're clingy, too. See what I mean?"

It was clear that I was a teaching tool who couldn't win. In conversation, in bed, in the lobby, anywhere. But Melony was on a roll.

"In New York, you were so quiet. It was boring! And irresponsible. You didn't even pack protection!?"

She had me. I was an unprotected bore.

"So what happened between you and him?"

"He said he had to run an errand nearby."

"An errand?"

"So he walked me home."

A pile of bricks. Ugh! In the privacy of her own studio apartment. *It ain't a score if it's not backdoor.* I couldn't escape Auggie's words. I pictured him from behind, mounting Melony on her roommate's recliner. His stone-washed jeans at his ankles, her silver glitter skirts to her shoulders. Thrusting and ramming and breaking and entering!

"He thought the blindfold was cool."

"I thought the blindfold was cool."

"But you didn't act like it when I took it out. You just sat there, looking scared."

It was horrible to hear myself described this way.

"Most the time, you're so down on America and everything, not like Auggie. He's so optimistic. He makes me feel like we're moving forward."

I must admit we were standing still when she said this.

Melony continued. "I just can't take it. I needed something to relieve the stress."

"But Auggie's the one who says America is one big Ponzi scheme!"

"I know. That's what Jonny taught him, but Auggie convinced me he's not really like that." Melony grinned. Her face lit up every time she said *Auggie.*

"He has had all this adversity to overcome, but he always knows things can get better. He is so optimistic and inspiring! And once he cinches a couple more deals, he's going to live on a cliff in Malibu. He said I'd be able to walk to the beach."

Malibu? Cliffside property? The Auggie I knew was broke

and afraid of heights. I couldn't believe she fell for all of that. I couldn't believe Auggie said those things to her.

* * *

Later, I interrogated Auggie.

"What do you expect me to do, tell her that America is one big Ponzi scheme? You and I both know we're fucked, but with chicks and customers, you never say anything like that. You've seen me in action. You see how I work. Did you ever once hear me tell a girl that everything's a scam and hopeless?"

Auggie had a point.

"You've got your head so deep in your asshole, you've lost your ability to communicate with women. Philosophy has turned your brain to mush. Professor, you need some deprogramming. We gotta get you laid."

"I. . . ugh. . ."

"And not by paying for it!"

So that was that. Auggie had this way of resolving our disputes and making me feel as if he were on my side.

Chapter 13
All In

A few nights later, I was home alone. I was resting on my couch when the phone rang.

"OK. I'm in."

These were the first words I heard, but I knew it was Auggie's voice. For a brief moment, I didn't know what he was talking about.

"In where?"

"I'm ready."

"Ready for what?" A *ménage à trois* with Auggie and Melony? The thought came, loitered, and ran.

"Your idea, Prof. The job. To take him out."

I was still digesting the information about Auggie and Melony's indiscretion on or off the changing table. I wasn't in the mood for righting any of the ways in which Auggie had been wronged.

As if reading my mind, Auggie continued.

"Look, Prof. I'm sorry about Melony. I don't know what I was thinking. But what's done is done."

"Hmm," was all I could muster.

"I wasn't thinking. That's the truth. The truth is I'm never thinking. I'm like an animal." Auggie's voice quickened, as if he were running out of time. "I'm just an animal. Responding to urges. Grabbing at whatever I want. Whenever I can. Do you think I enjoy this? Being *me*, twenty-four seven—"

"Auggie—"

"I was fucked over by my mother and my stepfather. They beat me and raped me. Locked me in a closet and threw me in a group home. Twice, and both times full of *schvartzes* who smelled weakness and attacked. Beat me up and kicked me when down."

"Auggie—"

"Everything they'd been taught about the 'collective white man' was true for all I knew. It came to the surface in the juvenile pen. They took their vengeance out on me. I was accessible pale prey in the kiddy joint."

"Auggie—"

"No interruptin', Prof, okay? Let me just say this. My life has been hell, and you're one of the best things that's ever happened to me. Just knowing a guy like you. A smart guy with respectable work. Decent and humane and doesn't get too bent out of shape when I bang his girl by accident."

"Auggie—"

"You got ideas and I understand all you're trying to do for me. I'm sorry I banged your girl. She latched on. They do that sometimes, so I felt obliged to feed her the Hebrew hog. Yeah, I wish I could take it back. If I could stick my wocket back in my pocket, I would. I'll make it up to you anyway I can. I promise."

"Auggie—"

"But your idea. It's a good one. There's no justice anywhere. My bangin' her backdoor in the storage area for frozen foods is proof of that."

On the inside, I still fumed, but I let Auggie continue.

"So let's let bygones be bygones, but not forgive the unconscionable. I'm in. I want to whack the old man. My stepdad. Put him down with some so-he-can-rest-forever medicine. You and Jonny can loot that fucker blind. Pillage and plunder 'til you get your fill. But I'll tell ya one thing. I'm not gonna let you or Jonny get the kill shot. That's my job. Understand?"

"Okay, okay. I understand. But I've been interrupting because I have to go to the bathroom. I'll call you right back."

And I did.

Three weeks later we were back in Jonny's trailer, hatching the plan. Maybe the murder was my idle musing, my thinking out loud, but Jonny was the one who could teach us how to execute.

Part II

Prefatory Quotation:

"Man is not an island."
—Thucydides, *History of the Peloponnesian War*

Life Lessons from Jonny November 9

The key to a good stakeout is a clean car and a clean thief. I don't want you in a hot vehicle or something rented by a guy who's been touched. But I'm talking emissions, too. You don't want dirty fumes to draw attention to your automobile.

A dirty thief gets caught. A guy doesn't bathe, he's looking for trouble. In the stir, you walk around stinking up the joint, and the brothers take notice. Not good. The next thing you know, five of 'em force you into the shower and make you suck on much more than the suds. But no drop-the-soap jokes, please. Forced penetration is overrated. It's not fun, even if you're in a relationship. Even if you're the enforcer.

Hey, snap out of it. Remember that ninety percent of the guys on the inside are nonviolent offenders. Except for your rare shower-rape scene, violence comes from the state—cops, guards, soldiers, etc.—beating up old men and murdering innocent women and children. So most of these guys aren't going to force you into prohibited anal-cavity activity, pump you up in the back alley, whatever. Sorry I just played up that angle. That's the sensational bull surrounding prison, not the common reality.

But they are gonna scrub you down. Make you pray to the gods of Dial soap and Suave shampoo and genuflect afore the lord of Listerine. So if the guys on the inside are this aware of enforcing the no-funk rule, imagine what police and folks on the outside would do. Remember, the fuzz are looking for the easy write-up, a nonviolent offender they can pinch without showing steel and ammo. That could be you for offensive odor.

I knew a guy who was on a stake out for three weeks. He was watching for when the wife would be with her lover. Her old man wanted my guy to off 'em both while they were screwing and make the whole thing look like a lover's quarrel gone out of control. My guy is on the case, twenty-four seven, and he starts cutting corners. He doesn't trust nobody to sit in for him, so he doesn't have time to leave his car. No shower, no bath for weeks, so his funk is working overtime. He and his wheels become positively more pungent than an Indian kitchen. So, finally, what happens is that the mark catches a whiff.

In fact, it's the boyfriend, one of those effete types you're sure is behind door number two on the down low even though all you see him with is hotties and strumpets by day. The first time is in passing at the neighborhood delicatessen. My guy is ordering Genoa on pumpernickel, with pepper jack cheese and coarse ground Dijon, but his odor is outperforming his salami and mustard when the mark walks in. The mark only wants milk but is visibly disturbed by my guy's stench. He holds his nose with his fingers and suppresses a moan. When he receives his change, he dashes for the door.

It's within twenty-four hours the next time my guy returns to duty, but the wife and boyfriend are gone. No coming and going. No nothing. After a full day he reports this to the husband, and after two full days he goes right up to the house and slips inside. No occupants anywhere. They cleared out. Neither he nor the husband who hired him ever see the wife and boyfriend again.

How do I know it was the funk?

Get this.

The private investigator gets mailed to him a week later a package, and inside are deodorants and Italian colognes. No name. No return address. Simple as that. *Capisce?*

Chapter 1
MasterCard Marxists and 403b Feminists

Auggie and I had resolved our differences, and now we had a common purpose. With Jonny, we had a team captain, a take-charge guy who knew how to execute a crime. Organized by our leader, the plan took off.

I began to count soft green dollars. With Auggie and Jonny, I'd stumbled upon a way to escape the itinerant teacher's life. I'd be out of the adjunct game and on my way to the good life. Who could know how my life would change with this burst of moral and economically advantageous murder? I imagined a decent apartment and a quality pre-owned automobile. Would I even want Melony if I had the funds to attract some age-appropriate competition?

I knew my money wouldn't come from teaching in the fall. Between Melony and the plan, I'd forgotten to fill out my course-request form and had been abruptly shuttled to last in queue. There'd be no classes for Professor Vittinger unless multiple philosophers were to croak, catch mono, or land full-time gigs. None of which was likely, so it was my last lecture then, or at least my last class for the foreseeable future. I droned on about some crazy shit, ignored the precocious inquisitor in front who had a bad habit of sounding smarter than me, and collected the final essays. Then, I dismissed the class twenty minutes early and flipped the bird to the ceiling's corner security camera before heading out the door. I tossed the papers in an imposing green dumpster on my way to a faculty meeting on retirement planning. With our plans and Auggie's promise of a generous share in the winnings, I knew I'd be retiring soon, and I wanted to make sure my plans were in order. I was tired of taking philosophical positions on not working and looking forward to living it.

As I strode across campus, I was interrupted by loud yapping and yammering. I heard shouting commotion. I looked up and saw stinking, old Shalamov with his head and torso halfway out the window. He'd been an adjunct in philosophy since I was an undergrad, and he reeked of tobacco and unwashed wool suits. Oversized outfits he'd wear even during summer session. Now he was screaming at a woman below in the courtyard.

"I'm doing this!"

"You coward! You couldn't do it if you tried. Stick your head back in the classroom and teach those kids."

"Fuck you, bitch."

"Don't talk to me like that!"

"To hell with our marriage. It's been a disaster since day one. I've reached my limit!"

He was out on the ledge.

He was off it!

Head first.

Swan dive down.

Splat.

Blood and body parts all over the courtyard. A foot dangled from a leg with a femur high in the air, almost perpendicular to the thigh it belonged to. Arms hung limp from a torso as if the limbs hardly belonged to the body at all. I blinked twice, twisted away, but couldn't *not* look long enough before staring back again. I felt horror, delight, disgust, and pain, all the extremes that make us so.

His wife screamed. Her "help!" and moans and cries of "bloody murder" sounded like five hundred women, an abrasive cacophony of menstruation and genocide.

A few moved in to help her and attend to the body, but I had to press on. So I moved at a brisk pace, a fast walk faster than a jog.

Inside Antioch B, I was the last one seated in a room full of aged professors. It stunk of baby powder and urine. Stale decades and Depenz diapers. How could anyone reek of so much age and decay? The incontinent crowd had a way of ruining retirement for those of us who'd never see it. Or at least we'd never see it as it appeared in the television ads for annuities and long-term care for the affluent capitalist.

At the front of the room, a foppish fellow in fine threads, my age or so, was discoursing thusly:

"You see, you have several options as to where you can donate your organs. Three local hospitals are partnering with us, but we also have an eye on the international community. Organs can be safely transported and installed in impoverished bodies all over the world. Whether your fetish is for the Asian subcontinent or sub-Saharan Africa, we can help your organs make a difference overseas..."

As Mr. Fancy Pants droned on, I looked around the room at all the sad, meaningless, and soft professors. It was all desiccated vagina and limp, leaking cock. These were my would-be sort-of colleagues' privates were I to remain at Urban State.

It occurred to me that I was mistakenly attending a meeting only for regular faculty. Tenured faculty. Job-secure cows with retirement and dental. Nearly dead 403b feminists and MasterCard Marxists who would never think of me as a genuine colleague.

I quickly searched the room for any signs of unattended or rotten teeth. I felt a sinking inside, a realization that I was the sole man among them without a substantial retirement plan. Years ago, I'd opened a Roth IRA, and I'd managed to add a few hundred dollars every other year before growing weary of this plan to fund the retirement of my high-fee broker. After that, I resumed my weekend routine of throwing my contribution down on the bar. In Philly's dive bars, fifty bucks bought ten drinks, tip included, enough for an entire weekend for me.

But now it sunk in. I was broke and penniless and doing the dirty work for these hairy, disgusting Foucauldian cow fucks; they'd been sucking on the teat of tenure for thirty years or more while the marginal, aka me, kept the mongrel hordes at bay. In a flash of brilliance, I saw myself with a couple of AK-47s hidden under my trench coat and *Catcher in the Rye* in my back pocket. No, fuck that shit. I gave myself some Nietzsche, Marx, or some other philosopher dicked over by his academic department, and in his name, the revenge would be mine.

And then, I remembered the plan. The justice I'd soon be serving to Auggie's fucker of a stepfather. Compared to an actual molester, these tenured capitalists were innocent. What a bunch of redundant scholars and sedentary nobodies with nothing new to say, so they invented oppressions, juxtaposed jargons, smiled at each other, and pretended their lavish benefits and salaries were earned.

Their sins were financial—against entire generations of naïve parents and duped teenagers—but they hadn't shoved their dicks up any ten-year-old asses. Not to my knowledge, not typically, at least. Alas, I had to admit this much, and I winced at the hypocrisy of my envy. But nevertheless, they lusted after that next closed-end fund to supplement retirement, no doubt one that looked the other way when crimes against nature or children were committed in the name of their holdings. And always, at school, their hands were out, greedy fingers eager to take more money for fewer students any chance they could get. There was guilt here, too.

They deserved to be fucked with a little.

So when Fancy Pants stopped speaking and asked for questions, I stood and delivered:

"I say, why not go for broke? Why wait when you can end a life now and society as a whole can profit to such a great degree? What this man is talking about is only the tip of the iceberg. Let's face it. We get a lot more bang for our buck, and younger organs to boot, if we let go, say, a little earlier than expected.

"Voluntary euthanasia is at the cutting edge of retirement planning. Much more than a last lecture, it's a way to ensure that your organs live on to help others. Which, presumably, is why you chose education in the first place. To serve society. Perhaps for some time now, you waxed ambivalent over the capitalist educational model; perhaps you merely want out in a well choreographed, professional manner? Well, we can help. By choosing immediate release—i.e. death—and signing all of the proper documents, we can help your organs live on. You will be dead, but your liver and heart will be serving the poor and disenfranchised.

"Just imagine what we can do for your money once we've removed you from the picture. All those erratic choices you made about stocks and bonds, the anxiety of selling high and buying low. Well, dear madams and sirs, we can put an end to all of that. Oh, some of you will say that you were indexing all along and using a retirement tool to match your age, and well, yeah, that may be true, but do you seriously think we would let you in on the really good stuff? Of course not. We can make far more with your money on our own than we'd ever allow you to earn."

The old cows looked aghast, the ones who weren't half asleep or dreaming about dessert. My speech was an eye-opener to these professors accustomed to staring at mutual-fund prospectuses with their GLO eyes.

But I knew I was leaving, and held no truck with any of these "benefits," so as a final act, I cried, "Where do I sign?"

Fancy Pants produced papers, and I signed on the X everywhere it mattered. I saw to it that should they endeavor to track me down, they could turn me upside down, shake out my net worth, and donate my bloated bladder and failed spleen to the needy and darker-skinned classes.

Then, with alacrity, soon after I dashed from my retirement planning, I called Melony.

"I wanna fuck."

"Come over."

I could tell I was improving already.

Chapter 2
Where Sperm Earn Their Suicide and Eggs Play for Keeps

She smacked me off when I fought to ride the caboose, but then she kissed me on the cheek and whispered "missionary" in my ear. At first, she made me follow her up on the bunk bed, the one she shared with the roommate she hated. The balls of my toes ached on the round metal ladder steps, and I felt dizzy climbing toward heaven. At the top, I saw a single built for one coed unimpaired by a wanton, lustful older man. When she recognized that the bed wasn't large enough, I felt relief.

After our descent, we got to work on the carpet. It was time to add extra shag to the area rug. So we took off our clothes. Methodical more than romantic, but within a few minutes, the jacket was on and I'd snuck through the bushes to regions unknown. I was on the inside. Where it counted, where sperm earned their suicide and eggs played for keeps.

But the hidden corridor of power was too roomy. No friction possible. In the vast labyrinth, I felt near disappeared. To be frank, I didn't feel like I was inside anything at all. It was more like an empty room with missing walls. Some other guy had broken in a few weeks back and stolen the furniture. There was nothing to hold onto, nothing to rub against.

Was it me? I measured at least four and a half inches and up to five on a good morning, so even if below average, I didn't deserve to feel quite so small and humiliated. Was it the condom? It said "ultrathin" on the package and that it was made for her and his pleasure alike. Maybe she was unusually wide? I couldn't say, but I noted that she looked at me and smiled throughout the entire experience. By all appearances, it was great for her.

Finally, I tried as hard as I could. I pounded away until my lower back and abdomen ached severely. No doubt, a menacing scowl revealed itself on my face. By the time I finished, my lower abdominal muscles were so sore that I was certain I'd gotten a hernia. Or worse. It would have been easier to politely remove myself and rub it against her knee cap.

She was kind, even generous, in her understanding. "I wouldn't want to do it wearing a condom either, Michael."

Oh, really?

"A friend of mine told me it's like having sex with a glass of water."

For a moment, I found myself in philosophical deliberation on the best way to get inside the glass without spilling half the contents although I knew that wasn't the point.

We fell asleep in each other's arms, sort of, although in fact, as I dozed off, she got up to go to her computer, and my last memory was of her typing away furiously, no doubt an e-mail to a friend about how the old goat couldn't perform.

Where else was I to turn but to Auggie for discussing such sad affairs as sex without friction? Did I know anyone else who would speak of such things? Who would understand at all?

"See, that's what I've been tellin' ya, Prof. Ya gotta go behind the scenes. Sneak down the alley and enter through the rear. It ain't a score if it's not back door."

After that conversation, it became my obsession. I wanted to investigate the steamy underside, or other side, of sex with Melony. Sure, it bothered me somewhat that here, too, perhaps Auggie had been the trailblazer, and I would be following his lead. Lucky to arrive on the scene as a second and not a twenty-third. But I also wanted something better. Something different. And new. Tight. Like real fucking, or at least what everyone imagined that intercourse was supposed to be like.

Life Lessons from Jonny November 10

I once had it too wide, just like you say. Same exact scenario. See, what I didn't tell you about was the other time there was this girl on the porch. If she was twenty-one, I'm a stone-cold killer. Well, you know what I mean. Anyway, I hope she was over eighteen, and I know she had an infant on her hip when she opened the door. Thankfully, fast asleep.

Someone else had knocked or broken in or whatever before I showed up on the scene. Dig? So what the hell, maybe I could still snag the big box on the porch on the way out.

She just puts the sleeping baby down on the California king-sized. Tells me, "Don't worry. At this age, they can't roll over."

I'm doing my prep work, and I get my pecker protector out.

Yeah, never leave home without it. You need cash, keys, and a condom in your wallet 'cause you don't know what the hell you're gonna find on the outside.

She nods okay, and I'm wondering how we're gonna do it, but she drops her sweatpants and there's nothing on underneath. Then she just leans face-forward at the foot of the bed and shoves it out. What's a guy gonna do? That's enough to get me in the mood. Yeah, Big Pharma can kiss my ass. No Viagra, Cialis, or any other old-man corporate grease required to get this engine oiled and in gear. She's going "goo goo" and "gah gah" to her tyke while she starts swishing her bottom around.

I get the hint and I'm firm as kosher bologna, and I'm in there enjoying the ride. Feeling pretty fucking great about the whole business, and I get a little rhythm going. Pause, thrust; pause, thrust. Before you know it, the old guy is making milkshake, and it's over. Everything is A-OK until I pull out and see blood-red liquid all over my balls. Then, I notice it's on the shaft, too. And soon, dripping onto her beige shag carpet. "Fuck!" I scream. In disgust, I run to the first sink I find, which happens to be in the kitchen and full of dishes. But I'm desperate to clean up, so I grab the dish rag, the only one I can see, run some tap water, and start rinsing off. I squeeze the juice right over the morning's cereal bowl—"Nice to meet you, Lucky Charms with sweet surprises."

She's moaning in the background, part, "Geez! What's the big deal? Afraid of a little blood?" and part, "Please go to the bathroom sink! My mom will kill me if she finds blood on the kitchen towels!"

I'm cleaning up as fast as I can and hoping I can snag the box on the way out. You know what? She let me take it. She just walked. Didn't ask if I'd call or swing by again or nothing. The baby started crying in the background and that distracted her. So she flashed her tits real quick and locked the door behind her. I grabbed the box, ran to the van, and drove away.

I turned on the radio in the van, and it's that whiny talk-show fag, and today, he's doing some special on making twenty dollars last a week. One of those financial feminists is on the show with him, and I get to remembering his spiel about heterosexual guys—what we call men—and how, basically, we have to eat it to prove we're straight. And also, we have to eat it even when the monthly payment is due because real gay guys swallow so some disgusting analogy like that which doesn't even make any sense. What an ass clown. Makes legal tender, big bucks, for saying that crap live on the air, telling you, me, and the rest of the world what their eating habits should be. That we gotta lick the bowl, even when the cherry sauce is dripping down the sides. But hey, it's a free country, so more power to him. Just don't buy into any of his crap or you'll feel even worse.

Anyway, Prof, I've been there. Don't feel too bad about all of it. You deserve high marks for banging a young chick without paying for much more than a room and theater. I just started paying direct to simplify my life. I had to "compartmentalize" as the chicks would say. *Capisce?* But whenever I'm at the henhouse,

I make a special request. No gravy on top, please. If the hole is red, then Jonny's not in bed. Then, I wink and Madame Chen laughs at my jokes. She's one I'd marry, but whenever I ask, she always moans and says, "I know you playboy, Jonny Boy. Spare me headache."

Chapter 3
Pooling Resources

It was time to let the books go. Not just mine, but everyone's. Whatever was in the office. If I was selling recent review copies chosen as textbooks by current officemates, so be it, but I was almost positive that ninety percent of them hadn't been touched in years.

From my wallet, I found three cards left under our door by the textbook resellers. Of our nine hundred odd titles, they bought seven for fifty-five bucks. I packed up the remainder and took them down to the sidewalk outside the university. A Sunday sale of used books. I hawked and cajoled and chatted up prospective buyers and managed to move thirteen titles in two hours for the whopping sum of twenty-three dollars. The remainder I left in boxes outside the library. I tucked my sixty-six dollars into my pocket and moved on. Within an hour, I sold the office computer to a white guy in geek plaid and horn rims who didn't ask questions. Forty bucks. I couldn't find anyone to take the furniture.

Back at Jonny's the three of us discussed our resources. I produced the wad of cash. It was less than I wanted, but I hoped it would impress. At least it impressed me until Auggie told us he went door-to-door selling how-to-pick-up-girls tapes and made over a thousand dollars in commissions.

"It's crazy, but it wasn't just the loner guys. A lot of those types are hard-up for cash and couldn't afford the product. But the housewives and single women were eager to learn more. I got an invite inside eleven times, five times seated on the couch, three times offered coffee, and twice I closed the deal. I could have gotten laid if I wasn't all business."

"Nice work, kid."

"How'd it go for you?"

Jonny November pulled out an envelope and counted one hundred dollar bills.

"Who'd you rip off to get that kind of dough?" Auggie needed to know.

"Nobody."

"Then, how you'd get it?"

"Cash withdrawals of my credit cards."

"How many cards do you have?"

Jonny got up, limped out to his car, and returned with three opened packages of playing cards. But instead of withdrawing fifty-two cards in red, white, and black, he dealt a long hand of twenty-some units of plastic braille. Gold, silver, black, red, and even an aqua-colored Visa with dolphins swimming in the background.

"Whoa," was all Auggie could muster.

I gulped and sighed.

"So, we got the dough to do this right. What do you say, gentlemen?"

Jonny crossed his arms over his chest and waited for us to speak.

Life Lessons from Jonny November 11

"How I'd do it?" is what the professor asked. Well, I had ten cards in my sock drawer already. And I had a system. Separate the socks; darks and lights is a common tactic here. Keep all the cards in a stack under the darks, and whenever you max out a card, move it to the lights. A key to maxing out the card is to get as much cash as you can. Before they notice. Remember, it's still a free country—well, sort of—and there's no debtor's prison although I've been reading news stories that suggest otherwise. As long as we got government bailouts for hedge-fund assholes and insurance-firm fascists, too big not to fuck us over, America won't be too quick to lock up the rest of us. You say we already have the highest incarceration rate in the world? Well, yeah, but never mind the white-collar sociopaths. Look at all the dipshits, mooches, and crazies we got running around in this country, and explain to me how we keep our prison numbers so low.

Anyway, be sure to get the cash. Cash is king, you better believe the Chinese know that much although they're screwed too because betting on American T-bills sounds worse than betting on con artists and screw ups like you and me.

So when I knew the plan was a go, I raised as much cash as possible. Over five weeks, I received fifty new credit cards. The new cards were good for total cash advances of about twenty-five grand. Yeah, they tightened the flow of easy credit and access to real money. I used multiple aliases and social security numbers, but for safety's sake, I don't want to see you playing with this kind of fire. The novices are always the first to get burned, and I don't want you to wind up like me. Tagged with a record and forced to make a life of it. You gotta pay to plastic, maybe, but I'll do my best to keep you out of the federal pen.

Chapter 4
Choose Your Weapon

Around Jonny's plastic patio table, in his trailer's kitchen area, we further refined our criminal plans. Philosophy had left me with too many questions, but Jonny had all the answers.

Michael: "OK. So I brought a sword back from the conference on ancient Greece. It's a replica of the one Alexander used to cut the Gordian knot."

Auggie: "You want the kill shot to honor an ancient pedophile? No way. We need a shovel. Steel and wood. Something to knock him out with."

Jonny: "Nah. I'm gonna do it with this."

In a moment's notice, Jonny pulled off his left leg and raised it to his shoulder. He pumped it up and down like a warrior and beamed at us, his accomplices.

Chapter 5
The Car

With our cash, a sum of seven grand, we shopped for supplies and transportation. Despite Jonny's prosthesis theatrics, Auggie and I selected a steel shovel with pointed tip, and Jonny picked out the most inconspicuous stake-out car we could afford. It had to be roomy and somewhat common, and although the three of us all survived 1980s police shows, we knew our car should be from the 1990s or newer. In the end, we chose between a fifteen-year-old Toyota Avalon XLS and a nineteen-year-old BMW. The Toyota won when the curbstoner showed us a full-sized spare tire in the trunk and dropped the price by five hundred dollars. Auggie seemed as pleased as punch with the price we paid while Jonny noted that you never see similarly aged American cars on the road.

It had a black exterior with taupe leather interior. "No dents or dings," "all highway miles," "everything runs perfect," and, "air blows cold." The only blemish was a lavender stain in the middle of the front bench seat. I saw ancient Greece, Jonny said "Florida," and Auggie muttered, "You can't take Leroy anywhere without him leaving a mess." In a world of pinkish pale slobs, he was the only white man I knew with a clean apartment.

Life Lessons from Jonny November 12

Myself, I was mainly just a curbstoner, but I knew a guy in the joint who worked special financing at a legit dealership. W-2s, health insurance, the works. He got it because he had a pal on the lot, and they ignored his sheet. Or that's what he told me. Anyway, they'd scour the auctions looking for big American cars they could sell, and they were hard to find. Hot or cold, anything with room for six that sat lower than an SUV was in demand, and folks were paying a premium for pleather and vinyl interiors. Land of the Prius, this was not.

My guy rose through the ranks and soon he was promoted to used car manager. From there, he went to work, skimming off both sides of the transaction. He'd get two bills a pop to buy the car that the wholesaler wanted to move off his lot. Then, he'd falsify the buyer's order before delivering the invoices to his primary employer. He was taking in three grand a month *before* any legit commissions owed from his regular jobber. Anyway, he drove a platinum-package motorcycle until the cops snagged him for statutory and sent him back to the pen for his priors.

Stay humble, friend, and as clean as you can.

Chapter 6
Stake Out

A week later, I found Jonny November whacking off to an image of Melony on my way back to the Avalon. He'd ordered triple crème and sugar in his coffee, and as I was passing the cup through the window, I saw him in the act. Left hand deep in side pocket, right hand holding her photo. It was the one I kept in my wallet, and after he cleaned himself up and apologized—"Michael, you're quick on your feet; good trait for a watch dog"—he produced the leather pocket-sized along with a quick explanation of how he divested it from my person. "You weren't looking, so I stole it." I slid Melony back in her slot, and checked for my credit cards, cash, condom, and photo ID. Then I shoved my wallet deep in my sock.

So we would wait, two guys watching Auggie's stepfather come and go with his younger wife and little girl.

The three of them left the condo together very rarely, at most once a day. What we learned is that Auggie's stepdad's wife would walk her to preschool and Auggie's stepdad would pick her up. Because the wife returned home later from work, we saw that the stepdad was with her alone for a couple hours each day.

"The fuckin' pervert," is how Jonny put it.

Indeed, we never knew for sure what was going on during that time, but it gave our imagination even greater chance to justify what would be our crime.

"When we tie him to a chair in the basement, before we light his balls on fire, I'm going to beat him senseless with this."

Jonny would pull off his left leg and show me how the prosthesis could be used as a weapon. By this time, I'd drifted so far from any moorings the examined life could provide that I found Jonny's violence of the leg rather enticing.

I admired its techno-plastic, flex-factor design.

Later in Auggie's apartment, we would discuss what we saw.

"The kid is there, but the wife's not around for a couple hours every afternoon."

"Fuckin' pervert."

"Amen, Jonny. Amen."

* * *

Back at Jonny's trailer, I placed the can back behind the camper cooler and listened to Auggie's insistence. "We can't kill him in front of the little girl! She'll wind up scarred, just like me."

"Relax, Auggie, it's a kill, not theater rehearsal. There won't be an audience. We'll make sure the girl is in another room."

"No, that won't work. I won't do it."

"I have an idea." I didn't know where this came from, or why it had come to the point where this was my manner of thought. I suppose I was intent on action and was playing an imagining role. I allowed my thoughts to flow and, thus, freely I discoursed:

"Melony. She's the bait. We set it up as if your dad, I mean your stepfather, meets her by accident. Then we have her lure him back to her studio. On her couch. Then, we kill him from behind. Before he even cops a feel. She can use her blindfold."

Auggie: "I want him to see my face before we kill him."

Jonny: "I like it."

Auggie: "The fucker has to know who killed him."

Jonny: "That's easy. I conk him over the head with my foot. Knock him out. Then, we take off all his clothes and tie him to Melony's recliner. Gift him a golden shower, or shit on him if we want. When he wakes up he smells our feces and sees our faces and you slice off his dick. With a death shot to the head, put him out of his misery a minute or two later. How's that?"

Auggie: "I've never had friends as good as you guys."

Here was where I hoped my innocent question didn't break the mood. "But how do we convince Melony to go along with all of that?"

"She banged your best friend," Jonny said. "She feels guilty and would like to pay you back."

"So I'm supposed to convince her to help us murder his father?"

"Hey, Michael, it was your idea in the first place. You got us in the mood and now you want to bail out?"

Auggie had a point there.

"Relax, Michael. A lot of young women, twenty-somethings, like this sort of thing. It's adventure. As long as she knows it's just revenge, I'm sure she'll help us out."

So that was it. Our threesome would accept one more.

Chapter 7
In It for the Money

I'd attended a selective liberal arts college, trained at respectable research institutions and even completed a dissertation for a doctoral degree. In our shared office, I'd tell new adjunct hires I was ABD, so they wouldn't feel their own situation was so hopeless. If they saw a ten-year veteran adjunct with a PhD, they might lose hope of securing a permanent job. It was the least I could do, as a good American, to remind the young that we were an innocent and optimistic country where everyone was entitled to a fulfilling career. To make sure they understood that PhD stood not for "piled higher and deeper" or "Pop has dough," but in fact the degree meant "professional happiness desired," and at the altruistic colleges of democratic America only the angry or sad ones need not apply.

But where had that experienced teacher and reasonable soul wandered off to?

These days, I was loitering around supermarkets and plotting murder with a pussy hound and a flimflam man—seven and a half semesters of college between them—listening to stories of Auggie's sexual seductions and Jonny's life on the lamb. I thought perhaps what I needed was to pick up more classes, but I'd tried that in the past. Teaching five or six at once kept me out of trouble, busy as Hegel if burdened as Nein, and it also left me exhausted and forlorn and feeling as if philosophy had betrayed me. I felt brain dead from using my brain too much. Fried. Spent. I had no time for any advanced thinking and found myself betrayed by the same clichéd thoughts and in-class discussion builders that "philosophers" from coast to coast were using upon the undergrads underneath their supervision. What would Nietzsche do? Hand out a piece of blank paper and ask them to write the questions? Could you argue that live football or pop music proved that virtue was not always in the mean?

If I could become so quickly reduced to a mindless money-grubbing capitalist, grabbing as many courses a term as I could, was there any point to advanced education at all?

In my younger years, I was quiet, but I was never entirely an outcast. At least, I didn't see myself that way. I liked to read, that much was true—but from an avid reader, I'd become a supermarket degenerate?

Was it just a matter of all the normal guys pushing ahead, desperately searching for someone to marry, so they didn't wind up alone past midnight at the grocery store, hoping to run into some other weirdo or loner? Now, here I was bringing my twenty-three-year-old—a former student, no less—into a plot to kill Auggie's stepfather. A part of me felt like I must be worse than Humbert Humbert, which was rather ironic because it was a disciple of H.H. that we were looking to murder. For a moment, I tried to picture Auggie's stepdad reading Nabokov's masterpiece. In my head, I sat him down at a desk, then on a couch, and finally lying down on one, but I couldn't picture him reading the novel. In fact, I couldn't picture him reading anything aside from the business section of a daily newspaper. Or, possibly, in a doctor's office skimming whatever dated gossip rag was available.

But the fact that our mark raped kids and didn't read was no excuse for my own involvement in his murder. Or was it?

* * *

I tried to remember what my life was like when I was nine to twelve years old—when Auggie was getting the worst of it shoveled between an uncaring mom, a dead dad, a molesting stepfather, and piles of "Negro" boys left to rot in civilization's storage spaces. Its institutions for abused and troubled children.

But I had trouble remembering anything at all about my life at that age.

I wasn't yet involved in serious reading. For me, that wouldn't come until sophomore year of college. Likewise, I'd exercise upon occasion, swimming or pick-up basketball, but I was never on any sports teams. Band? Nope. Orchestra? I hardly had the talent or discipline for delicate classical scores. Television and video games? I saw them claim the eyes and brains of some of the finest teens I knew, at least in my neighborhood, but they were never the ticket to my destruction.

The facts were that I dabbled. I did a little of this, and a little of that but never overindulged. It was as if I had no focus. Or passion. It was all so moderate, two-parent mediocrity, so fucking banal as hell. I remembered those years as a remarkably happy time of my life. It was precisely an antithetical life when compared to Auggie's, and for that solitary reason, I felt someone like me owed him one.

Or maybe I just wanted to kill? To mash in some guy's face with a rusted steel wrench or shove an ice pick up his ass.

That was another way of looking at it.

Hmm. What would Melony think about that? What would Jonny say?

* * *

Of course, I was in it for the money. The burglary would pay more than the murder. Increasingly, during idle hours in the Avalon XLS, I'd find myself fantasizing about what I'd do with the dough. Where I'd go. What I'd buy. Even which charities I'd contribute to. I found myself thinking of that fucking Frenchman, Michel Foucault, who used his prize money to buy an expensive, if secondhand, Jaguar. He even went through a period where he'd buy clothes to match his fancy car.

Indeed, he earned the money by writing iconoclastic, groundbreaking books, revising power for future generations who'd go deep into educational debt puzzling over what he was talking about. My winnings would merely be gleaned from murder, but we'd both be philosophers with cash in the bank.

A sports car did not appeal to me. Travel, in style, did, and I saw myself in a wide range of overseas destinations from Bern to Budapest to Bangkok to Beijing. Perhaps, with Melony at my side, I'd expand my horizons and see the world.

"Let Me Explain"
by Melony Sorbet 2

As soon as they told me, I knew I'd do it, but I tried to play hard to get. I'm a girl. It's in my nature. I need to be pursued. So I bargained over my place or yours, and made sure I'd get a glimpse of all that money wasted on a molester. In Auggie's stepdad's house, I imagined expensive paintings from contemporary artists, a safe behind a pen-and-ink or underneath a copper statue. Sticky fingers at the shopping mall in high school, but I wasn't planning on stealing anything. Well, maybe I'd snag his watch if it looked like it'd pay for textbooks in the fall. It was like the coolest idea, like one of those "efficiencies" Sarah Palin is always talking about. We wouldn't need judge, jury, lawyers, or bail bondsman. We'd eliminate all the middle men; we'd save time and money and execute justice. Auggie's stepdad would get what he deserved, so I agreed to play the part.

All my life, I dreamed of starring in the movies—you know, opposite Brad Pitt or Adam Sandler; I'm not as picky as Michael says I am. Not picky with my men anyway. (Sorry, no offense.) So, you know, this was going to be like the movies. Acting. And it would all be for a good cause. That man did horrible things to Auggie, and I bet he was doing horrible things to his daughter on weekday afternoons. Starting the affair with the younger woman while Auggie's Mom was dying with cancer doesn't bother me as much. At least his women were over eighteen, the ones I knew about. Besides, if he didn't have a taste for the young stuff, how could I be involved in the kill?

So I've decided to take the role seriously. Like this is my first stop on my train to fame and a starring role. I told Auggie and

Michael that I'm willing to perform. I'll do anything to make the plot more realistic. I was once in this small play, just a church-type performance that would never get performed at Sunday service. I was the female lead and the guy directing it encouraged me to go all out in make-out scenes with the male lead. He was married, but I didn't care. Sometimes his wife would watch rehearsal, and she looked pissed. It turned out the director was best friends with the male lead and his wife hated her husband's best bud. Before the play, I mean. But hubby was a good kisser; I must admit that much. And it was fun to piss off his wife.

I know whatever I do will be for a good cause. No one deserves what happened to Auggie. Isn't that why we care about wounded kittens?

That was the thing about Michael and Auggie. They made me feel like a part of something, like I was on a career track, and going the right way. The guys my age were mostly obsessed with sports or off with their guy friends. The loner ones were weird, quiet, or all about video games, and the ones I dated never liked my friends. I was always lonely, even if we were in the bedroom. It was never the worst of times, but never the best either. ESPN was always on television, and during the act, it felt like the young buck was reading *Maxim* on my back. At least with Michael and Auggie, they could see my face. They knew it was me in the room.

Chapter 8
Playing Dress Up

We bought Melony new outfits. She wanted the same styles, spaghetti-strap bebe, hot pink glitter miniskirts, etc., and she made me go with her to try the clothes on. So we spent an entire afternoon wading through the discount mall, searching for a set of costumes. I sat with an aged mass market of Kaufmann's Nietzsche. Yes, reading *Beyond Good and Evil*, I waited for two hours in Ross, Dress for Less. Every five minutes, she'd interrupt my puzzling over a passage or aphorism to appear before the facing mirrors and demand of me an opinion. What could I say? How to express enthusiasm for something I had no knowledge of? Clothes were clothes, and I must confess I had a taste for the skimpier ones on a younger woman, but how directly should I express that to Melony? So I sighed and shrugged and felt relief each time she walked back to the changing room, and I could return to underlining my text or scribbling in the margins.

By early evening, we'd spent our hard-earned cash on assets numerous and tangled enough to be considered an entire wardrobe in less developed countries. Our packages included polka-dot miniskirts, fluorescent tank tops, faded Daisy Dukes, sparkling camisoles, pastel summer dresses, and tight-fitting jeans. It was all we would need to execute the plan.

Chapter 9
Placing Melony on the Mark

In less than a month, we had Melony at the sandwich shop where Auggie's father went to get his daily Reuben. She was positioned at the end of a full case of prosciutto, Genoa, Muenster, and provolone. A barrel of shark-sized kosher dills to her lower left, a full selection of condiments by the register she operated. She was the lunch-shift cashier. Jobs were hard to come by, but not that one. The guy was too lazy to make his own sandwich. It was no wonder he married for money. Twice that we knew of.

Melony saw Auggie's stepfather five lunches a week, and within a month, she had the date lined up. Lunch at a middlebrow dine-in-only on her weekday off. It was a restaurant that served all the global entrees one would expect, fusion this and pan-Asian that, an entirely globalized menu of multicultural pasta or rice. Nevertheless, it amounted to nothing more than mediocre food. Thai tortillas and tofu burgers with peanut sauce, all of it with the calories on the menu, enough to terrorize Melony, but she was intent on playing her role to the fullest, and she insisted she wouldn't dress romaine or iceberg with barbecue sauce.

"Let Me Explain"
by Melony Sorbet 3

He was fat. Well, not obese, but close enough. He had one of those guy stomachs that flops over his shirt when he tucks it in with a belt on. Like he hadn't seen his prick in the shower since 1993. And his clothes were gross. The black T-shirt made him out to be a joke. He was a fat guy over fifty who thought a tight muscle-T could make him look twenty-five years younger. As if it wasn't obvious he was a white whale hiding hairy folds of blubber underneath. And his jeans? Like gag me with a wilted, leaking old-man dick. They were designer, yeah, but Jordache, from the last decade, maybe two. Like a dork, he'd roll the bottoms up, the way they did it in the 1980s.

All the same, he wasn't entirely without positive qualities. At the restaurant, he pulled my chair out, so I could sit. Before that, he opened all the doors. And he paid for both of us. I winced when I recognized that his tip was less than ten percent. Yes, it was completely embarrassing, not just to be paid for, but to be paid for by a cheapskate like him.

I had money. The problem was that money wasn't everything, and I also wanted a lot more of it. What I really wanted was adventure, and this little role-playing gig was certainly that. Once I got paid by Jonny November I could go to the Jersey shore or Vegas or anywhere anytime I wanted. I didn't even know if I'd take Michael or Auggie with me. I had to admit that I had a soft spot for those guys, and I loved the attention. I'm hip to *ménage à trois* and other kinky tricks, but it was still kind of yucky always having to look at a guy even as old as those two.

You can imagine my disgust when I saw Auggie's stepfather

through the water glasses, chewing with his mouth open. Saliva practically dripped off his lips, and his tiny red tongue darted in and out like a lizard's. Who would want that pink salamander inside her salt box? His eating noises were beyond gross. I mean "disgusting" doesn't begin to describe it. Like you'd prefer a starving hog with a plate of pig slop seated and slurping across from you.

But back to the beginning of the restaurant scene. He smiled and stared at me, until the menus arrived. I looked up and down and finally settled on my trademark iceberg with barbecue sauce. Yeah, I know I promised the guys I'd order real food, tofu or pad thai, so that's why I added green peas on top for protein. Auggie's stepdad ordered a veggie burger well done with blue cheese and mushrooms. Jonny would call that a fag burger if there ever was one.

Okay, so that's not what he ordered. He was surf and turf all the way, lobster and rare steak. Japanese style. I don't know why I lied about the blue cheese, but I guess it was like I wanted them to know he ate food that stunk. To wash down his ocean roach and red meat, he ordered a gin and tonic. He told me what he'd order before the waiter arrived, a cute guy a couple years ahead of me at Liberty Tech. I guess he wanted me to know I could get whatever I wanted, which in a way is nice even if it's just to fuck me over, his wife, or all of our children, past and future. So if he's drinking, I'm drinking, and so I ordered a coke and rum, yum, and requested the potatoes and salmon—moist and pink, so he wouldn't know I was completely grossed out by his fresh-from-the-ocean-cellar entree. The lettuce was only my dinner salad.

The waiter left, and Auggie's dad stared at my tits as he asked me about school and my future. He said he wanted to know all about my dreams and aspirations, and, like, if I hadn't met this guy through Michael and Auggie, I'd probably think he was just like any sort of older, parental type. Let's say avuncular, so it can sound almost legit. Of course, this was all save for the fact that he *prolly* saw me as almost too old to bang.

Chapter 10
Lunch with Mr. Wrong

Back at Jonny's trailer, Melony gave us the lowdown.

"That's a fag burger if ever there was one," muttered Jonny.

"Then he asked me if I'd like to come back to his place!"

"Bingo is his name-o!"

Auggie and I both gave Jonny a confused look.

"Relax, guys. Not what we wanted for this date, but it means the guy is putty in our hands. Melony can set the date now, so we can be prepared."

Oh?

"Waiting for them inside." With that, Jonny unstrapped his prosthesis, pulled it off, and raised it like Excalibur, high over his shoulder. We waited in suspense, wondering if he was about to karate-chop the table or take an imaginary big gulp. When he tired and put his right leg down, we could breathe again. *Whew.*

Auggie nixed my replica-sword idea, but despite Jonny's theatrics, there was no way I'd go in with anything less than a shovel.

Chapter 11
Robbed

Jonny used a platinum Visa card and Melony's barrette to pick the lock and get us inside through the rear. *It ain't a score if it's not backdoor.* We snuck in as quietly as we could, entering into the kitchen. I loosened my grip on the shovel, and took a look around. Late model stainless steel appliances with an unremarkable microwave, coffeemaker, and toaster oven on the counter. It was all newer than any ever found in my rentals, sure, but nothing special. Auggie opened the fridge and whispered, "Crap. Nothing but Chinese leftovers, condiments, and half a case of root beer." He opened the freezer wide, so we could all two pounds of fish sticks and a couple quarts of ice cream.

We moved through the kitchen and into the dining room where we saw a wooden table with a bowl of fruit in the middle. Apples, bananas, and pears, some brown past ripe and none of it polished. Jonny unstrapped his leg, held his ear lower, and rapped the prosthesis on the table.

He muttered, "It's not hollow, for a secret stash, or even hardwood. Must be chip board under the surface."

We shared a group sigh and continued. We each readied our bag for looting. Jonny found the stairs and moved upstairs to look for a safe.

We found all kinds of furniture and decoration in the modest-sized living room. Pastels, light blue and yellow, but also mauve and beige in the background.

A painting of girls by a water lily pond hung above a desk, and I saw all six as children Auggie's stepdad had molested. It was possibly a Renoir or Manet, but only a print of such. As an original, it would be worth millions. On the desk underneath the painting sat a bowl of crayons, dozens of them in various stages of use, from untouched to broken to only a nub that remained. By the bowl appeared a drawing, mainly with purple and yellow, and it looked like a half-plucked balding Big Bird performing a striptease. A ballet tutu at knee level, but no genitalia, thank god. I thought of the children lured in by Auggie's stepfather and wondered if the kind man sent them home with their drawings. I shoved a fistful of crayons into my pocket.

Auggie picked up a wooden object. It was one of those items you buy at a tourist-trap souvenir shop. A duck on wheels. He sniffed it and put it back down. Then he removed a lavender flower from a vase and licked it. After that, he lifted a large seashell, beige and white, to his ear, and checked for the ocean's roar. No sound, so he held it under his nose and inhaled. His tongue darted out, took a quick lick, and retreated.

From there, he snooped around the ground floor. He was sniffing everything. Furniture. Wall art. Vases full of flowers. On the first floor alone, Auggie's stepdad had five vases, but none of them struck me as particularly expensive. Indeed, they were the kind that came for free with a dozen roses sold over the internet, those deals where the shipping is padded to jack up the price.

Jonny limped back downstairs. "No cash, no guns, nothing but discount jewelry. In the master bedroom, all he has is a twenty-seven-inch tube. The old fashioned kind with a generic channel changer resting by plastic digital alarm clock, the kind you buy in a drug store."

My millions slipped away.

"This shit's no good," said Jonny while gnawing half a banana from the fruit bowl. "Nothing here but chump change and plastic crap." On impulse, Jonny dumped the apples and pears on the carpet, stepped onto the table, dropped trough, bent down to squat over the empty bowl, and left a dump for the next fellow to eat. Firm and steamy. A protest movement against pedophilia and the fact that Auggie's stepfather was too cheap to leave some high-ticket items around to make a thief's job worthwhile.

"Don't worry, I just want him to catch a whiff before we kill him. I'll clean up my DNA before we ditch."

Jonny looked like a man who'd shat in a coffee can for months and finally had a chance to squat on a bowl. Too bad his smile wasn't worth a million bucks.

Chapter 12
Cluster Fuck

We were trying not to breathe, when we heard steps. Keys rustled outside the door. The turning of the lock, and the door opened. Melony's little "Hee, hee" as they entered the foyer.

"You did not."

"Did so," said Auggie's stepfather, mimicking a child's cadence. "Say, are you up for that glass of wine?"

Bingo. I tightened my grip on the shovel.

As soon as Auggie's stepfather walked past, I leaped from behind the kitchen island. I raised the shovel above my head and screamed at the top of my lungs. Then, I lunged.

He stepped to the left and sent me sprawling into the dining room. *Shit, I missed the fucker!* But I heard him fumbling with the lock to the back door. Before he opened it and escaped, Auggie ran from the dining room and smashed the Renoir or Manet over his stepfather's head. Even though I knew it was a fake, I winced with pain of financial loss. Auggie crouched low, leaped, and grabbed him around the neck. His stepfather struggled toward the living room, as Auggie dug his fingers into his face and covered his mouth.

Melony, quick as a cat, pulled out her perfume and got him right in the face.

"Argh!"

But she got Auggie too.

"Motherfucker!"

The two of them were entangled and screaming, and I was certain anyone within two hundred feet could hear the commotion.

I suppressed shouting, "We're screwed," and then saw Jonny leap out of nowhere and begin shoving them toward the kitchen. After rising and regaining my balance, I bent low in a rugby stance and helped force them back into the kitchen. By grabbing onto the refrigerator handle, Auggie was able to escape his stepdad's clutches, but the force of his momentum sent stumbling out of the backdoor.

On instinct, I drove the pointed end of the shovel deep into the molester's chest. I fell backward, but Jonny, thinking quickly, pushed the shovel in deeper and turned it almost ninety degrees. No doubt his innards got swirled around because maroon goop leaked out.

In shock and terror, I stared, and collapsed with the weight of my action.

"He's dead," proclaimed Jonny.

I killed him. Just like that.

"Michael! What about our plan? We were going to keep him alive. Torture him."

"I don't know."

"You stole my show, Professor."

"Relax, Auggie." Again, Jonny. Our voice of reason. "We're okay here. I'm going to check outside and see if anyone's looking this way. I doubt the cops have been called, unless someone saw Auggie flung into the backyard. But no one sees nothing. Usually."

Jonny poked his head out and returned a minute later. "The coast looks clear, but you can never be safe. We need to abort. Abort the mission. Forget the shit. Just take the cash and cards from his wallet and scram."

The house smelled of death and shit. I felt the shock of murder and the loss of a jackpot. I shuddered and yelped once before Jonny hissed, "Shut up, Michael." Melony was whispering about the stench, but she seemed to be intact and functioning. She didn't appear to be markedly effected by the brutal slaying. Auggie was upset, but it was hard to tell if he was bothered more by not getting the kill shot or by not collecting big money. Jonny produced almost a hundred sixty bucks from the stepfather's pants, and handed us two twenties each.

"Okay. Time's a wasting. If you don't see our mug shots on TV, meet in my trailer in four weeks. If you do see our faces or my face, then all deals are off. If I collect any dough, I'll find a way to locate everyone and pay out."

Jonny told us to leave in one-minute intervals and to head in separate directions. Lady's first, so Melony disappeared, holding her nose. When Jonny motioned me toward the door, I didn't need a second hint to escape the scents of shit and death. I hurried out as quickly and quietly as possible.

Auggie's Revenge

Part III

Prefatory Quotations:

"What in the name of God could humanity be if man is an example of it?"
–Guy Davenport, "The Haile Selassie Funeral Train"

"To the corporatist henchmen running higher education. You're too stupid or delusional to see what you are, but I hope God isn't as ignorant and selfish as you. Fuck you."
—Jonny November

Chapter 1
Funny Faces

I'd killed a man. This much was true, but surprisingly the remorse I felt was manageable. Yes, I would run away from my image in my bedroom's full-length mirror. There were moments when I could not look myself in the eye. On the other hand, there were times when I found myself staring, in appreciation first, and then like a lunatic. After smiling widely, I'd bark like a dog. I'd repeat these barks twenty or fifty times at a spell, and alter my audible call to a growl. I'd bring my hands up to my face and make funny faces. Thumbs in ears. Fingers splayed and bowing up and down. But still, I could catch myself and return to some kind of normalcy.

Keeping to my squalid two-room studio left me with time on my hands. So I invented a little game with these funny faces. I would give them each the name of a famous philosopher. For example, the Kant became a naïve but repetitive motion that involved repeatedly shoving my thumbs up my nose. I felt no shame that nothing about it suggested "categorical imperative" or "perpetual peace." After that, I did a Nietzsche, flailing against a dying horse. I'd slap myself hard against the cheek and force myself head first into the sink. Like a coward, each time, I'd catch myself just before my forehead slammed down on the steel faucet.

What did I make of all this narcissistic staring? Was I certain that what we had done was just? Did an evil man, a molester of children, deserve his brutal death? Could my indulgence at the end in fact be a sign of good karma? Through murder, had I, in fact, altered the cosmos for the better? Was this then a variant of an eye for an eye? A red heart for a tush?

I'd learn soon enough that karma, as a concept, was debatable, but if there was such a thing, then "good" could hardly be the best modifier to describe my own.

Chapter 2
Just Like on TV

Yes, they were onto our scent, so to speak. Or so I assumed. It was a combination of sniffing dogs and the latest technology that did me in.

A few nights before I'd found a card in my door. It was above the lock and wedged in the crack and from one Detective Polite who upon the back penned, "Give me a call."

I, of course, did not. For the next day or two I was a walking bathtub of salty perspiration. Could the card mean anything other than that we'd been uncovered? There was so much shameful sweat sliding down my body that it felt as if my shoes had been soaked in the Red Sea. What would happen? When would I see Melony?

After one and a half sleepless nights, exhausted, I finally collapsed into a coma-like state. It was past three in the morning, and I slept the sleep of the world weary drunken philosopher. A heaven on this earth had come to me at last.

So I was terrified when I heard a loud smash, like a cannonball had ripped into the window. An aftershock followed, a loud *kerplunk*, smashes, pops, and plops. I was jarred from my dream state and wide awake. Had the Philly police moved quickly to extreme measures? Were they ignoring all manner of collateral damage and bombing me out of my studio apartment? Was I but another Philly denizen to get burnt to a crisp inside his own home? But they only did radical shit like that to black people, no? I rented in a mixed neighborhood, but white enough to avoid such attacks from our leaders. It couldn't be state-sponsored violence, right?

I stared at my walls, searching for a huge break in the window or a tear through newly exposed brick. I saw nothing and was for a moment confused. Away from the wall, I cast my eyes downward, and tried to reimagine what had just occurred. Could the crash have been the end of a nightmare? Something terrifying I could not fully recollect?

Exposed by street-lamp light coming through my tall windows with their broken shades, I noticed a few books on the floor. I squinted and saw Kant's *Political Writings* straddling an anthology of Russian nihilism, and several mass market copies of Kaufmann's Nietzsche translations—*The Genealogy of Morals* and *The Birth of Tragedy* combined with *Ecce Homo*. These were my copies from my undergrad years, and I couldn't remember any recent perusal of these texts, but I was soon distracted by more books. Machiavelli's *The Prince* was squished under Plato's *Republic* and Aristotle's *Politics* and *Nicomachean Ethics*. Foucault's *Discipline and Punish* sat wide open, face down and pages splayed. When I squinted I saw a nail piercing the spine of the black cover. The nail came from a long, black piece of pressed wood, and other pieces of wood, exposed nails, and books were strewn all over the floor.

That's when I figured it out. My tall, narrow bookshelf had finally succumbed to its teeter-totter existence. In the middle of the night, it had collapsed and crashed to the linoleum tiles of faded black and white, a checkerboard that the frugal landlord had laid over the torn and abused original hardwood floors. I turned to the wall and sighed with relief, as I saw the full-length mirror had survived unscathed.

I didn't count myself among the superstitious and was unsure if an unharmed mirror meant good luck, but I was able to fall back asleep with ease.

In the morning, I left the broken shelving where it lay and ignored the hundreds of books strewn across my floor. I found myself staring at the crucified Foucault, but never felt the urge to tear it away from its nailing and resurrect the prison book as best I could.

* * *

A few afternoons later, I was interrupted during a sleepless, anxious *siesta*. Three loud raps sounded on the door, and I knew my luck was gone, maybe for good.

The knocks acted as a forklift and got my ass off the couch and decidedly in gear. I did what I'd seen in countless movies and television dramas. As quietly as I could, I snagged my cards, cash, condom, and keys. After sliding into my shoes, out the back window, no score, I jumped. Like a cat, a clumsy, drunken one, I landed on all fours on the first floor's porch roof. From there, adrenalin charged and seeking safe harbor, I shimmied down the drain pipe, slid off midway, flopped ass first onto the backyard patio's concrete, and cut through the backyard bush and bramble. As quickly as a late thirtyish philosopher could, I climbed the six-foot grated fence and at the top tore a gash in my shin from the exposed edges of aluminum.

"Argh! Fuck!"

I had no time for further expletives, and so wincing in pain, I nevertheless maintained my composure, leaped down, fell knees first, and fucked the world thrice over. From there, I gathered my appendages and ran out the back alley. I hooked a left and ran away from my apartment.

When I didn't see seven police cars at the next corner, I rallied and felt a slight surge of optimism. For once in my life, the criminal had escaped.

Chapter 3

A Newly Minted Man of Action

As soon as I hit the street, I knew I needed to access an ATM. I'd have to withdraw as much cash as possible for fear that they could freeze my assets. So I jogged, sprinted, stumbled, stopped, and finally tried to catch my breath for a few seconds before sliding into a corner grocery a couple blocks away. On impulse, I looked at the corners of the ceiling for security cameras, and as soon as I found one, I turned my head down and marched to the rear ATM. The third-party machine was working, and I paid six dollars in fees to withdraw the maximum. To hide five hundred dollars on my person, I split it four ways among either front pocket, my wallet, and under the sock in my shoe. I ran a couple more blocks and across the Parkway and boarded the first bus that arrived.

Expecting the usual crowd of Auggie's tired, overworked "Negroes," I was surprised to be greeted by pale and plump types in late spring pastels. As it turned out, I'd landed on a purple bus. It was one I'd read about, for tourists enjoying the scenery from Old City's historic sites to a winding route within Fairmount Park. I tried to appear as inconspicuous as possible while wracking my brain for a good place to get off.

Trying not to stare at the lone babe on board, a thin thing in lavender halter and pink shorts cut above the cheek, I had an idea. I got off at Fairmount Park's Please Touch Museum and determined to walk to Chamonix Youth Hostel. Away from the museum, I strode past fields and onto a walking path bordering a leafy wooded area of the park. To my left, on an open field, I saw the entire world on display in a soccer match. "Football," I thought to myself. I'm supposed to call it football if I am to overcome my prejudice and provincialism.

I took a path that cut through the forest and got me closer to the hostel.

One hundred yards ahead and on a field to the right, I saw a feisty game of ultimate with men and women on both sides. A Frisbee flew toward me, and I saw a long legged young woman dash after it, and out of the blue, out of nowhere, a stout young woman in a full sprint leaped high into the air and tipped the flying disc away from the first girl before she could complete her two-handed pancake catch.

As a newly minted man of action, did I now identify with the leaping girl, running from behind to overtake her prey? Not at all. I felt scared, like a guy on the run from the law. There was no Leopold-and-Loeb arrogance about my current predicament.

Past the ultimate fields, in a bizarre fit of doubt and fear, I gazed upward in every direction. I searched trees and telephone poles for security cameras and even the sky for unmanned spy drones from all the major players—from the to Amazon to Russia and China. I shuddered when I saw the pale bulbous likeness of the Urban State philosophy chair hovering above me until I realized it was just a fluffy graying storm cloud.

I continued on down Chamonix Drive, and to my left I noted tennis courts. Up ahead, the scene and scents changed, and I came upon a barn and a few horseback riders. A minute or two later, I was at the front desk, inquiring about the price of lodging and food.

It was post-9/11, but it was no trouble securing a room in the youth hostel. The young bearded fellow was quite the gentleman, and I was soon safely ensconced as one of six in adjoining two-room triples. For a moment, it reminded me of freshman year of college, reading Plato and Rousseau with a penlight as one roommate whacked off, grunting like a caveman, while the other memorized his STEM facts and snored like a king.

At present, three other beds were inhabited, and a long-haired reed-thin t-shirt-and-jeans-type held our attention. He'd been around the block.

"Dude, I lived outside for a year. It toughens a man."

As an evening shower raged outside, we then listened to his exploits, from panhandling in Berlin to sleeping in Central Park in Manhattan to banging rich ass after working as an impromptu translator in Beijing bars courting American investors and China's *nouveau riche*.

"Dude, the owner's daughter was an insatiable freak. Past 3 a.m., she'd crawl in my window and leave scratches all over my body."

But most of his lecture stuck to the topic of roughing it, and his words sunk in. Inspecting food for rot or mold, studying grassy areas for feces and glass before you set up camp. Most of it seemed like sound advice, what I needed to hear under current circumstances.

That was how I came to make a public garden my home, and thieving for vegetables my trade. On a tip from the long-haired fellow, I wound up living in corn stalks north of the Parkway. I was grateful that among the droves of yuppies gentrifying the Art Museum area, there was a large contingent who wanted it somewhat back to nature despite also desiring a central city address.

Chapter 4
In the Public Garden

On the run, I was unable to visit Melony, and if I ran into Auggie anywhere I knew I'd have to duck or walk in the opposite direction. Under such circumstances, I had time to ruminate. I was no longer slave to exhausting paper-grading or mindless discussion with unphilosophical undergrads. I no longer flipped through quasi-theoretical secondary texts, like a madman, matching quotations and identifying tags in search of a peer-reviewed article with which to pad my C.V., in hopes of making progress in my field. (The truth is that despite my badmouthing of the tenure-track class, I always held out hope that they would one day welcome me into the fold. Even as I drifted farther into adjunct teaching, knowing full well that whatever I did it would never be enough, this yearning for tenured respectability remained.)

But for now, even my responsibilities to enlighten and entertain Melony were no longer.

I had free time, time on my hands, extra time, hours I could call my own. This was my chance to ruminate, to think, to philosophize, dare I say it. I could sneak into a bookstore with a coffee shop, do my best to stay awake and appear non-homeless ("homeful" or "properly homed"?), and have my fill of the magazine rack—general interest, academic journals, scriptwriting, all of it.

It was there that I stumbled upon an article in an obscure journal called *Tension Headache*. I'd never heard of it before, but it offered tasty morsels of radical thought—from center right to radical left and all the moist side dishes in between. I was drawn to an essay called "The Talibanization of the Southeastern United States." In it, the author described conditions for young men, eighteen to twenty-nine, in that region of the country. They weren't good. An accelerating high school dropout rate grew as a parallel curve to rise in gun ownership and the increasing burdens of student-loan debt for those able to pursue college. The new improved globalized world was proving to be a disaster for men on the margins, and white American males were now no exception to this rule. The best among this gobbled up and discarded generation could hold down what remained of our manufacturing base and other blue-collar assignments. But even these "successful" types were jaded.

Far from embracing the pseudo-intellectual libertarian theology or a philosophical anarchism, they were intent on avoiding government entirely. Although an older generation who'd described shrinking it down and drowning it in a bathtub or sink could be seen as their father figures, they in fact had more violent plans. They were banding together and collecting weapons, and they were ready to storm the cosmopolitan centers and attack the loci of state control and thought. This meant government buildings, but most of all schools. They were going to cut off electrical currents and wind-based energy generators of the universities, capture the women researching and professing there and return America to its origins—a pre-Edison moment when slavery was alive and women were at home and breeding hands to help out on the farm. And all men, white men at least, were created much more equal. It was a return to a white male dominated Jeffersonian utopia— except for the fact that anyone who dared mingle with the slaves in this go-round would have his business cut off and his balls beaded into a necklace and wrapped around his ears.

So the revolution was on its way, and scary men would soon fight their way back to positions of authority, but this didn't lessen my feelings of guilt. I looked up from my magazine and saw a beautiful young Asian woman, dressed to the nines, look away from me. Even in my current state of homelessness, it seemed I had enough going to attract their eye, and I could this attribute only to my increased facial hair.

It was something I'd been noticing for a while now. Increased numbers of Asian nationals throughout the city. Young women with bank to buy coffee in public at all the usual spaces—bookstores, coffee shops, food courts, and everything in between. They appeared all over Collegetown as well as center city. A steady rotation from crowded affluent cities of the Far East, twenty-somethings intent on exploring the Americas via two to seven years of U.S. grad school. Their parents were the *nouveau riche* of Nanjing, Taipei, and Busan, and able to pick up the heavy nut for travel costs. What more, I saw that I could catch their eye and hold their attention. I looked almost normal and had a pulse. They cared enough to smile slightly and pretend they weren't aware I was staring back.

I was in demand and could snag the girl with a promise of a green card. A male, American, in possession of most of his hair, an apartment—well, not quite—but citizenship and straight teeth. At least, there'd be curiosity until they demanded to see my dossier and learn that I was a man who had ditched his contract work to become a murderer of all things. I remembered fondly, then, what it was like when I had my apartment and steady adjunct classes. My life before the murder.

Such thoughts brought me back to Auggie and our late-night discussions of dating in the world of glocalization and diaspora.

"Professor, you've got functional parts and working papers in the land of lower population density. You think we got smog in Philly, well, ya gotta go live in one of these Asian cities—Beijing, Toronto, Shanghai, and Tokyo. It's that simple. You look harmless. You might even be a nice guy. . ."

At times, Auggie could make me feel valued, even *desired*, in a way my academic employers never did. If I bothered to attend departmental meetings, I'd come away feeling like a doofus.

". . .and I'm the only one who knows how demented you really are."

"Demented?" Wasn't that worse than doofus?

"You laugh at all my 'Negroes' and '*schvartzes*,' don't you?"

He had me there. *Ugh.*

How I missed those aimless conversations with Auggie, all of his crazy stories, his neurotic and paranoid vision of our capitalist democracy, his "ain't a score if it's not backdoor," which he always claimed was patriotic, too, and all of his dreams for the future.

I heard myself replying, "So they'll marry me no matter what I'm actually like?" Auggie had a way of making me feel like a product or a tool more than anything else. But I must confess, he made me feel valued, even *desired*, in a way my philosophy bosses never did.

"Prof, there's millions of these chicks stuck in overpopulated cities. They're screwed. If they don't want to suck cock of some connected crook in power—a stub-dick asshole, no doubt— they'll be trapped living with their parents or marrying some sad bum—one of those deformed button-pecker dudes who has to eat shit for forty years just to scrape by. Have you seen how ugly the men are in Asia? How they smoke and work themselves to death just to survive?"

Coming from short and bald Auggie, this kind of conversation was an amusement indeed.

"And they sleep on the floor. You can offer them an apartment, a bed three feet off that linoleum crap your landlord put down because the cheap bastard wouldn't invest in new hardwood floors when he bought the place."

"Yeah?"

"You even have cable television and internet. All-you-can-eat utilities in the land of the free. You know, your hair is flat and your teeth are yellow, but you're really not a bad-looking guy. You should smile more."

Auggie had a way of making the global world order seem all so much more depressing—a complex labyrinth of chutes and ladders dominated not by love and friendship but by green cards and citizenships and marriage as a business transaction. Even after murder, my sentimental side proved strong. I didn't want to see the world this way, and yet, the possibility that as long as I could keep a job I could get free, hot sex from multiple women— well, this would have been a life I could lead, and now I could see that I'd thrown good opportunity away with one deed.

Was the article not proof of everything that Auggie was talking about? The lack of women and good jobs and resources that was hurting all of us. That seemingly was one reason we were driven to kill. We didn't just hate Auggie's stepfather because he was an evil abuser, but because he had money. And he flaunted it.

I looked up again, searching for the young Asian hottie, because I was drawn to money, too, but she was nowhere to be found. It didn't matter as I'd ruined all my chances anyway. So in grief, I buried myself in magazines.

Life Lesson from Jonny November 13

Yeah, right. You were hoping I wandered off, that maybe you wouldn't have to deal with the likes of me again.

I scare you a little. I know that. You look at me, and you wonder what you're looking at. Ugly face. Bald head. Deep grey bags under either eyeball.

It's okay. Avert your eyes. I won't be offended.

You look down, you see the missing leg, and you turn away entirely. So what?

But the thing is that you want me to be successful. Maybe you don't want to look at me, but you want me to be happy. Food on the table, running water, hot and cold, and heat in winter. Internet access? Why not? Maybe even cable TV.

You want your government to take care of me. To get this done, you don't mind donating your own time and dough either. It takes me off your mind. If you see me outside the CVS, you'll look the other way, but as you do so, you might toss me a couple quarters. Maybe a dollar or two if you're feeling generous that day.

You're a good person, and as such, you don't want society to forget about me.

So I persist. In America, I survive. That doesn't mean the country itself isn't road kill. Due to die off soon. But, hey, for now, we're still here, so don't sweat the small stuff.

Chapter 5
Men of Goodwill

Warmer weather was keeping me alive, but stealing from the vegetable patch was humbling, so I tried to take as inconspicuously as I could. No more than one ear of corn per stalk or tomato on a vine. A few urban farmers would return by nine each morning, and so, I would be sure to clear out at least thirty minutes earlier. At first, things were not so bad. I had cash on my person, spent sparingly, and aside from the obvious—no job, girl, apartment, etc.—I never felt as if I was going without.

But to see if the case against me was progressing, five days into my new life *au naturel*, I snuck into an ATM, tested my card, and had it declined. "Fuck," I muttered softly but aloud. I kicked the machine, screamed in toe pain, saw that there were people in line behind me, and silently sulked off.

I could only suppose that whatever few hundreds I had left had been frozen by the authorities.

From there, a more difficult period began. Even the villains, the world's worst people, the one percent, what have you, imagine themselves to be the heroes of their own stories, and I saw myself this way. I, too, could be a hero or protagonist, and not some mere bystander in the greater drama of someone else's life. It was awkward to see a murderer as a hero, so I had to constantly remind myself of how Auggie's stepfather had been selfish and evil.

I didn't want to draw anyone's attention, so I did what I could to disguise myself. I grew my hair long and avoided eye contact. One afternoon, unbearably horny, I ventured to the peep shows at 22nd and Market. I'd never visited before, so you could say that Jonny and Auggie had gotten the best of me. That I was gone for good. For all I knew, Melony would prove to be my last unpaid-for poke, but I could still drop a few quarters on a peek.

But on the way to leering and shame, I came upon a group of men milling about in the alleyway behind the corner Goodwill store. They surrounded what appeared to be a hi-tech dumpster. On closer inspection, I noticed that it was no dumpster, but rather, a Goodwill bin for clothing, canned foods, or any nonperishable item the humble bourgeoisie felt it necessary to contribute to the hungry, tired, and poor of Philadelphia.

A man and a woman in a station wagon drove up and double-parked on the opposite side of the narrow street. The vehicle was aged, but it appeared well maintained and had intact *faux* wood paneling along either side. The humble pilgrim behind the wheel opened the door, rose from the driver's seat, and walked to the back of his vehicle. He pulled out two large dark trash bags. One, he threw into the bin, but with the second one, he distributed the contents to the people waiting.

This was a crowd of mostly black gentlemen. Most appeared older than me. They were tired and sad in the eyes, and with deep facial wrinkles, either from abuse of the system, the needle, both, or something else altogether. They were rough around the edges, unkempt and in need of a soaking.

I approached closer and saw that not all of these were men, and not all were homeless. Or, I should say, this is not something I could know, but that some of them appeared well groomed and as if their hands and lives in some ways had been protected from the elements. And so I joined the group. I was at the end of the queue, but the driver with the bag still had a few items left. It seemed as if he was judging what remained against what would be best for me. After a moment's search, he pulled from his sack a pair of purple sweat pants with a Minnesota Vikings logo, and with full eye contact and slight warmth passed them to me. Alas, I hated football, always have, America's game as violent symbolic sodomy. The pants were too large, and I knew I would never wear them.

"Thank you, sir." I nodded and received these alms for the poor.

As soon as the benefactor returned to his wagon and drove off, a small man, sinewy and girlish, dove into the entrance of the official Goodwill bin. His legs contorted and twisted until, within minutes, he disappeared.

Minutes later, as if by magic, the other black bag was flung back into the alleyway. Smack in the middle of where we waited. I expected an anarchic attack on the satchel—the biggest, meanest bullies with the most pronounced tattoos and prison records grabbing first—but in fact, I saw nothing of the sort. The men waited patiently until the small man popped back out. They clapped vociferously for this Robin Hood, who, playing his part well, took a few bows for the crowd.

He then moved the bag, hauled it over to a man, and said, "Professor, could you divvy up these materials?"

The "professor" was older than the others, also thin, and he wore wire-rimmed glasses.

"Ok-kay, th-then." His stutter was matched only by his quivering fingers and shaking forearms. "La-la-let's duh-duh-divvy up these cl-cl-cl-cl-clothes."

He came to me first!

"Thuh-the fuh-fuh-first will be la-la-last, and the la-last will be fuh-first."

It bothered me not in the least that I was now number one.

I had gotten the dregs from the bottom of the other bag, and now he was going to correct this injustice. He took a glance and soon found something special near the top. Blue jeans. Levi's. What I hadn't worn in years, but what would be suitable now. Perfect, in fact. After checking the label, I saw they were only one waste size too large, thirty-eight, and the length was close to my thirty-two. I would alter my dress and still look okay. One could never leave appearance completely off the table. I wanted to feel comfortable but needed to look cool. Or at least remain somewhat within societal norms.

I shared a slight smile with the kind, stuttering man.

He moved to the next patron of the Goodwill bin, and I lingered and watched as others received Jesus's offerings. A few crossed themselves and other mumbled prayers. Everyone was grateful to receive new clothes. A couple hours later in a 30th Street Station bathroom stall, I was thinking of his generosity as I changed into *my* jeans and with care made sure I transferred all of the stolen crayons into new pockets.

* * *

I'd like to tell you from that point on, a permanent change occurred in my thinking about the order of things. Whereas before, I bounced around among nihilism, anarchism, libertarianism, or just some confused notion that life hung in the deconstructive balance, whatever that meant, now I saw my ideas drift toward something more egalitarian. I recognized that we were a society of equals.

God no, I didn't become a Christian, and if your next guess is that I embraced Islam, then you've got the wrong guy. Socialism? Communitarianism? Communism without forced collectivization? That may be what you'd like to believe, that one of these theories became my ideal. But the truth was that while sharing clothes reminded me of my readings of Marx, I remained a skeptic, not a believer. I didn't philosophize being homeless as living in a state of nature. Out on the streets, I thought mainly of my own survival.

But I did chuckle when thinking of how these idled workers or nonworkers, descendants of the motherland, Africa, whom I saw sharing clothing, food, and Christianity could ever return me, at least momentarily, to Marx, he who saw nothing of use in religion and possibly even loathed Africans, Christians, indigent people, and everything these men, in a way, were.

But still, there was decency, perhaps, in Marx's ideas of alienated labor and the means of production, so under this new influence, one day, I tidied up as best I could, and after selling stolen vegetables, I headed for the local burrito chain. It was corporate Mexican owned by wealthy white shareholders and led by an overpaid CEO. Quite naturally, the operation depended upon local labor, mostly alienated blacks, to survive in the competitive marketplace of college taco and salsa.

I was striding with purpose when a wall of TVs caught my eye and slowed my pace. I stopped and stared. There must have been four rows of five televisions each, and on all twenty screens, a professor was lecturing. His male understudy, perhaps a teaching assistant, pointed to power point slides that appeared to have sexual instructions on them. From missionary to doggy-style, he was leading us watchers through our positions. I stood and watched and after several minutes ascertained that this was a contemporary classroom. The professor was teaching a televised MOOC to millions of viewers across the globe. The course was in Prostitution 501. It was graduate-level hooking for the indebted masses. As a final thought, he informed the viewing audience that a progressive society was taking shape, and we would all soon be able to sell our bodies legally in every left-leaning region of America.

When the screens broke to a commercial, a shiny cosmetic woman explained that everyone watching each episode and completing the weekly quizzes and field work would receive a certificate in Applied Prostitution—choose up to four from male, female, bi, poly, and trans—as well as a shiny paperback explaining where specific maneuvers taught in the class constituted legal work, both in the states and overseas. In the spirit of all-American inclusivity, and legality, no one would be turned away. From this, I gathered I was merely viewing one of many mini lectures and this one happened to be oriented toward folks looking to get ahead. What would the corporate university think of next?

Moving on, I found my favorite burrito joint, and pushed through the glass door and straight to food. I stood in line, trying to appear as regular as possible—not as a homeless murderer, but more like a grad student in philosophy or comparative lit. I hoped that I would be served.

For the truth was that Melony was not all I missed about the middle-class world of conformity and work. In fact, this place had a salsa verde that I was absolutely bonkers for. Tasty green stuff I would sit and savor and mingle with sour cream, guacamole, Monterey jack cheese, and refried beans.

I stood behind three others, and soon two more waited behind me. Would the queue protect my interests? I'd be just one customer cog in the fast-food wheel, and there'd be no problem or complaint. Standing and waiting, I ignored the faux Mexican wall art, and perused the seated clientele. My eyes were immediately drawn to a young woman in the corner. She was a Collegetown classic—a white privileged undergrad reading her well-packaged Vintage International trade edition of Michel Foucault's *The Order of Things*. I'd never read it although in the itinerant world of casual labor, in a bookstore between campuses, I had perused its first few pages, front and rear, along with its exterior blurbs and cover design.

What would mighty Michel think of this irony—he who put the Marxist dogmatists to bed for the last time, shifting the intellectual discussion away from the drudgery of strident and binary economic class warfare and toward something more discursive and Dionysian. Sexy and new. What would he think of this contemporary moment and the lay of its land? A young lady in the corner of climate-controlled corporate-chain America, reading his words in a translation from the French. It was an edition pimped out by a multinational publishing conglomerate, a book sold to eager, if alienated, graduate students all across the United States.

Not five yards from the glass window where she sat was the same garbage receptacle where I had watched and later berated the crusty punk girl who had been scrounging for scraps for herself and her dog.

Yes, what would a Marx or Foucault think of all that?

Thankfully, I snapped out of it. I could no longer afford to linger and think of philosophers or ideas. Socioeconomic paradoxes or the vagaries of capitalist places and practices. I was on the lamb and on the run. Desperate to survive and escape was no abstraction. In the real world, I had to look past the murder, flee my apartment, and figure out what to do or where to go next.

Life Lessons from Jonny November 14

So you want me to tell you what a Jew is? "Define a Jew"? Or, this is a game show, and you're telling me my only shot left is if I take Jews for a grand or seven c-notes?

Okay, this is what I got. If you don't like it, fair enough. Remember I'm only a half-breed.

A Jew ain't only a religion, and it ain't a race. It isn't an ethnicity, and you aren't disqualified if you're good at spreading mayonnaise on white bread or bad at money or good at sports or bad at guilt. It ain't about whether your mother is Jewish or your old man converted or both parents fasted on Yom Kippur. It don't matter if you were *bar* or *bat mitzvahed*, or if your grandma's recipe for chicken soup kicked Campbell's ass, or any of that.

It ain't about a toe in Israel, or an opinion on Palestine, or an uncle who died of a heart attack in Brooklyn or Queens, or a family story from Ellis Island, or an aunt who was murdered by Nazis or Russian *pogromchiks*, or whether or not three-fifths of your person is scared shitless of Auggie's *schvartzes*, or at least the young bucks you see walking with guns out and half their pants down.

It's got nothing to do with advocating for communism or capitalism or wearing wire-rimmed glasses, goatees, or any of that. You can take any position you want on dividing or unifying Jerusalem, women at the wall, living in the settlements, leaving Long Island, or pulling a Kinky Friedman and keeping your dick wet in Texas.

No way. It ain't about whether you banged your mom, *schtupped* your sister, or salivated when you imagined the possibilities. Are you nuts? You sure?

Okay, so what's a Jew?

A Jew is when you boil a whole package of Hebrew National Beef Franks to feed the alleyway dogs because you're that kind of decent human being. No, you're not a Jew if you feed the dogs. Some Jews are frugal and some are generous, and that's got nothing to do with it whether or not they banged Mom or Sis. You're a Jew if you let the boiled water sit and when it cools a couple hours after feeding time, you drink it. At least half of it. A Jew drinks the hot-dog juice. Gargles and swallows. Doesn't spit the liquid out. That's a Jew.

Chapter 6
Into the Garbage

As things went, my pocket cash dwindled while eating and selling stolen vegetables dried up entirely. Or I should say, I was caught red-handed one evening, sneaking corn and tomatoes into my satchel. They had been onto me all along. Legumes had gone missing, so they had formed a town watch, a vegetable lookout if you would. In only a few days, they'd found me. Of course, I tried to beg off, to insist that it was a one-time affair. But then they showed me photographs. In them, I was swiping fruits from the earth on successive days—five to be exact. They understood times were tough and for that reason they had chosen not to prosecute, but they then demanded a week's worth of my labor as compensation. They would feed me a meal, too, during this time, and even permit an extended stay on the dirt blanket. But after that, I would have to clean up and get to a homeless shelter. The normal channels, they insisted, were effective in dealing with men of my kind. Oh, how little these people knew! Would their attitude have changed if they realized they were interacting with a philosopher-murderer? A man capable of leading students into Plato and men into crime?

So I did my time, yes, I did. I weeded and planted for a week with these crunchy souls and their granola sandals. The sun was hot and the labor was hard. I was forced into an awkward position where communication was required. These sunnily disposed Americans—optimistic believers in the next day, our future and aspirations—demanded that I show some positive change in my demeanor. They wanted to know that rehabilitation was possible. I did my best to act reformed, if only so they could feel satisfied with my progress.

* * *

At the end of my sentence, I found myself back at the garbage receptacle; if you've read this far, then you know exactly which one I mean. How fondly I remembered those days. Yes, I was bitter, but also fully clothed and allowed to visit a girlfriend fifteen years my junior. Back then, I was regular and working and had a roof over my head. Where was I now? Haggard, unkempt, and sleeping when I could in an urban vegetable patch.

Famished, I dove into the garbage like a rabid mammal. I sifted through the empty coffee cups—plastic, paper, espresso-sized, etc.—and shook each one, listening for the splash of liquid. If even half an ounce remained, a tablespoon of liquid, sugar, and coffee, I downed it right away. Soon I had a bit of a caffeine buzz, and my sifting accelerated. Whenever I saw an empty carton for food—cardboard, Styrofoam, plastic, what have you—I opened it, shoved my nose in, and sniffed. If nothing about its contents made me retch, I peered more closely, looking for signs of movement. Despite all the ranting against lazy government employees and unions, I knew that good men, honorable men, picked up the garbage each evening. No matter what one heard about this occupation in the past, these were sturdy no-nonsense black men mostly, church-going folks who neither drank nor smoked—at least not on the job. So I could trust that yesterday's trash was gone, and the day's "catch" would be fresh.

I chanced upon half a turkey burger, sniffed, and opened the wheat bun for close inspection. By some act of God, this one had been denied mayonnaise or any fecund, melted cheese product. The burger sat squished beneath pickles and onions. This was not my favorite when ordering from the menu, but alas, as a beggar, I had no chance to choose.

I bit in to discover that in my celebratory joy, I had guessed wrong and that in fact, I was chewing on some kind of macrobiotic vegan soy concoction. It tasted mainly like tofu, garlic, and dirt, but despite its hardness and cardboard aftertaste, with my hunger, it was all fine by me.

Standing and chewing, I felt a slight return of sorts—not to health or dignity exactly. But something positive came to me. I could only assume it was protein from the burger. I looked up and noticed, then, that numerous young adults were sneaking glances at me, and some were gaping in awe. On instinct, I checked my fly and saw once more that the zipper was open. But they were not gazing at my groin, no. Why were they staring? Was a man digging in the garbage so rare? Why didn't I feel greater shame?

I realized that I was digging through public waste and slop for leftovers I would then devour like a wild animal. I'd made progress from classroom eating from the garbage, mainly for show and to be provocative, to the real thing. I was certainly on a slippery slope, but to what end?

* * *

I ceased digging and stopped eating leftovers altogether. Because I wasn't stealing either, I saw my cash slowly disappear until I was under two hundred dollars. The c-note I kept under my sock for an "emergency" was now a twenty-dollar bill. What had become of me? Where had I picked up "c-note"? Obviously, it was Jonny and Auggie, more than Nietzsche and Foucault, sloshing around in my brain and out of my mouth at this point.

Sitting on a fallen tree in the forest of Fairmount Park, I found myself crying tears of hopelessness. I felt lonely and desperate for a connection. Melony would never see me in my present state, and I didn't know what to do. But then I remembered the plan! Return to Jonny's trailer in four weeks! Jonny was our team captain. Our fearless leader. If I were lucky enough to find him at home, I would demand his advice. And my share of the winnings from our kill. In the moment, it felt like my only chance.

Life Lessons from Jonny November 15

"Shut up and listen to your teacher." You heard that, right? It's good stuff. If you get it good, pre-K through twelfth grade, you're likely to make it into your twenties with no priors. But be careful with that college stuff. Look at Michael. He got all caught up in philosophy and the smiling professors kept admitting him. They throw him a bone, an adjunct course or two each semester, and it keeps him in the game, makes him think that if he embraces a lifetime of learning it might lead somewhere.

But like most of us, he winds up dragging. Falling behind. Ten years later, and he's still got no dissertation. He's teaching college at two or three schools, living hand-to-mouth, eating meals in food courts in between afternoon and evening classes. He's adrift. Advanced degrees lead to advanced debt. Seven grand in the bank and he doesn't know where his next meal is coming from.

Killing time in the stake-out car, Michael told me about an officemate. Duffleman, Cyrus. A complete whack job. So fucked up from these adjunct overloads he's turned inside out and upside down. The kind of guy who'll get his tongue halfway up a lady's asshole but cringe when receiving his coffee from an Indian. The corporate model has these guys screwed in the head.

The capitalist knob jobs in charge of higher ed could care less. They smile widely, tend to their own retirement account, hold out their hand and accept Michael and Cyrus's no-bennies work and everyone else's tuition and fees. It's a sucker's play. For the most part chicks and black folk got it worse than the rest, so you can wake up in your late thirties, as itinerant labor in the knowledge economy and feel even more like shit because you started out with the white man's advantages.

Chapter 7
Tired and Tapped Out

As shabby as I appeared, it was easy to navigate through Camden's thrift-store corridor, the main retail strip. Beggars and whores and dealers avoided my gaze as they panhandled, leered, and provoked outside the long line of Dime-Marts and Dollar Burgers. I walked through, and I made it past all the destitution and prostitution and into the trailer park. In the back corner, I found Jonny November's water-stained half-broken trailer. But then I realized that waiting outside and knocking was too risky. I needed to get inside. It was then that I remembered the door had a broken lock, so I pushed myself in and blurted out: "Jonny!"

Nothing but silence.

I looked in the other room. There was no one around. I knew the bowl was missing, but nevertheless I checked the bathroom. No one home.

Back in the kitchen, I saw a note on the table:

Dear Professor,
Michael, I'm sorry that this is all there was. I searched for as long, and as well, as I could, but a few minutes after you left, I heard a siren. I didn't know if it was coming for me, but what could I do? Remember what you saw on the television, me and the white van, etc.

A vision of the fornicating bears flashed through my head. Next I saw the football player without arms and legs. But then I remembered seeing Jonny removing holiday gifts from the porch. Jonny had been touched. That was what he was reminding me of. I kept reading.

My gut told me I had to skedaddle. So I did. Sorry I can't tell you where I'll be by the time you read this, but I hope you get somewhere just as safe. Now it's time to get out of dodge. You've got to ditch Philly anyway you can. ASAP!

Remember to eat this note before you leave the trailer and if you need to wash it down, there's soda in the fridge. Put on the glove before you touch anything and then take that too.

Also, I left you some pocket change. I figured you'd only show up here if you were broke and lost about where to turn next. Enjoy it but spend wisely, on necessities, etc.

I gotta scram now. Good luck, bro.

By the note, I saw a suede glove for a left hand and the cash—a couple twenties, a worn fiver, a near-mint ten, and a few crinkled singles. Several SEPTA tokens and quarters, too. At least I wouldn't have to walk back over the Ben Franklin Bridge.

Doing my best not to touch the table, I picked up the money. I handled it with care, and pocketed it all. On second thought, it would be safer to store the dough about my person. Separating bills as I'd done in the past, I wound up with a couple singles in each front pocket, the five and ten in either sock, and the twenties by my front toes of either shoe. The coins and tokens went in my right pocket, too.

I grabbed the glove, shoved a finger into each leather digit, and clumsily picked up the note. It didn't exactly cause me to salivate, but I had been hungry. That was a reason I came here of course. I moved to the fridge, and with my glove hand, opened it. Sure enough, two bottles of root beer. No electric, so it was warm but serviceable.

I removed both plastic twenty-ouncers and placed them on the table. I opened one quickly and spray flew everywhere. So much for leaving a clean slate behind. After the ensuing fizz dissipated, I put the paper in my mouth, and chewed. Within minutes, it was a big clumpy mess that stuck to the roof of my mouth. I gargled with root beer, but that didn't help.

It was just as I began wondering why there wasn't a note and cash for Auggie, when I began hearing voices.

"Ya gotta tear it into tiny strips first."

Yikes! "What!?"

"The note. Not the cash."

As I turned around, I recognized the voice, and then saw, why, yes, it was Auggie, and no one else.

My mind went blank as I instinctively interrogated.

"What are you doing here?"

"Just scouting out the joint. Things are getting a bit sticky at my place. Complications with a couple girls down at the supermarket. I'm worried I'll have to start banging 'em both, and I'll need extra cash to rent a room some nights. Could get expensive and exhausting, and one of them is a freaky liberal chick. Boulder tits, no bra, and bushels of hair under the arms. Her legs are a forest that could win a fight with a lawn mower. I think she'd like believing she was giving head to an abused orphan so poor he lives without running water. Her kind is drawn to me like a Negro to cheese sandwiches."

"Shouldn't it be a mouse?"

"Yeah, whatever."

"How can you even consider dating under these circumstances? How can you even consider talking at all?"

"Oh, they already checked me out. I'm the abused stepson, remember?"

"That's it?"

"Well, if I ditch, that makes me look guilty, right? So I stayed put."

I experienced a shock of envy from this news, that Auggie knew exactly what to do and how to handle the situation.

"And I passed the lie detector. I had a great alibi, so I'm good to go."

"But you were there."

"Prof, does anyone else have to know that? Of course, it wasn't true, but it cooled the heat. I suspect all of my experience lying has paid off because I'm getting better at it."

Auggie had a point. So this was what it had come to. I was fraternizing with liars and deadbeats and men mooching off the system and then some.

"They haven't been following me the last two weeks, so I'm on schedule as Jonny advised. But it looks like our gold didn't come through."

I winced as I remembered how little I'd shoved into my pocket a minute ago. But Auggie was cleared. He was living in open view, whereas I was hungry, thirsty, tired, and in need of a week's soaking in a bathtub. I hadn't shaved since skipping out the back window. I was stealing vegetables to survive and shitting them out behind a bush in the park. It was then that I envied Jonny's coffee-can system.

I focused again on Auggie, who stood arms akimbo with a confident, satisfied facial expression. He was taking it all in and waiting for me to return serve just once.

"So where do you think Jonny ran off to?"

"Well, he *drove* off I'm sure, and if I were a betting man, I'd lay my cash on heading west."

"San Francisco?"

"He hates Northern Cali. Says it's all dog shit and minorities unless you got huge dough to live with Whitey Goldfarb, Desi Patel, and Chairman Mao in Silicon Valley."

"So?"

"My guess is Hollywood. LA. The coastal region, not inland where all the FOBs land and procreate with what's already there. Marina Del Rey is the dream, and Jonny is running so many scams, he'll make it happen."

So Jonny was smart enough to take his own advice and ditch the Delaware Valley. But what could I do? I didn't have money to repair my car or even get far by bus or train. My more pressing concern is that I was a wanted man. Or, at least I was stuck in Philly without an alibi.

I lost my composure and told him about the last month of my life lived in city parks and vegetable patches.

"I'm sure my belongings have been impounded and the apartment cleared out. I'm living in dirt, between cement and ripe tomatoes growing on the vine. These conditions are untenable. I don't know what to do. Or where to go. I can't go back to Melony. My grizzled look would gross her out. What should I do?"

"Relax, Prof. That's the first thing you gotta do. Wait until the case grows cold. Like on TV shows, a cold case. They forget about you, or they keep you on file but slowly lose interest. That's real life, not Hollywood. It'll take a few years, but it'll happen. And you stay clean, so they never suspect you of anything. That'll be easy for you since you're not a criminal."

"But I killed a man!"

"Relax, Professor. You done good. He deserved it."

"A few years!?"

"Yeah, five to ten years ought to do it."

"Ten to twenty!?"

"Yeah, twenty to ten, but then it'll feel like you're a free man."

Auggie smiled as if he had granted me a Get Out of Jail Free card, but it was then that I wanted to strangle him. If I put on the glove, they'd only have half of my prints around his pale, stumpy neck.

He was telling me that living on the lamb, if not always on the run, was to be my fate for what remained of my middle years. I could kiss goodbye any semblance of normal routine—work, job, woman, etc. My life would be sneaking around and pretending to be someone else. Another man might find this opportunity to slip into another life as stimulating adventure, a great escape. But I felt terrified.

When I was finished contemplating my own sad fate, I noticed that Auggie had disappeared. Out the front door? I checked Jonny November's broken clock and hypothesized it must be late afternoon. I was tired. Too tired to heed Jonny's advice right away.

All I had energy to do was flop on the couch. From my lower position, looking up, I saw that Jonny had a slither of a bookshelf high above the opposite wall, nestled in the corner. Against the wall were a couple dozen books wedged between the corner and a bottle of Jim Beam filled to the brim with pennies.

Before testing the television to be sure he sniffed cable from a neighbor—and presuming Comcast didn't beam it into the trailer park for free—I stood up again to inspect the books. I saw: an old copy, torn red cover, of *Let's Go U.S.A.*; in a similar state, a worn and weary copy, purple cover, of *Let's Go Europe*, and again, worn and weary, a paperback Bible whose faded spine offered Old and New Testaments. Last, there were a dozen mass market paperbacks, and after a swift perusal, I realized they were all mystery and crime novels. Last, in the corner, was a copy of *Lew Hunter's 434, A How To Write a Hollywood Screenplay*.

That we had the same taste in how-to guides seemed like a strange coincidence. On the other hand, wasn't everyone hoping to escape their circumstances through Hollywood fame? I picked it up and leafed through and saw underlining and asterisks and check marks in the margins. It was my copy! I turned back to the front and saw scribbled under my inscribed name these words: "Relax, Professor. I pinched it when you weren't around and left it here for fun. But no worries, Jonny's resourceful. If we're lucky, he'll sell film rights for our story and pony up some make-up cash."

I grabbed a few of the novels, read first paragraphs, and stuck with a Western that had sex and death on the opening page. It took me ten minutes to fall asleep.

Sleeping in vegetable patches must be no bed of roses because when I woke up, it was pitch dark. But I was exhausted and had no trouble returning to sleep and waking again to a bright slither of light coming in from the crack in the shade of the lone window. It must have been early daylight.

I lay there, immobile, craving a cup of strong coffee. And a sanitary shit. A shower, even if the water were a yellowish color or brown as the Schuylkill's summer tan.

But how would I ever rebuild my life to access these things?

I remembered that I had enough cash to buy coffee twenty or thirty times before the dough was gone.

After that?

Who knew?

I found myself moved to tears over my plight. It was simple self-pity sliding down my cheeks. Where the hell was I in life?

I was a criminal, a murderer, on the lamb and the run. I was haggard and unkempt and sleeping in a thick forest of urban vegetables while supplementing my diet with pissed-upon meats retrieved from the same garbage receptacle where I'd berated the crusty girl with a dog in her bicycle basket. Imagining the young woman on the bike reminded me of the trip with Melony to see a show on Broadway, and soon, the tears became a torrent, a storm of watery regret. I'd had a charmed life—work, apartment, a girl fifteen years my junior, all the wants and needs known to middle-aged philosophy man, and I threw it all away to fight for Auggie's justice. I was worse than Diogenes the Dog. A hypocrite who couldn't handle the hand-to-mouth existence of squash-vine life.

The crying went on and on and when it became too much, I left Jonny's trailer in search of the coffee that for now I could afford.

Chapter 8
Caught Red Handed

But again, what could I do? Where could I go? Despite Jonny's note, I couldn't escape Philadelphia. It seemed too risky to spend all my petty cash on carfare. A different section of the city was all I could think of, and so instead of returning to the Art Museum area I headed west for the outskirts of Collegetown.

At 48th and Warrington Avenue, I found an urban garden with even more fruits and vegetables, and better sleeping conditions in its hidden alleys. Early on, all went well. It was easy to bed down on secret dirt, and the garden's fruits and vegetables were plentiful enough that no one noticed a missing cucumber or tomato.

By the end of my first week, I would even, at times, forget that I was a wanted man, and life became a bit of a routine. Something I could cling to as daily comfort.

Sex was the one thing missing in my life, and no matter how hard I tried to forget it, I couldn't. Thusly, in the middle of the night, I found myself thinking of Melony, her bold white behind that could almost pass for a black girl's. Her perky tits and that time on the rug when she let me inside. It wasn't a "score" by Auggie's accounting, but how could I hope for better?

I grew so lonely that one evening when no one was around, and the coast seemed clear, I grabbed a squash and red pepper off the vine, don't ask, and set to work. I had my pants and underwear completely off and folded at the base of the veggie vines looming above and protecting me from public view. I was almost home free, so to speak, when I heard a loud, "What the fuck!?"

Two leering hippies, no shoes and cruel smiles, found me under the vine, two-fisting. They hovered above, and I felt the wrath of their unwavering eyes. When I came up for air, my back side was covered in soil and mulch. They saw the tomato crushed in my writing hand and its juices bleeding all over *mon stylo*, and they turned away in disgust. No matter how aggressively I'd taught all the postmodern conditions and deconstructions of the things in themselves—singular, right? I know—to contest their version of events would be hopeless.

But they were kind, if condescending, and they marched me to a garden meeting that was summarily to adjourn that evening. It was inside an F-space, what had once been an A-space, yes, now for feminism but then for anarchism. The irregular chairs we sat in were of wood, metal, cloth, and plastic. Folding and sturdier models colored red, brown, black, and white.

Discussion ensued of weekly proceedings. The operation was well organized. The urban farmers sounded highly educated. Some worked, many did not, and I was left imagining that they were once undergrads, too, educated people in the greatest country on earth, growing their own food to survive.

For my case, a tribunal was formed. From behind tall bookcases stacked with gender and oppression, three judges appeared. They were a man and a woman perhaps ten years my senior and a younger woman who looked familiar. Where had I seen a peach spaghetti-strap top below hair a swirl of orange and purple? *Ahah!* It was the very same crusty punk I'd seen grabbing from the garbage weeks ago. After she recognized me, she gave me a cat's snarl and hiss. A dirty look and a haughty leer!

I knew my day of judgment had finally come. I was or was not on the lamb from the proper authorities, but this pretty thing here was going to see that I pay.

In a flashback to the incident, I saw myself as a monster, mean and cruel. I'd far surpassed my area of influence to give the garbage sifter a piece of my mind. Where did I get the authority to tell this young woman how to live or what to eat? I was an itinerant knowledge cog at best, a murderer at worst, and I too had tasted and taken from the same trash receptacle. Oh what a hypocrite. I'm certain the shame washed across my face. Perfect timing, as this tribunal certainly required a guilty man.

"Order! Order!"

The long-locked, white-haired hippie addressed the room.

"We know times are tough. We are producing our own food because our government has failed us. The food stamp program's switch to a card effectively lets people experience less shame when they shop for groceries, but it does not resolve the underlying issues. The quality healthy food that all Americans deserve—organic, free range, and local—is still unavailable to all of us getting by on the card. To get enough sustenance, we're stuck choosing among Monsanto and a host of other poisoned mongrel grains and fruits."

Ahah!

So this was it. There was a philosophical bent to the proceedings, or at least an assessment of personal ethics in the face of governmental "efficiency." I liked it, as I knew better than to praise Monsanto. I'd never approved of the corporate-farm flatulence from my old officemate, Cyrus Duffleman.

"So that is why we have come together to build our urban farm. But one among us this evening has taken advantage."

He shot a look in my direction.

"We have caught an interloper. We're all about free love and free expression, but we also know the garden is off limits for hanky-panky. Particularly if the suspect is also a tomato thief." The man's tone become slightly derisive, and I detected a hint of irony. It was as if he was mocking me, but also the proceedings. Perhaps he did not believe in tribunals? A jury of the people, small as this one might be? Or maybe he saw me for what I was. A peculiar masturbatory thief, one who no doubt belonged in much tamer surroundings. A long-locked unwashed today, but one whose complexion and manner still suggested I belonged to the cubicles. To the bourgeois concerns. The world of work, rent, bills, and the rest of it.

His staring caused everyone to turn and look at me. I felt extra caught. Shame and self-loathing.

He resumed. "We need to assess the guilt of this man. After that, we determine his punishment."

Fervent discussion ensued of my theft and manipulation. It went back and forth, and I was impressed that I was allowed to stay and bear witness.

The crusty punk girl got in her two cents: "He is one of those rude 'civilized' types who thinks he is the one who needs to save us."

After an hour that felt like an afternoon, the final pronouncement came.

"As rehabilitation, you will live with us for two weeks, tend the garden, and perform additional chores. Susannah will host you in her bunk." The leader pointed to the crusty punk who, once more, sneered at me.

Chapter 9
To the Precinct

Believe me, this was far from some happy utopian ending, where the unwanted murderer wound up living among the communal people in a state of bliss, an alienated man come to find his heaven on earth, rejuvenated by a crusty-punk girl, down at the crossroads confessing to all he did wrong. In fact, Susannah hated me. I was as bad as her beef-eating father and not unlike the old man and her uncle combined. He was a tenured professor who'd continually compare her life to the last dull dead pale text he was reading. Thusly, Susannah tortured me with nitpicky criticisms of everything I was doing wrong. I didn't know how to weed or use a hoe or whether or not cucumbers and green peppers were ripe for picking. This made me miss my BBQ-sauce-and-lettuce Melony all the more.

After a long day of her nagging, a relentless spewing of constant criticism, she told me we could do it if I ate her first. I must confess, I'd never made it inside to the peeking place at 22nd and Market, and I was still horny. But when she shoved it in my face, I saw a hairy monster that scared me shitless. It disgusted me even more than the fact that I had murdered a man. So each time she flashed bush, I'd scamper in fear to the far corner of her third-floor front in the commune's shared Victorian squat between 49th and 50th on Florence. She'd watch me run and laugh at my cowardice. After a week of this, she grew bored and upped the ante. She swung her bottom to lure me in, but then as I scurried toward my backdoor score, she'd make a quick one-eighty and shove fur in my face. For thrills, she'd add a long sonorous queef that I could taste on my tongue. Either way, I'd retreat, terrified, as she cackled and farted. This went on for two weeks.

When the month came to an end, I was grateful. I was sick and tired of the constant dialogue. The give and take. The chatter about all manner of radical baloney. Even if I believed in much of it, voted for most of it, when I bothered to vote, and recommended it profusely during class discussion, it was a nightmare listening to these unoriginal "theorists" and practitioners of left-wing ideologies. It was unfathomable how they could stand to listen to each other, if in fact, they were listening when they weren't interrupting or taking the cucumber mike. My taste for something more nihilistic or multilayered never wavered, whether or not the crusty punk was threatening me with her uncombed cavern or not.

Of course, I didn't tell her that, and we had seven more meetings after the first. Yes, I counted.

But there was no permanent life for me among these people. I was not one of them, and I knew I must disappear.

* * *

I came to see that I should turn myself in. I had no life on the outside. I was stripped down—no apartment, no work, no purpose. How much longer could I go on, sneaking into libraries, waiting in line for hand-me-downs, eating from the garbage, swiping communal tomatoes, and waiting to get caught? I was just one homeless man among the masses—a parasite begging for society's scraps.

In jail, once more, I'd have a routine—"three squares and a cot," as Jonny would say. I'd be surrounded by a violent throng according to the movies, but by ninety percent nonviolent offenders according to any left-of-center publication. Either way, I could adapt and survive, and I wouldn't have papers to grade. How hard could it be compared to a life sentencing to the lowest rung of academe?

Besides, I'd read the classic writing from prison—Boethius, Machiavelli, Gramsci, Primo Levi, and MLK's "Letter from a Birmingham Jail." Even Hitler needed his jail time to write *Mein Kampf*, indeed, a far larger loser than Heidegger, but at least he did his time. My hope was that some quiet with a stiletto would be awaiting me as well. I could plead guilty, act as if I understood the charges and get fifteen years at the most. They would have to take into account the crimes of Auggie's stepdad.

Even if the courts failed to find inspiration in our collaboration, the men in jail might respect an accomplice to an avenging son, fighting for justice in a brutal world. They killed child abusers in prison, so they might see me as the opposite: A hero protecting the innocent. A self-starter who made plans and took action. This was the American way.

Once behind bars, I'd get on a writing roll and produce copious quantities of text. I'd pen a treatise or two, publish books, and build a C.V. I'd tell my tale in a memoir as well, and some university with a bold hiring initiative and radical approach to jailhouse philosophy would hear in my story a tale of heroism and intellect, and hire me to teach the prison house of philosophy, advanced learning in the field. They'd understand my plight and welcome me into the fold. The university always had room for irregulars, as long as they published upon occasion.

The sleeping quarters would no doubt be a step above the city parks and gardens I'd been tenting in.

* * *

In the cover of darkness, I snuck away from the communal garden as soon as I paid my price. I tried to be as quiet as possible, but Susannah woke up anyway. She flashed bush, gyrated, and cackled as she saw me collect my clothes, shove my feet in my shoes, and ditch. It must have been past 3 a.m. when I trudged up Baltimore Avenue toward campus, and hooked a left over on 40th. I made a right on Locust and headed straight through Locust Walk. It was the safest route, and I hoped I appeared enough like a meandering graduate student not to draw too much attention. I passed under the red conical sections that formed a looming statue. As a boy, when these were first installed, I'd play in them with my sister. The cones were hollow, so we ran through the spooky sections. A fierce wind tunnel was known to haunt this extended campus path, but the air was still on this cool June night.

I went over the 38th Street walking bridge and paused at the top to admire Philadelphia from a higher view than I'd recently been exposed to. An occasional car whizzed by underneath as I stared north, at Powelton Village, and beyond. From such summit, I descended down between Ivy Green Business School buildings, and social sciences and the old fraternity houses. At 36th I veered left and walked by the broken button statue outside the university library. Inside I would sit, read, sleep, and dream for so many hours as a younger adult, a graduate student. Because they required identification and a photo image, I hadn't been through the oversized glass doors since I climbed out of my bedroom window when I heard the police knocking. From 34th and Walnut I meandered through Liberty Tech University, a campus under continuous construction expanding into e-galaxies far, far away. I walked by the 30th Street Train Station and onto the Market Street Bridge. At the Goodwill Store, I hooked a left on 22nd and walked under the dark underpasses. I avoided waking several homeless people sleeping under cover of the train tracks headed to Suburban Station, and strode through the expensive Logan Circle condominiums and houses.

I walked across The Parkway, all the way to the precinct on 22nd just below the Wawa Food Market. I got to within one hundred yards, and then, exhausted, I sat on a mangled, damp, bench and closed my eyes. But at this point, I was too awake to fall back asleep, and I stood again and walked to within fifty yards. I stood there and watched. Three officers came out to chat and smoke cigarettes, and I stood and observed them, but they hardly noticed me. Did it seem strange to stare at the police in the middle of the night?

I guessed not, as they didn't approach me and ask why I was there. Two of the officers went back inside, and the remaining cop lit up a second cigarette and stood taking in the night air. At one point, I thought I could hear him mumbling. Maybe he was using a wireless speaker phone or reciting a song or prayer? He turned, and he must have noticed me because he waved! Were the police accustomed to being stared at by homeless men off

The Parkway? I did not know. All I knew to do, in fact, was to wave back and try my hardest to grin.

* * *

So I walked away. The smoker outside the precinct had such little interest in me, the indigent man gazing at him from afar, that it was both boring and insulting. It made me feel inadequate, like I wasn't enough of an outcast or murderer to get noticed by the police.

I returned to my usual haunts and dwelled for a few days. I slept downtown and even tried panhandling. "Thank you, sir." "Yes, ma'am, I will take your advice." "Just say 'no,' yes, sir." "With you generosity, I know can make the transition!" "Sorry, I don't perform stupid human tricks for shiny quarters." I made enough each day for two wholesome fast-food meals. With a regular sliced tomato and dead leaf of lettuce squished between fake meat and a sesame-seed bun, my vegetable theft became a thing of the past.

It came to me that I wanted to make a larger impression. In philosophy or murder or some area in which humanity would stand up and take notice. But I'd wound up in everything, from thinking to writing to love to life, making no impression at all.

Even when I left the precinct, I felt no piercing stare on my back. There was no one there monitoring my movement, onto my scent, hunting me down.

Then it hit me.

Perhaps I was not a wanted man?

True, there had been a policeman's card in my door. But that could have been for anything, right?

I had heard knocking, but that may have just been my harassing landlord. He was always scheming to play one tenant against another or to spit some venom about the dope smokers living a floor below me. Perhaps, as was his custom, he only wanted to collect the rent a day before it was due.

There was nothing better to do than check my old apartment. I would return and see if there was yellow tape all over the door and windows. I'd seen this in the movies and also in my departmental floor at Liberty Tech. A past boss, an academic philosopher, had been fired and arrested for child pornography not long ago. The authorities had found the stuff all over his desktop. It was mixed in with Heidegger and mingling with the postmodern riffraff and continental crowd. The police took his computer and dusted the keyboard for prints and DNA. Traces of semen, or so I was told. They then left us with yellow tape all over his door and permission to gossip like good citizens of the land of office employment.

In my disheveled state, I wandered back to my old apartment. I was determined to look around. Sneaking in the back way seemed like the safest bet. Thus, I returned via the same alleyway from where I had escaped with my life and meager necessities. I knew my present state was a bit alarming—long, wild locks of hair and a full fluffy beard—so I tried to be as inconspicuous as possible.

One thing in my favor, of course, was the anonymity of downtown living. So many of the residents in the neighborhood were single dwellers and no few of these were strange. Weirdos and *isolattoes*, intent on keeping to themselves. In center city, eccentric types owned homes, or at the very least, they inhabited meager efficiencies with working utilities where they could lay down and rest after another weary day. This meant that the genuinely indigent homeless—in a word, me—could blend in with the crowd. My long locks and pungent odor were not necessarily abnormalities in a community known for its irregularities and nonconforming types.

One evening at twilight, I returned down the back alley. I walked along the metal fence where I had scraped my hand in my frantic escape. Only this time, I was slinking slowly but regularly, pressed against the fence to stay in the shadow. When I looked up to my left, expecting to find my open window and torn shade, I was shocked to see lavender beach towels. I walked ahead, anticipating that my unit was in fact in the next house down, but alas, I saw the same oversized rainbow-colored curtains that I'd known from the past. Why, of course, time waits for no man and my apartment had been rented by someone else. My next thought was of my possessions, my valuables. In this case, of course, these were only my books. If there were a new tenant, then presumably they wouldn't be splayed all over the floor. But had they all been collected and shoved neatly into milk crates and cardboard boxes? Or could they all have been thrown away? There was no other option, then. I had to ring the bell of my landlord or the new tenant.

I chose the tenant and rang the bell.

When she answered the intercom, I tried to explain that I had lived there before. She said she didn't want any. I restated my purpose, and she quickly stifled my clarification by stating that she had been told the unit was brand new. The black appliances and strong smell of varnish supported that notion.

"Do you know what they did with my stuff?"

"What stuff? There was nothing here when I moved in."

With that, she hung up.

So that was that?

I had disappeared from the world of working people, the middling classes, grovelers after health-insurance copays and three-percent raises, and there was no trace of me. I was no longer counted on the employment rolls. Being more or less x-ed out of civilization reminded me of Dr. Karl Othar, an adjunct in communications, who seemed happy as a clam, content with his role in society. One night after teaching three to five classes, he fully exposed to the world his euphoria by posting to social media a photo of his brains plastered against the wall just before changing his profile settings from private to public. Was I happier away from the pressures and obligations of society and work?

I saw this in terms of Auggie's life. It was different from being trapped in a closet, tortured and physically abused. In fact, I had my freedom of mobility. There was no claustrophobic moment of someone stuffing me into darkness or forcing me to do things against my will.

I left my building puzzled. Confused. What at all was *mine* about the building? I couldn't say, and I was also unsure of what my next move should be. It occurred to me again that I might not even be wanted at all. That I could clean up my act—shave, change clothes, etc.—and rebuild my life. I'd go somewhere else.

In my more positive moments in the classroom, I'd insist upon the greatness of free societies, and how the beauty of America is that even with modest credentials, if life grew genuinely dull and tiresome, you could abruptly alter its terms. You could find a job in another city and move to this other place. Scrub yourself down, change clothes, trim facial hair, and present a fresh, clean you. No one would know you there, and you could become someone else. You could pick up a bit of work, and begin anew. The majority white students I taught didn't want to know how difficult such a transition would be for Auggie's "*schvartzes,*" so I always left that part out.

But I still needed to know why the detective's card had been left in my door. That was unusual to say the least.

I realized that in our plans to execute Auggie's stepfather, I'd become myopic and had lost track of the daily news, all the murder, fire, war, and worse. All that kept us together and bound in imperfect, if collective, humanity. Our shared commitment to mutual destruction. Perhaps some other man's crime had led to the police officer's card in my door?

Life Lessons from Jonny November 16

I'm talking to you, kid. You want to go to college? You want to learn? I understand. You got a big plan, grad school, the whole bit. Maybe philosophy, just like Michael? You imagine some dream professor's life, where you sit around in a circle jerk with all the other little Heideggers, reading last century's Nazis and Jews off the student-loan dime. Whacking off to the total debt amounts—seventy-seven grand for undergrad plus a masters, over a hundred large with a PhD. Ask Auggie's buddy, Professor Michael, to see how that turned out.

This is America, so one generation devours the next. Never forget that. From saving Private Ryan *my ass* to the Vietnam draft to student-loan burdens in the twenty-first century. The old masticate upon the young here, and with impunity. They rip into twenty-something flesh, tear muscles and tissue, and gnaw at the carcass of the next America. Okay, don't let me get carried away.

I wanted to go to college, too. Maybe even hustle a chick-magnet major like English or sociology. Yeah, I stuck around for a few semesters and change, but for guys like you and me, it's not affordable. Seventy percent of us finish with thirty grand in debt. What does that get anyone? A hole that much larger to dig out of is what. If the debt doesn't kill you, imagine suffocating from all the bull-dyke omni-fag "discourse" in the seminars. You start choking down all that crap, and before you know it you're spent. The deep majors aren't safe for any guy with his pair intact and prepared to use it in the traditional manner.

How do I know "discourses," you ask? Good question or not? If you hit the books for a couple years, read the papers, live around colleges your whole life, and keep your eyes open, you can't help but pick up some of the lingo and misuse it with the best of them. What the hell is "performative" anyway?

So yeah, you want to learn? I want to learn too, but how do we do it? Read on your own. Think on your own. You need a syllabus? A piece of paper that tells you what to read? Okay, we'll play professor and student. Send me a piece of paper and an SASE, and I'll send you back a list of books. After you read them, I'll write you another list. You want to ask questions? Send them in writing. Specific ones only, please. It'll be a correspondence course. We'll keep in touch, or better yet, for advanced study, I'll get Michael to write you a list if you need better books. You see Michael? You see what he's like? That's what advance schooling does to a guy. You want to wind up like that?

Those elitist hypocrites up at those schools, Michael's bosses, God bless 'em. Hey, I'm liberal, too. Legalize hooking and weed and let the other guy fag out free and easy, and leave more poontang-titty for the rest of us. I'd vote gay, not *goy*, if I thought it was safe to show for elections. But I got priors, and I don't need to know what else they got on me. Forget my known unknowns.

But I know I'd never vote for any of those capitalist frauds with their hand-me-down lives. Yale lawyers and Harvard MBAs, prep-school Oreos and vanilla-wafer white boys with sympathy for us, the masses. Fuck that. I don't want their pity. They're all so full of shit. You know what I mean. Yeah, up at college, their appointed friends smile at us, teach us the sanitized PC approach to assessing history, and tell us all to behave and wait for our opportunity. And work retail part-time and minimum wage while we do so.

Fuck that. That works for them. Not for us. Maintain the status quo. Train the sheep to stay asleep. Prop up the establishment and all those old money dirt bags. El Y.T. and his golfing buddy, Jimmy Got Green. They go into business and politics, where they slam the rest of us where it hurts. Thick and deep in the wallet. They don't do jack shit for a regular guy trying to get ahead in the world.

It's like how Europe did Africa. They exported Christianity to the Dark Continent as an instrument of pacification. Don't let them fool you. Jobs? Careers? Yes, for the top kids, the well trained ones with the brains upstairs, it all works out, particularly if they smile endlessly and work their parents' connections. But for the rest of us? No fucking way are we gonna leave college with anything other than egregious debt. Government loans, credit cards, all of it. So go to college if you want to hear a few lectures, hang in the library, and check out the latest in careerist support bras. Stand around a pony keg of piss water, a yard of cock on game day watching corn-fed farmers' kids kill the quarterback. Tailgate grilling and booze and all that. Yeah, if that's your thing, do it.

But if you're like me, and the system is already stacked against you, against most of us, then college is not the right move.

Trust me, I know. I've lived around colleges my entire life.

Chapter 10
The Library of the Free

Determined to investigate, I chose the main branch of the Free Library of Philadelphia as my research center. Despite my present circumstances, as I approached Logan Circle, it gave me quite a thrill to enter into the same library I had grown up in. The grey slab marble of the ancient building reminded me of better days. I remembered all the afternoons as a teenager when I would visit to read and explore. I would walk down from my middle school on Spring Garden Street, and spend a couple hours in history, philosophy, and literature. Back then, the free library's aged texts still circulated.

Alas, no one was reading books these days. To my left, I could see the stacks were full of books but bereft of browsers, and as I passed, on my right, I could see that the folks in the lending section were searching for music and film. Now I walked up the wide stone steps at the center of the interior and moved to where they kept the computers. In my zest to remain hidden, on the lam and out of view, I hadn't been to a public internet station in months. It then hit me that my e-mail could be backlogged—a mishmash of students' laments, dating-site and investment spam, and all the daily reminders I received from years and years of browsing online.

At the computers, I saw that a line awaited me. There were grown men mostly and so many looked homeless that for a brief moment, again, I felt a sense of common purpose. It was a place where I could belong, but so many were darker skinned that I felt like an outcast even here. Nevertheless, at the desk with a seated librarian in charge of dispensing internet-access blocks of thirty minutes each, I wrote my name on the list. After that, I sat and waited to be called.

There were so many of us indigent folk, sitting there and waiting for a computer. Was this the fate of the public library system? I wondered what would happen to Nietzsche and Hegel and Feuerbach and even Heidegger, yeah, that asshole. Should I not first walk down the hall and around the corner to pay a visit to my old friends in philosophy? I could attempt to lift up their spirits with a reminder that some of us still cared.

My number was called, and I was assigned an internet station. For the moment, I forgot about dead white epistemologists, phenomenologists, pessimists, and supremacists. I turned to the worldly task at hand. Sitting down at a computer, I checked my e-mail. Universities first, then personal e-mail and social media last of all. I was behind by a mere 10,529 messages. In my haste to plan the perfect crime, I'd gone offline and somehow, after overcoming the initial nagging of internet withdrawal, the thought of going back on had not occurred to me. Now I skimmed and scanned and saw there was a single message from Melony after the last time I saw her.

I pointed, clicked, and read:

Look, Michael, what we had was fun, and you introduced me to some interesting guys. i'm so glad I got to know Auggie and all about his story and what you did for him is so great. But like, I have to move on with my life. You and I are headed in different directions. You're sweet, but I can't really keep you in my life right now.

i'm sorry. I mean like what if you get caught and go to jail? how would that affect my career? Those prisons are so icky and they're full of the yucky kind of black boys and i'd feel really bad if I was too grossed out even to visit you. I don't even want to think about the gross food they serve in those drab cafeterias and the cockroaches and water bugs scurrying around the place.

So like this is it. Auggie told me he knows a guy in Hollywood and he's going to help me get there. i need to be around positive people and I need to feel as if my life is going forward. I'm sorry, Michael. That was really sweet and brave of you to take care of

Auggie's stepdad and i hope you get better at sex and everything.
Good luck, sweetie.

ox,
Melony

I paused, felt sad, a bit humiliated, but for whatever reason, it wasn't too hard to press on. The relationship was ridiculous, really, and I should be lucky I escaped romance without any embarrassing hair loss or erectile dysfunction. Melony, or any girl Melony's age, would have been too much for me in the long run. So I laughed and cried inside, and chuckled aloud, wiped away a tear, and turned to the other messages.

There was one from Jonny November that began, "This is only to let you know I have your e-mail. Delete this and then remove from the trash can after you read." It was dated the day before the murder, and its concluding line read, "I hope you spent the twenties wisely." This last bit caused me to consider that there could be cash in my wallet. When I looked down and to the left from the corner of my eye, I spied that the scruffy fellow next to me was staring at pornography. I was briefly reminded of catching Cyrus Duffleman viewing the same years ago when we shared an office; he looked so humble and humiliated, shame and urgency at once written across his brow. At the time, Duffy said, "Sorry" softly as I laughed in his face.

This time, I stifled my giggles and disgust. It was soft core, exposure above the waist. The fellow's arm and shoulder were moving. Looking down, I saw that his joystick had popped out, and he was manipulating the controls. It was discrete save for the fact that his zipper was open and from my angle, I could see the exposed, offending weapon. It could even pass for professional jerking off. Not that I should count myself any kind of expert on the matter. Disgusting. Alas, even the homeless had loneliness and sexuality.

The shock of revulsion got me on task, and soon I was combing the local news. I searched for all kinds of terms—"police dragnet," "center city crime," and that sort of thing. Through the miracle of the contemporary internet search engine, it took me less than thirty minutes to find what I was looking for. There had been a series of rapes downtown, and I understood instantly that could explain the card in my door.

For the most part, Philadelphia did as good a job as any American city at keeping its criminals separate from the "good people," but occasionally, a sweet young pale professional, taught to overachieve and pity the masses her entire childhood, would wind up bringing a ne'er-do-well into the fold. As in, into her bedroom. An underachieving male of another stripe, who once he was gifted a taste of the good stuff would decide to go on a binging trip. Once hooked, who can say "no" to high-rent zip codes, down comforters, silk sheets, and grad-school ass with premium coffee in the a.m.?

In this case, the culprit was described as more or less my height and weight and potentially my complexion, and in fact, there had been a dragnet in center city among those living in the inferior, discounted studios and junior one bedrooms like my own. I found this information in an article dated six weeks ago, and I sat at the computer, stunned and amazed. And frightened.

I feared then that not only had I murdered Auggie's stepfather, but that I had completely lost it. The gift of Melony had turned me into a serial rapist! It had come too easy, and I had taken advantage. I darted my head about to make sure there were no authorities lurking near the library technology. No one waiting to arrest one of us for rape, murder, multiple crimes, or worse. The chicken choker right next to me was going on as usual, with increased vigor, and I realized this must be a less regulated place. Once library patrons got past first-floor security, there were no police anywhere in sight.

Then, it occurred to me that perhaps I was not a multiple rapist, so I resumed my searching for news. Presto! Within fifteen minutes, I discovered a more recent story stating that they had apprehended the culprit. A man had confessed!

Not guilty! I was free at last. True, there was still the murder of Auggie's stepfather to reconcile, but at least I hadn't also violated innocent young women.

I read then about the accused (or I should say, *the confessed*).

He had been brought up in a troubled home in troubled times. The usual in poor parenting and hard times. Depression, violence, and regret. He had joined the armed services but was later expelled. No, it was an honorable discharge, but he had been given an unsatisfactory rating. From there, it went downhill. He had shuffled from one job to another. He'd get laid off, or he'd quit after sticking around long enough to get passed over for promotion. Before his confession, he had little trouble with the law although his girlfriend noted that he did have a temper. Once he was thrown out of a bar after a round of pool. Which he had won, along with one hundred dollars, although he didn't like the way the loser had handed him the money, out of order and dropping it on the table without eye contact.

I wondered about his childhood and found myself considering to what extent the confessed rapist had been abused. Physically, emotionally, or in any other way. Were there traumas similar to what Auggie suffered? I saw him locked in closets, beaten, and molested. I could envision what likely had determined this man's fate.

Although I did not see him as innocent, or rather, *excused*, not for the rapes at least, my thoughts did then turn to all of the accused, the criminals in jail carrying their childhood traumas like albatross strewn around their necks. All the poverty, abuse, abandonment, violence, poor schools, drugs, alcohol, ignorance, injustice, and more that had shaped their lives. It was all one big corporate capitalist ass-fucking, all the frozen and fast food and dollar menus and laid-off fathers and men who left before they got fucked over by someone above them or the entire system. There must be millions just like Auggie, and very few ever had the luxury of seeing their molester killed in cold blood with the help of his friends.

But where did that leave me?

Even in my meager efforts to survive, still my thoughts were of Auggie and those like him—all of the young, wounded, and traumatized Americans. My working life had been built on a pile of their tuitions and tax dollars. I was supposed to stand behind the lectern and tell them that this is America, the land of possibility and philosophy, and that everything would be okay despite increasingly high college costs and educational debts that would be a burden to repay. The state schools were as suspect as the rest in their compliance with structural classism that admitted the wealthiest first and made college least affordable and accessible to the children of the poor.

These children were innocent, and I could only see the state as totalitarian and oppressive, an illegitimate, unlawful hegemony led by and for a wealthy elite. The more money you earned, the more of a metaphorical molester you must be. Sure, the rest of us had our rights and our votes. But did it matter? True, I up until recently had a toehold in the world of legitimate work. In the past, several institutions of higher learning, apparatuses of the state, did offer me legal, taxable tender for my efforts at brainwashing, I mean teaching, future contract-slaves, soon-to-be 1099ers tending toward eligibility for food stamps and Medicaid. These future freelancers kept me employed, so I had an ability to subsist, to tread water, in the brutal seas of the American economy.

That was my thinking in the moment. Was it accurate? Was it flawed? Was America lying and cheating all of its own abandoned and abused children? What could America actually do to help them? What did murdering a single stepfather solve? What else could I, we, or anyone do?

Life Lessons from Jonny November 17

Listen up. This is important. Train yourself to go without, but if you got to have it, I understand. Chinatown will satisfy your needs.

Madame Chen runs a respectable house—nice girls, clean rooms, soap by the sink, etc. You go to Madame Chen's and you ask for the yellow tail. That's where I took Auggie for his eighteenth birthday. Maybe if someone'd taken Michael there, he'd have his head screwed on straight about the rest of life's crap. Madame Chen deals straight, not like most men you meet on this earth. She's got the freshest fish in Chinatown, and I guarantee that she will not disappoint. But if you need it a little spicier, check out Lady Tran's down the block. Narrow alley, windows painted black. She runs a professional establishment. I know, the name sounds Vietnamese, and that's what makes it so good to eat at. She's got the feistiest red snapper within a hundred miles. Top-tier tilapia and premium squirrel fish. Ask for extra oyster sauce or sesame oil. Cash only, okay, and remember to wear a jacket because she doesn't charge extra for crabs or sea crawlers. Yeah, it doesn't make sense that the best fish in Chinatown is Vietnamese. That's Philly. Go figure.

Hey, remember that when you're getting your nunchuks waxed at the House of Tang, lay off the chopsticks Charlie humor. White-man rhymes about slanty-eyed pee-pee Cokes were never an aphrodisiac. Be polite and respectful. Tip well. You treat the girls right, you get treated right. *Capisce?* Once you go Asian, there's no other persuasion. But spare me the Chinese stars and all that kung fu and karate noise. Sounds like you're a lover, but Jonny's a survivor, not a fighter. The wushu kicks and chain whips aren't for me.

Chapter 11
The Liberty Bell Plot

After a few weeks of perfect June weather, low humidity and sunny, with temperatures rarely past eighty degrees, summer roared in with a soaking. Evening rains brought morning mist, and too soon Philly was hot and humid. The sky would fill up like a million-pound water balloon and burst into drenching storms.

Seeking shelter in indoor public places that didn't kick out the indigent, I thought of Auggie and his promises of making it out to the coast one day. His vision of blue skies, scenic cliff-side property, and waves crashing onto the sand. It occurred to me that he might be there. I hadn't seen him in any of my recent perambulations around Philly. This had been his dream. His goal. And perhaps the dead stepfather had finally caused him to take action. I envisioned then Auggie on the beach in a Playa or Marina Del Rey, walking arm in arm with two young playthings, his conquests out west as easy as apple pie, the girls finding his goofy pick-up lines to be just what the doctor ordered.

But where did that leave me?

I was a homeless man perspiring on and off the hot asphalt of Philadelphia. For me, meeting Auggie had ultimately been the train wreck that ruined my life. True, his pick-up routines in the supermarket had no doubt inspired me to snag Melony, but I couldn't hold on to her, and alas, as we know, he had taken her first. He changed my life. Yes, under the influence of Auggie and Jonny November, I was led to quit my stale day job and kill a man. Unbelievably so, it had been my idea! For a moment, then, I was caught with the notion that in fact, it had all been some kind of scam. That although it had been my idea, somehow it had all been turned around and gotten upside-down and that I had been manipulated by Auggie and Jonny, as in some sort of sting where the real crooks lead the innocent man to his demise. Before I'd met them I had steady work and enough "change in the till" to feed a spare six-inch hoagie to the homeless.

But where was I now? And what was I worth? There had to be something more for me on this planet. Something dangerous and daring, something I could do before I turned myself in.

I became obsessed with doing something then—yet, again—not only for Auggie now, but for the millions of Americans trapped in the system of capitalist abuse. Something daring and bold. Cathartic and rewarding all at once.

My obsession became the bell. The Liberty Bell—a symbol of all the promise that wasn't in this land of destroyed childhood, false hope, and promises beyond reach. They used the word Liberty as if we weren't all confined to the prison house of parents. As if the state itself were not some oppressive father violently abusing and molesting and violating his citizen-children. This was the America all about my city. This is what I saw and knew.

* * *

So I made preparations. I researched the options. I studied the charts and went to the websites, for legal explosives, semiautomatic weaponry, and such. I felt young again, like one of my students, alienated nineteen-year-olds searching online for bombs and IEDs. I bought straps and vests. Detonators and electronic devices. I read books and took notes. I listed and grouped. I studied and learned.

One soaking hot summer day, I went to scout my location. As soon as I walked outside from the 5th Street Blue Line Stop, I realized something was amiss. I hadn't passed by here in quite some time, and it seemed like the lay of the land had changed.

At first, I couldn't find the Liberty Bell at all, and I feared I had forgotten its location. But across the street was Betsy Ross House, and nearby stood several brick colonial buildings. Hadn't this always been our bell's vicinity? I walked toward some new structures—brown brick and glass—that I couldn't remember from the past. There was a long line outside, tourists presumably, and I couldn't help but discern that over half were Asian. They had a manner and dress that suggested not homegrown or hyphenated, but rather authentic visitors from overseas. Could this be our sacred bell? Surrounded by foreigners with wealth to fly far for vacation, and intent upon waiting in a long line to catch a glimpse of history?

I approached and stood behind this line of several hundred strong. I caught a whiff of Beijing sweat. It was the strong odor of men from a non-soaping culture, a colony of unwashed underarms and groins. Yes, as dirty as Diogenes, and I was judging the stench of others. But I needed to know for sure that I was in the right line, so I ignored the pungency of Asiatic sweat and asked as politely as I could, "Pardon me, sir, are you waiting to see the Liberty Bell?"

The man right ahead of me turned back with an awkward expression on his face. He looked fearful at first, as if I were *his* foreigner, a barn sleeper, some Uighur come to pummel his face and steal his camera and currency. So I tried to smile, an expression I couldn't remember having had for weeks. It may have looked awkward, but it was enough. I repeated, "Pardon me." That got the man grinning and smiling and soon he was poking the gentlemen in front of him and saying something in Mandarin, Korean, or Vietnamese. I'm ashamed I was unable to say for sure, but within moments, they produced a gentleman from near the front of their group and more than one fellow nodded affirmatively and said, "Good English."

So this was their translator.

I asked my question again.

"Yes, yes," and the gentleman pointed to the front of the line, "This is the line for the Liberty Bell." He smiled at me, and I smiled at them, and everyone smiled, and no few of my new friends engaged in some vigorous handclapping. Brief small talk with the translator established that Mandarin was their language that I could not understand, but I was a good man helping with the English.

With that, I realized that I'd likely need to adjust my plan.

But I was stuck with these Chinese. It would be too rude

to turn away now, and even though I'd discovered there may not be anyone after me after all, I still didn't want to attract too much attention.

We waited. Beads of sweat clung to our brow. The alternating moods of anticipation and patience. An hour passed, and we passed two armed security guards, Park Rangers no less. We were frisked, and we were at the bell. My entourage of Chinese grew excited. I could feel their passion. It felt contagious. I was drawn into their world.

To a man, they took out their cameras. To a man, these were expensive ones with lots of megapixels and sophisticated displays. They grouped together by the bell. I saw what was happening, and I interceded. I offered to take group photos. They discussed for several minutes, and acquiesced.

One by one, they passed me their cameras, and I took two photos with each. I could imagine them all downloading onto Flickr in the evening and sharing their work. After each click, they all smiled. I was accepted into the group. I was their friend. This meant that I then had to pose, not only in the group, but with each man separately. The American friend. A quasi-philosopher turned murderer, but good enough for foreign tourists nevertheless. They invited me to American Fat Burger to share beef, beer, cholesterol, and thick wedge fries.

But I had to escape. I hadn't spent this much time with people in months. Frankly, I knew I had misanthropic tendencies, but this was too much. Their stench, far from forgotten, seemed to linger and grow stronger. I knew I stunk, and yet I was ready to retch from *their* odor. So bidding as fond adieus as possible while trying not to seem too abrupt, I made my final waves, smiled, and escaped.

Back outside, I looked around. Indeed, things had changed. I found myself walking north, toward some large new buildings I had never noticed before.

I approached and soon saw that I was staring at The Constitution Center. It was an impressive edifice of grey slab and glass walls. I then recalled news of such a building being built. It was something I'd read in a paper or seen on television. A new structure to house visual and audio exhibits of our nation's early history and paperwork. The economic trend was toward tourism, more and more restaurants and retail. A booming downtown ground level with empty office space rising high above.

We were manufacturing memories. An imagined history of our great nation. The Liberty Bell and Betsy Ross House and such were not enough to satiate the needs of the global traveler intent upon early America. Private companies had gotten in on the action, too. Duck tours, Freedom Museums, and cross-dressing Ben Franklin tour guides. Wigs and skirts, that sort of thing. So the state saw what the private sector was able to accomplish, and moved in on the action. I'd read that it took five years to get past political red tape and to tear down the abandoned structures and put up this new one.

President Fern didn't come to baptize the building, but his Homeland Defense Secretary did. Governor Ed Cliff was there, as were thousands of protestors. In fact, I had come to the event and that was probably the last time I'd visited these brick buildings and cobble stones. Had I been so myopic in my concerns that day that I missed the renovations of the Liberty Bell?

Anyway, the celebration was crowded. Bodies pressed against each other in the summer heat. Hawkers were getting five dollars for sixteen ounces of bottled water. At the time, it had reminded me of another event at the same location that I had gone to years ago. That one had been for marijuana legalization and had attracted a crowd of a few hundred suburban dope smokers come to enjoy high times in the city. I'd been weaning myself from undergraduate Hegel and one-hitters but still of a mind to check out the scene. So as I listened to Governor Cliff express his fine thoughts about the Constitution, Philadelphia, protecting our freedoms, and brotherly love, I pictured him dressed like the youthful leader of the pot smoker's rally fifteen years previously. A big fatty and a few roach tweezers on his person, in the middle of his speech, I saw Cliff rolling a spectacular blunt, toking long, flying high, passing the twig, and saluting these freedoms that our armed forces allowed us to inhale!

But now armed security, in grey and green, manned the main entrance, although there was no crotch-goosing or any kind of frisking. I wandered right in and had a look around. There were far fewer tourists overall. I could only suppose that looking was much preferred to reading, and the exhibits here were heavy with text and short on artifacts. A few original documents in a sea of contemporary facsimiles.

It took me only a few minutes to know for sure that I had found my location. The Liberty Bell might be off limits, but I could still blow up the Constitution, or at least a quality replica of such.

Life Lessons from Jonny November 18

Okay, back to school. I'm just glad Auggie and I saved Michael before he drifted into a permanent state of adjunct professor. The news is out about those guys now. Mostly oppressed women, fucked by patriarchy—yeah, you and me, right?—and the guys are defeated males to the nth degree. They slave and slave and slave and can't pay their heating bills and never have enough for new glasses. Forget about a decent restaurant meal or being able to afford fifteen minutes at the house of tang. Adjuncts are overworked, exhausted peons. Even for the girls who dig the pity-party routine, they aren't chick magnets. In a good semester, they get a few smiles, maybe a giggle, or a few coeds thrusting forward or bending down in their little peek-a-boo tops. But that's it. Hell, most adjuncts feel lucky they weren't arrested for drooling or groping after a long day of exposure to the younger set.

They all wanted to be writers, but their last flailing grasp of fame is to wear pants that crease or fold so as to accentuate a bulge. They parade about in front of the room showing off a just-pretend schlong to young impressionable minds who've already seen far wider snail behind the thong. Kids today are quick and contemporary. They take a photo and post the professor's man bun on Snapchat so their friends can add derisive comments to the image of the corduroyed ghost dong. Students can be merciless. Maybe we're right to fear the next generation.

Chapter 12
A Greater Evil

But by then, the Rural State case was all over the news, and I began to connect it to my crimes—the murder of Auggie's father but also my affair with Melony. True, the latter wasn't the same as a sixty-seven-year-old with a ten-year-old kid. Melony was "legal," so she could vote and drive, serve and get served; in fact, she was almost old enough to rent a car. She was a year younger than the young woman they'd caught a President with, and they had little trouble convincing the voting public he was a child molester. These were my students, who as small children had been taught by television that their President was, more or less, a sex offender even though the intern in question was old enough to rent a car with her own credit card. Imagine that.

I followed the story of the end-zone abuser on the internet accessed from library computers and various TV screens throughout the city. I learned that one didn't need a television in the home, or even a home, to keep up-to-date on all the big news.

I'd hit the men's conveniences at Liberty Place and ignore the suits on either side shoving twenty dollar bills in my face, as I stood at a urinal aiming as straight as I could and minding my own pee. For twenty dollars, I wondered what services were rendered even as I'd lean away from the hand with the dough. Was I supposed to stretch it out and wag it or take the pin-striped, pay-per-penis man in a stall and let him play whistle on the weasel? Drink from the fountain or merely measure for size? Was I such a failed capitalist that I'd refuse easy money when I had none?

I'd dash away from these mishandled transactions, and find my way to the corner of 17th and Walnut where I'd peer through the glass walls at televisions of an internet bank's café. Malarkey looked to be about the age my father would be if he were still alive. His varied expressions covered a range of emotion. Bewildered. Shamed. Laughing it off. Befuddled and confused and sometimes visibly agitated. At times, he looked very much like a child, and a scared one at that.

I grew angry.

Finally I tired of Malarkey, the clown, fed up with the university's lack of action, its ignorant and money-mad mediocrities in charge as well as our own complicity in the events—how we all craved football, and when we were tired of gridiron violence, we wanted to see a guilty man on trial getting the death penalty. If we couldn't get death, we wanted the maximum sentence in the maximum security prison, a life as horrible as it could be with rapes and sodomies far worse than the ones he had committed, and without the accompanying gifts of bowl tickets and autographed balls. We followed the Marlarkey story, waiting to read about abused black psychopaths sodomizing white patriarchal power by any means possible. Hold the glove, and with extra backdoor end-zone dances after the score. We wanted everything that might take our minds away from our own miseries and failings.

I turned away. I moved to another news page that is, an international one, and here Malarkey had a thumbnail in the corner, showing he'd proved his worth to the globe. But what dominated the news—just below the various police actions, militarizations, wars, trade disagreements, cyber thefts, and corporate frauds—was the international case of Darius Mélange. He was accused of leaking state secrets from all the major powers—from nuclear nations to financial firms—and he was also being extradited back to his native Denmark where in Copenhagen he faced charges of deviant intercourse with minors, thirteen counts, three orifices each, and thus trumping Malarkey's twelve or nine! The latest was that he was seeking asylum in Israel claiming his grandfather had saved thirty-seven Jewish children during the Holocaust and had demanded free Galician Toukhes massage from none of them. But the Israelis were unable to confirm that Mélange the

Cobbler in 1942 was at all related to Mélange the Cyberspatial-secret-leaker pedophile in 2012, and they were in the process of removing him from their embassy's conveniences—indeed, the small window in the bottom floor men's room where he'd become stuck in his escape from his escape—and helping the Portuguese police escort him to a secure airplane bound for Prince Hamlet's old haunts. Another cursory search revealed that Mélange choice delicacy was female and tended to average three-and-a-half years older than Malarkey's boys. Unlike Malarkey, there was no indication that Darius considered himself to be in love with any of his victims. It was pretty much a repeat hit-and-run on the teenybopper set.

I drifted away from the news, intent on avoiding any progress on local archdiocese silence about the international cabal of papal abuse. Or news from Hollywood about unacknowledged allegations. Or the nine children from eight women that the latest sports celebrity had failed to pay child support for.

Indeed, there seemed to be an awful lot of this stuff. It was all over the news and in the home and workplace. Auggie's stepfather, my victim, was only the tip of the iceberg in a world largely dictated by the terms of the abusers—the filthy old men in power in nations and institutions—churches, universities, hospitals, and corporations.

And then it hit me. The constitution was an ancient artifact, a dead document from America's past. Forget all that symbolic bullshit! I was already a slightly less than premeditated murderer, so why not try to make a difference while I still had my freedom, while I was an unwanted man as best I knew now. My life, my usual life, was effectively over. I'd never be able to work again, not in any normal capacity. I'd killed a man and eventually the authorities would find me and lock me up. Besides what was my life, as in the sum of my experiences, worth anyway?

Before entering the PhD program at Urban State, I'd attended Rural State and escaped, albeit barely, with a piece of paper that said M.A. in philosophy from a department funded entirely by the millionaire head coach of the football team. Sixty years before me he had retrieved an undergrad degree in ancient philosophy from an "Ivy of the Great Lakes region," and he held life-long respect for the liberal arts. I'd been toiling as an adjunct, boinking a twenty-three-year-old, and doing a poor job of it at that. I was a murderer whose life was increasingly covered in rape and molestation of the underage set. Was there any point in not continuing on the rather dubious course I'd somehow arrived at by chance meetings in a supermarket? No doubt even if they never pursued me as a murderer, I'd lost any chance of returning to any life more decent than overworked adjunct-freelance slave.

That was how I arrived at the conclusion that I would kill again. It was somewhere between a want and a need, but it was real. Vivid and clear, perhaps more so, even, than the "facts" that informed the feeling. I would take revenge not only on Auggie's behalf but on behalf of child victims everywhere. And it was Malarkey who came to mind. Mélange was on another continent, and no doubt it would be a rather expensive puzzle for me to purchase a ticket and fly on a plane to England when I'd have to panhandle or worse merely to afford processing fees for a passport. Rural State football had educated me and was only five hours away.

It was time to return the favor.

Life Lessons from Jonny November 19

So I saw you walking downtown the other night. It was late, and you looked scared. Your head was darting back and forth. No, I didn't think you were expecting a terrorist, some ethnic anarchist with a dirty bomb and dark features. No, you were afraid of domestic darkies, young boys from the 'hood out and about, looking for trouble. Boys without fathers lurking in the darkness waiting on some unsuspecting fellow, and then wilding on a white boy like you. I saw your balls shrink and your neck pivot. Back and forth, back and forth. This, I saw. Yes, I did.

But you know what?

Those boys aren't the only ones playing a knockout game.

You know who plays the real knockout game?

Guys like this Malarkey character up at Rural State. It makes sense that big-time college football, stinking of money and greed, could produce such an evil fucker. That's right. Petting their knees and blowing on their stomachs. Tickling and rubbing and ass-dicking innocent little boys. Treating them like throwaway children. Born to single mothers in some lost section of Mississippi City, Pennsylvania. That's who's knocking out American kids with complete disregard for their future or even their humanity.

In the United States of No One Gives a Fuck, Auggie got knocked out, too, but he didn't stay down because he's a fighter. He's a great kid. Doing the best he can to overcome the odds. I helped him as best I could. The only way I knew how.

Chapter 13
A Guy Who Knows a Guy

I would need a weapon. There was no doubt about that. But how would I obtain one? I knew I shouldn't contact Jonny November, and I wasn't even sure of how to do so anyway. What I did instead was mingle in the library, looking for a guy who looked like he knew a guy, who would know another guy who would be the guy. The gun guy. But everyone was busy reading and sleeping and snoring and stinking, so I gave up and went back to the Goodwill bin and thanked god the spiritual leader was nowhere in sight.

I approached the first man who established eye contact. Like the urinal pervs, I flashed a twenty-dollar bill but then tucked it back in my pocket.

"I'm looking for a piece."

"Yo, I ain't no pimp."

"Pimp? I need a piece."

"Piece of ass?"

"Oh, I see. I'm sorry. I meant a gun."

"What the fuck you want that for? And why the fuck you asking me?"

Whoa. I'd gotten off on decidedly the wrong foot.

"Sorry, er, sir. I apologize for any inconvenience." For emphasis, I bowed repeatedly.

"Hey, wait a minute. No offense, man."

"None taken?"

"If it's a weapon you need, I can't help."

"You don't know a guy?"

"I don't know a guy, right."

We stood there together, sweating in the sunshine, eyes cast away.

"Okay, let's just say I may know a guy who knows a guy."

"How much are you asking for?"

"Damn. I don't want money. I don't want your money or any involvement. A rap sheet from twenty years ago is what got me to where I am today. I need to play it straight just to keep my debit card loaded up. By the way, would you need me to buy you any SNAP food?"

"Snap food?"

"You know, fruits and vegetables, maybe some healthy grains."

"I said I needed a gun."

"Oh, never mind. Anyway, what I need, white boy, is for you to promise over your up-to-no-good heart that you won't ever implicate me in this. You don't know my name, which you don't, but you don't know where I hang out, which won't be here once we're through. Got it?"

"Not a problem."

"Okay, then," and he moved closer and whispered in my ear. Just like that, I had a source and location, and he had my twenty.

A few days later, I popped onto the northbound subway, got off at Broad and Erie, and walked several blocks into black poverty until I stood in front of C&C's Pawnshop.

The place looked inconspicuous enough. Metal bars painted grey on the glass windows and door, but you could still see evidence of a smash and grab—a black plastic bag over cardboard in a lower left corner where someone had seen an item worth breaking glass for.

I patted my dollars in my back pocket, opened the glass door, and walked inside.

The place was dimly lit, and the pale flub of an owner was gruff, no smiles. Taller than me and much better shaven, his stern, if slightly vacant, visage communicated fairness and freedom to bear arms.

Within twenty minutes, he sold me a Saturday night special, taught me to load it, and recommended a shooting range.

Chapter 14
A First-Class Bullshitter and Razor Man

My weapon secured, I needed a route. Rural State was five hours by car or six on game day, so I wouldn't be walking. I counted my cash, not much, and went to Greyhound to inquire about pricing. A sign said no guns aboard the bus, no surprise, but a ticket would only cost twenty-three dollars. From there, I went back to the discount stores in and about The Gallery shopping mall and Market Street, where I found low prices on the items I needed: An "irregular" duffel bag; a three-pack of fresh, clean generic-brand socks, solid white; a couple pairs of surprisingly cheap designer briefs and boxers; a pair of grey-green khaki shorts; Brown Dickies pants; and two shirts, burnt orange and roan. The icing on the cake was a pair of summer sandals for the whopping sum of six dollars. For less than sixty dollars, I had changes of clothes and a bag for storage. Out of the store, and on my way home, I peeked inside a thrift store and found a used mustache and side burns that matched my dirty blonde hair. Score!

I spend a night in a homeless shelter my straw purchaser had called "safe and clean." It was safe at least, and I did get a thorough warm water shower. In the morning, hidden in a bathroom stall and moaning at times to feign number two, I struck a pose or two. I stuck the gun in my belt and in my shoe, but nothing felt comfortable. Despite my nihilistic tendencies, the possibility of having my ass blown off was not one I felt a need to entertain. So I placed my gun at the bottom of the bag, and moving quickly back to my bunk, took the new clothes out of their plastic packages, and piled them on top.

A block from the shelter, I found an affordable neighborhood barber. Melvin was a first-class bullshitter and razor man. Living near the shelter, he'd cut straight hair on and off for twenty-five years. In the course of a clean cut and shave for twelve dollars, tip included, I heard all about our city's failings. High city wage taxes, poor schools, overpriced housing on any decent block, inadequate public transportation and sanitation services. Dirty cops and corrupt politicians were a minor concern, and he didn't have much on inefficient social services or the shortage of qualified case workers. So, in turn, I updated him on child abuse, and why we needed stronger laws to protect against it. "Amen, brother," in solidarity he stated as a few seated old heads nodded in the affirmative as well.

I put on my glasses, and nodded approvingly as he used a handheld mirror to show me the front, back, and sides. Then, I popped up from my barbershop swivel chair, paid and tipped, secured my duffel bag, and headed off to the bus stop. The walk from Ridge Avenue back to the Greyhound stop was uneventful, but I took time to admire all the new condos and apartments that had been built over the years.

At the bus station, I strode straight to the men's room, avoided eye contact with a gentleman fumbling with his needle at the sinks while another stranger shat and groaned to the gods with his stall door wide open. I moved straight for the oversized stall, a luxury for the disabled, whose lock was thankfully intact. I took off the clothing I'd been wearing for almost a month, and donned the Dickies and the burnt-orange polo. It felt odd to be wearing clean clothes, but somewhat of a relief as well. Back in the waiting area, I noted that I still had twenty-three minutes before boarding time, so I hurried out of the terminal, hooked a right, and made for the back alleyway. There, I found exactly what I needed, a huge dumpster filled with garbage. I set down my duffel, and reached high to push my old clothes down as deep as I could. On second thought, I figured the thing to do was to untie one of those black garbage bags and stuff my clothes inside. Doing so, I suffered the stench of some lost soul's predilection for summer tuna sandwiches, but managed to wedge my old clothing underneath the bread crusts, tuna, and Fisher Price toy machine guns that had not made the cut in someone else's life. I retied that bag and shoved it deep underneath its companions. Gathering up my duffel bag, I walked back inside the station, and returned to the bathroom and washed my hands while praying the miserable needle man to my right would not inadvertently pinch me on the arm.

By then it was time to board.

I took a window seat in the middle and slid my duffel bag underneath. The bus wasn't crowded, and I thought I'd have the two-seater to myself when a few minutes before departure, a gentleman perhaps ten years my senior sat down beside me. He didn't look like a talker, which was good, so I nodded politely and closed my eyes. Five hours later we arrived at Rural State.

Chapter 15
Stakeout Redux

Popping a thumb and hitchhiking seemed risky, so I started off on foot. It was no easy task traveling inconspicuously through the five miles of fields and homes between the Silly Valley bus station and Malarkey's home. At times, I tried to duck and cover, and I rarely strode along any roads for more than twenty minutes at once. As much as I could, I bent and stumbled through a forested area, lush and verdant, and when I was strolling along two-lane highway, I'd dart my head left and right and even occasionally up into the air. I was paranoid and certain there could be a drone tailing me to Malarkey's home, courtesy of Google, the NSA, or some other upstanding citizen of post-philosophical America.

When I finally approached from the bushes and trees beyond the backyard, I collapsed and slept for several hours. Soon after I woke, I scouted around the house. There were two police squad cars parked outside during the day, but only one at night. I'd squat in the bushes hundreds of yards away and stare through binoculars I'd bought along with suction-cup rope and bullets my straw-purchaser told me I'd need. To secure my ammo, I spent ten minutes at a neighborly big box store.

It was hot July, and the mosquitoes were biting me, so I'd pause and put the binoculars down to slap an exposed forearm or calf. *Ouch*. About my body were insect wings and legs smashed against dried blood pasted onto my skin. I was behind bushes a couple hundred yards from the property, three houses away behind a worn, grey Cape Cod that was occupied by a couple so old they hardly seemed to move at all. Sitting in their bushes for hours, I'd only see lights in three parts of the house—an upstairs bedroom and downstairs living room and kitchen. Once I saw the elderly couple on their wooden swing on a side porch visible from where I was kneeling, but that was only for twenty minutes. I heard the old man mutter about the heat and they both limped back inside.

It was in their limited meandering—from kitchen to living room to the long journey upstairs—a full five-minute delay between the downstairs lights going out and the upstairs lights coming on—that I glimpsed what the end could be like, all the bed pans and pills and hot glasses of water and loss of appetite and wasting away. It came to me that Nietzsche's retreat to madness or Hemingway's blowing out his brains was the honest response to all that was to be anticipated about aging and losing teeth, mobility, and memory. My efforts here would not be in vain. That Malarkey's lust for young boys showed he feared death more than most, that he wanted to live, again and again, as it were, and that ending his life would be the fitting punishment, even as taking my own would be my just reward.

With only one squad car out front at night, and a patrolman who walked around the house once an hour, breaking in appeared rather straightforward. I would hide farther back, and I'd wait until the early a.m. when Malarkey would be deep in his R.E.M. sleep. Fifteen minutes after I saw the officer pass the backyard on his 4 a.m. rounds, I'd fling my suction rope and use it to shimmy up the drainpipe. Last, I'd hoist myself into the empty side room. This was where Malarkey's wife of forty-three years had taken her own life a week after she heard the news about her husband's crimes. From there, I'd act quickly and as quietly as possible. I'd burst into his bedroom, find Malarkey sound asleep, shoot him twice in the head, leave through the window, and sprint from the house.

Chapter 16
Chez Malarkey

It was time to act. I lobbed the suction-cup end of my rope high above the window, took several deep breaths, ran, and leaped at the wall. The drainpipe and aluminum siding were more slippery than I expected, and I slipped and slid, and fell off several times. How I struggled, falling back to earth again and again and praying my noises would not waken the neighbors, Malarkey, or the officer on the other side of the house. With a grimace, I finally found my way to the window sill. The window was stuck or locked from inside, so I smashed in a pane, found and turned an interior clasp lock, and held the window open wide enough to lift and wedge my body through and collapse on the hardwood floors.

Just then, opening the door and stumbling through was a sleepy Malarkey. He turned on the light and blinked rapidly as he adjusted his eyes. This was not in the plan. Ad-libbing as best I could, I grabbed my weapon and fumbled to get it pointed at my mark. He recognized me as a person, and on instinct, ran at me and dove. I fired and hit him in the lower side. He screamed in anguish, a fierce grimace lit his face, but his momentum was too much, and he crashed down on me, his full two hundred fifty plus pounds falling on my stomach. I felt an air-sucking punch and the weight of the world. My shooting hand was free, and how I wanted to fire at his hands, which were currently around my throat. Instead, thinking as well as I could, I rammed the gun's nose deep in his side and pressed the high-tech trigger. Once, twice, and after a third time, I heard him whispering in my ear.

"I don't know why you're here, but you sure as hell aren't getting my autograph." Then, he fell silent. But as if an afterthought, he added, "We're just molecules floating in the world. It's all meaningless. Don't expect to get any big answers here. Meaning of life stuff or anything like that."

Was he about to confess? I was too terrified to find out.

I gathered my wits, and I returned to my shooting. At the seventh release, I felt his fingers loosen from my esophagus. The pressure on my torso was great, but with all of my remaining might, I heaved Malarkey off of me and breathed a huge sigh of relief. I waved my weapon and whispered back at the dead man, "Know this now and well, motherfucker. There is meaning. There is meaning. You fucked little boys in the ass and the locker room and the basement and everywhere else. That's right. In every ass and office and orifice. You preyed upon kids who were forgotten by their fathers, the state, politicians, schools, and the rest of us. You used your power to take advantage. That's what I believe."

For a brief moment, his expression changed. The "no vacancy" sign disappeared, and it was as if the dead man was reacting to my words, understanding what I'd just said. I saw doubt, and recognition, and an instant of *anger* before a pavid grimace emerged as I pulled the trigger a final time.

Malarkey was no more.

I blacked out, and in an instant had a life's worth of dreams. My next *imagined* move was to shove Malarkey off me, rush down to the kitchen, grab his largest knife, return upstairs, and slice off his pants, so I could then chop off his pecker and balls. I cut off a strand of curtain, tied his evil triumvirate around my neck, and danced around his dead body like a spell-casting witch doctor. From there, I burst out of his house and went door to door looking for sex offenders. With Malarkey's pale parts around my neck, I flew across the state, touring the countryside in my *aristeia*, knocking on doors and demanding to know where residents kept their perverts. Some I threatened, others I maimed, and a few got off with a slap on the wrists from Malarkey's dead member. By daybreak, I had injured or humiliated at least three hundred men.

When I snapped out of it, I needed a moment to remember where I was and what had come to pass. Reality returned, and my second murder was part of it, but I didn't feel remorse. As I lay there, no longer dying, I felt glad to be alive. I didn't want to move, and my mind drifted through the events of the past year. I was lying on the floor in a spare bedroom with the second man I had killed. Less than a year before, I'd been gainfully employed in a respectable profession, albeit at a contract rate, and happily not getting laid but dating a young lady fifteen years my junior. Things had decidedly changed, and I could only wonder when my Raskolnikovian moment would arrive. Where was my guilt? My shame? My albatross?

In fact, I felt dynamic. Alive. I was far removed from my hero Nietzsche whose last effort at action was to collapse upon a flogged horse. I could only hope that anyone coming later to judge me would understand that this was about Auggie's revenge, revenge for all the Auggies, and not some misinterpretation of my favorite *uber*-philosopher.

Flat against the floor, I resisted an urge to mimic my dream state. That is, to find the right knife in his kitchen downstairs, and scalp his head and slice off his offending appendage and parade the trophy as jewelry about my neck. All the same, thought of such action produced a weird grin and giggles that took me minutes to suppress and silence.

After that, the usual doubts and fears returned. My mind wandered back to reality and my need to escape as quietly as possible from the house. Then I fell asleep.

* * *

From a sustained slumber, I woke to sunlight through the window. After a few foggy minutes of "Where am I?" and "How did I get here?" I panicked, stood up to dash, and sat back down to avoid anyone viewing me through the window. At last, I gathered my wits and any traces of me at Malarkey's, double-checking that I was leaving no glove or thumbprint behind.

When the coast was clear, I climbed up and over the same window, slid and fell to the grass, and lay for a moment on the ground. After enough time to note that there was already light in the sky, I made my move away from the house. I strapped my duffel bag around either shoulder, fell to all fours on the grass, and crawled like a worm to where the backyards met a communal golf course. When I chanced upon a man-made pond separating two holes, I put down my duffel bag, removed my second set of clothes, the grey-green khaki shorts with roan polo shirt, and put them on along with my mustache and sideburns. The sandals fit surprisingly well although it was then that I noticed the dew in the grass. But wet toes were the least of my concerns.

I stuffed all of my old clothes, my breaking-and-entering outfit, into the duffel bag, and then I scurried to the edge of the water, stood upright, and flung all my tools as far as I could. For an instant, I felt free. New clothes and a disguise. I remained low, duck-walking, until thirty minutes later I came upon the Rural State Recreation Center I'd read about in the campus guide. I found the bathroom where I'd planned on changing and felt chagrin for my hasty chucking at the lake. Wouldn't it have been better to trust a couple items to the lake, but to bury the others in the garbage receptacle here? Spread the evidence so as to better obscure the crime?

Chapter 17
Big Man on Campus

Years ago, as I limped past my final obstacles and completed a dissertation, I began my freelance academic's life. I'd still attend conferences, ever hopeful that I'd shake the right hand, exchange the right business card, meet the right department chair, and launch a career stalled in its developmental stage. One of Philly's rising stars of philosophy, a few years older than me, was swimming easily through his own academic success. It surprised me not in the least to learn that not only had Jacob graduated with the highest honors from Ivy Green, but he had moved on to one fancy postdoc after another until finally landing as the Leonardo Distinguished Chair in the Humanities at Rural State. (Yes, in fact, the champion football coach was funding half the liberal arts programs on campus, and for this distinction, a chair had been granted bearing his name.) A tenure-track slot, one that weighed in at a hundred thousand dollars, much more if you counted what the benefits and additional grants and speaking fees were worth. That he was also a straight white man cast a harsh light on the fact that my race, gender, and sexual orientation had nothing to do with my own academic and professional failings.

He was always friendly to me in passing—a smile, a hello, a few brief words in our shared interest in power and systems. So only hours after murdering Malarkey and merely minutes after a shit, shave, and thorough rinsing at the sink, when I ran into Jacob at the recreation center, there was nothing else to do than to smile and say hello.

He winced when he saw me. I wondered if I was shaking, and even after washing, I feared I reeked of sweat and dirt. But then

I remembered the mustache and sideburns and realized I must appear as a particularly downtrodden older version of myself to anyone who knew me from the past.

"Michael?"

"Jacob?"

"How are you?"

"How's your daughter, Jacob?"

After his early books on phenomenology and such, and then his advancements on power, as defined and deconstructed by Foucault and the French, he'd written a memoir, so the world could know his familial pain.

Jacob paused, undoubtedly trying to place whether or not I'd crossed paths with him when he had his little girl in tow.

"I read your book, Jacob."

It was a touching beautiful book about raising his autistic daughter, and it succeeded in humanizing the *meritocrat*, the industrious intellectual we had all seen hustle past us on the road of academic success. It made little mention of his wealthy roots or elite private-school rearing, but I shed tears when I read how the girl lost an arm in an incident with a patio grill. Jacob had dashed out for five minutes, to mail off a manuscript, and it took him over a year to forgive himself for leaving her alone. As a new man, he learned to blame the grill manufacturer, and even as he walked out of the courtroom two million dollars wealthier, he stayed true to his socialist principles and donated a full fifty-one percent of his settlement, after legal fees, to charities helping special-needs children in less developed countries. I grabbed extra tissues before reading the memoir's final pages.

"Oh."

"It was a good book."

Despite my present condition as an escaping double murderer, I smiled to show him how much the book meant to me.

"Oh, thanks, Michael." He looked away shyly, he was pleased and yet embarrassed to be receiving direct praise.

"You know, Jacob, most of us have only seen you as some privileged-kid genius, a boy wonder, perhaps with a bit of the kiss-ass about him, too. The book humanized you."

I wanted to tell him it made me feel like even more of an incompetent fool. Not only was I a failure in philosophy, career, and hotel-room sex, but I'd failed in pursuit of marriage and family as well, and I'd certainly never raised a child with special needs. Getting a twenty-three-year-old to Broadway and snuffing out two sex offenders was the best I could do in this miserable life. But I had to escape the conversation, too, escape the lobby outside the latrines and get back to whatever reality was left for a vagabond double-killer.

"Say, Michael, are you here for a teaching interview? If you like, I could put in a good word for you."

Oh, shit. Now I had to explain my purpose for being in a place as remote at this one, a rural university thousands of urbanites would have gladly travelled to for only one purpose. For the sake of a better-paying job. Decent wages and benefits with lower housing costs.

Thinking as quickly as I could, "Oh, that's quite alright. In fact, a cousin of mine is beginning graduate school in the fall, and I was just up scouting for housing."

Jacob's eyes glowed with approval of this message, and its evocation of extended family and graduate training. He smiled more kindly.

"Well, if there's anything I can do to assist, please let me know. Out here in the boonies, we're always looking to extend our family as best we can."

The word *family* stood and lingered. It graced us with its presence and wouldn't go away. It reminded me of Leonardo's molesting defensive coach and Auggie's stepfather and all the crimes and corruptions that prevented *family* from ever being what it was supposed to be for millions of children. Too often, the best our colleges could do was send these kids polite rejection letters or take them in, only to shove them off into the working world as wage slaves with thousands of dollars of debt.

Snap out of it, Vittinger!

I remembered once more I was a two-time killer, with blood just washed off my hands, and I had to escape. *Haha! Fuck! Haha!* It struck me as hilarious that I'd just shot a man seven times, and here

I was chatting in the student center as if nothing at all had changed. I nearly laughed out loud, and I think Jacob noticed the lunatic grin that appeared on my face and was suppressed as best I could.

"Is something the matter?"

Jacob looked at me quizzically.

"Oh, no, I'm fine. A thought just occurred to me. You see, I'm working on my first book."

As the proudly published author of at least nine monographs, Jacob smiled even more widely.

"Oh, how wonderful." His dimples creased as his smile beamed, and I was grateful I didn't grow a bone from the whole deal. Congratulations from one of the academic overlords. He was so genuine and kind that it was almost forgivable that he'd been born straight, white, male, and *rich*.

"Hey, thanks. Say, Jacob, it was good to see you, but I really need to shove off. You know how it is. I'm still teaching those adjunct overloads in the city."

"Yes, yes," and here I saw Jacob's expression turn toward a frown of concern for all the itinerant knowledge cogs teaching on pay-per-course contracts throughout the country. For a split second, I made my own connections and considered if the nature of this work was what caused me to kill in the first place. As well as the second.

"When the book is complete, perhaps I can help you find a publisher." As a leader of the precariat, he'd lend a helping hand.

"That's very kind, Jacob. Thank you."

Thank God there was no proffered palm, so he could feel how sweaty my own hands had become. We shared last warm regards, and then we stumbled awkwardly in the same direction up a short stack of cement steps until we turned in opposite directions, exchanged a final smile and hand wave, and were gone from each other at last.

As soon as I could, I turned a corner, and began striding as quickly as I could without appearing as if I were a murderer rushing from the scene of a crime.

Life Lessons from Jonny November 20

Yeah, another thing about college is those tenured professors. Yeah, so sensitive. I don't know what's wrong with people like that. They have easy lives and all the economic advantages. They teach one or two small seminars a term where they can say whatever they want. Their salary rides on student debt and middle-class mortgages, they have ample adjuncts to exploit and feel better than, they tell each other how brilliant they are, and yet they act like a bunch of cry babies. Half of 'em were born with a silver spoon. They have no idea of what it's like to be you or me. We're not talking about people who even visited bronze-plan relatives when they were young. The worst of 'em had to go on a field trip if they were going to view the poor. True, a fair number wind up with lazy, drug-addicted, or otherwise fucked-up children, just as any rich man would, but that don't excuse them from how they treat the rest of us.

The male of the species is a capitalist all the way. He'll smile widely about the sharing economy and MOOC you in the ass any chance he gets. You better believe he knows what he's sharing. Fuckin' doofus earning a hundred grand a year whose idea of social justice is for your tuition dollars to pay for his chance to orate over pedantic nonsense in lecture hall. It's more like the circle-jerk economy with these guys. Like I said, they're the little Heideggers of this world. No, they aren't killing anyone. They aren't Nazis watching colleagues lose their offices and get sent to the gas chamber, and they do wear their liberal armbands proudly—center left, Subaru or Volvo, organic coffee or tea, squash or tennis. They vote in every primary, and they read the ballot before they pull the lever or touch the screen.

But student debt shoots past thirty grand while adjuncts use credit cards to outlast the summer, and the best these tenured turds can do is post lefty memes on Facebook?

This one little Jew guy was a greedy, little whiner. I'm a half-breed, but I still gotta say it like that 'cause I get sick of *them*, too, sometimes. Yeah, I don't got it as bad as Auggie, but I know something's wrong with me. The way Michael began to act around us, whatever it is, I'm thinking it must be contagious.

Anyway, the Jew is one of *them*. Not the Jews or gentiles but the tenured professors. This guy writes a dissertation on railroad tracks in Nazi Germany. All the technical stuff with just a bit in the afterward about how we could have bombed the tracks and saved millions of lives. That's "we" as in us for U.S., the United States, not Nazis, Jews, gentiles, or Auggie, Michael, and me.

Got that?

Good.

So with the dissertation, he gets to tenure track when it was a lot easier to do so. The dissertation gets turned into a book, and five guys in his field read it and tell him he's a genius and write as much in book reviews for academic journals no one reads. Big chubby, right?

He builds a whole career off that book, gets tenure, the works. His nice match on the 401k grows to a tasty little nest egg. Thirty years later, at a state school where students would largely graduate debt free when he began, kids are now leaving with over thirty grand in loans while he's racked up almost a million dollars in his 401k. Imagine that the man has played by all the rules and done well, so what's the problem, right?

Think of it this way. He's become a millionaire off the backs of an entire generation of debtors and the six million dead from the Holocaust. His entire life's scholarship is all about studying trains that took people to death camps. He's a war profiteer who never ran a factory for munitions. The companies in his 401k stock funds handled that for him.

Do you see what I'm getting at?

You need more data? You want facts?

Fuck you. No, wait. That's a joke. But listen to this.

There's another guy who became an academic celebrity, a superstar, by studying black people. He's black, too, so in a way, it's just like the Hebraic millionaire. That's how they do it at the university, color coordinated, so they can tell you that's social or economic justice. College administrators love that shit.

So this professor is mapping and studying and popping out two-hundred-dollar book after two-hundred-dollar book, but what happens to the people he studies? They lose their jobs during a recession? He studies it. They go to jail? He writes about it. They get fucked harder and deeper by the collective white man? (Yeah, go figure, but that's you, me, Michael, and Auggie too.) He gets rich. He buys a small mansion on the mainline and pours the Beaujolais with his friends Vanilla Nice and Hugh. B. White.

You see my point. The whole tenured system is built on piles of pig slop and rotten eggs. It's putrid. Yeah, little Heideggers. They aren't ignoring Jews or anyone else being disappeared from the cubicle next door, but they aren't doing anything for the students either, class after class piled higher and deeper in debt.

Forget a million dollars in TIAA-CREF. This guy's got twice that combined as a net worth. It's in a 401k, Roth IRA, paid-off primary residence, and eight units in two buildings smack in the middle of the black slums he studies. Imploded projects turned into a city park for urban addicts and brothers on the down low right across the street from his substantial gross profit.

He sees the quarter, he picks up the quarter, but he sees a lot larger quarters than most of us. Dr. Sharp is the Magic Johnson of social psychology with a minor in applied real estate. Section 8, home-heating vouchers, and other programs have his net worth headed toward four-million dollars. Half the brothers in his buildings can't find a job, but when he tours onsite, the women shower him with hugs and kisses. The young ones glow like they want to make that motherfucker's baby.

Okay, enough is enough? Here's one more. Consider this prep-school queer theorist. Yeah, right, what the fuck is that anyway? Why does he get three times the bank of a regular type? It's some sort of philosophical thing for gay people. The false consciousness of bathroom stall dividers, the layers of the roll, the subtext of public hygiene, or something like that. But it helps if you're rich. This guy comes from thirty-five-grand-a-year prep school and private college at fifty-nine large per annum. Paler than mayonnaise on white loaf, he gets a free ride for undergrad from his folks and stipend plus fellowship over seven years until he finished his PhD. Just to be on the safe side, in case he is ever accused of not being radical enough, he taps white girl booty back door every other week so he can call himself a bisexual theorist at certain conferences. Avant garde, my ass.

So he's your top-shelf tenured professor, and he's teaching queer and black to the rest of us. He tells the students he's a sixteenth "African American," and he acts like James Baldwin is his special inheritance when you and I know that the real native sons are out here on the corner, exposed to the elements, trying to kick a heroin addiction, and licking snow queen's lollipop for five bucks a fix. That's the price of the ticket, my friend. Meanwhile this prep-school fag has a fancy condo, unlimited expense account for books, five grand a year for travel reimbursement, a free financial advisor, and unlimited insurance for his mental health.

Real gay black dudes, the guys on the corner, are losing hair and teeth while dying of pneumonia, hepatitis, and AIDS.

That's the college of oligarchical America, the no-fee-left behind up-your-ass of university *praxis*.

Where do we fit in?

We're squeezed in the middle, between old-money whitey running the ship and the totally fucked out on the streets. Those guys got no spark, but that's not our concern. Our outlook is neutral, but tending toward negative. The liberals in power aren't as mean as the corporate fuckers, but they make up for it by being even more oblivious. They're blind to the fact that their justice, access to education, only reinforces the class divide.

How do I know all about college and class injustice, you ask? Who told me about these tenured professors? The guy who snitched was an adjunct who lost his classes. Downsized, laid off, nonrenewal, whatever you want to call it. I met him in the slam after he got pinched for peddling knock off designer-brand travel tampons and other loose lady accessories outside the little girl's conveniences at major academic conferences. He was an impressive businessman who knew a lot about college. You'd be surprised at the mark up you can get for panty product when the progressives come to town. Desperate poor young women, hoping to land honest work making a difference. Employment with dignity, the life of the mind. All they want to do is presentations for professors, and my guy is there charging twenty dollars a snatch pad, with or without a PhD.

Yeah, it's a fucked up country, but stick with me, and I'll do my best to help you survive.

Oblivious professors and administrative ass clowns enjoy prosperity floating on piles of poop for the rest of us. Adjuncts like Michael subsist, students get debt-fucked and further screwed by textbook-gouging and fees to infinity. Throw in campus rape, suicide, alcoholism, and gambling on game day. A few schools even got star recruits punching coeds in the face.

That's the university. You go there to learn. Yeah, right. Tell me another one.

Chapter 18
A Thorough Escape

Three weeks later they arrested me for the Malarkey murder.

A better criminal would have imagined a thorough escape, but alas, short on funds all I could think to do was return to Philadelphia and search for adjunct classes at other schools. You see, Philly is the only place where I knew how to live, and these past few weeks, I'd even trained myself to survive there without an apartment or job. My goal was to get a foot in the door, then a room in a shared arrangement of some kind, and slowly rebuild my life. In fact, I'd just completed an interview for tutoring services at a Success Center at another school in town, and I checked the box that said "no" for criminal record. I was feeling proud of myself for having gotten so close to being back among the paycheck-to-paycheck, subsistence-wage workers of our city.

Because I wasn't in touch with anyone, I still don't know for certain how they got onto my trail. It was presented to me more as the cops always get their man, and it was only at the trial that I saw the surveillance video from the Rural State Recreation Center. Yes, it was that simple. I was as incompetent at murder as I was with romantic excursions to New York City, my philosophical career, indeed, my entire life. I only wish I could have avoided confessing to the first murder, but I brought it up within twenty minutes of my meeting with the detectives at the homeless shelter.

"I never meant to kill them."

"Them?"

Not only did they shake out Auggie's father, but they interrogated me for hours about numerous other cold cases, mainly men who'd gone missing who fit the profile of my victims—on lists of sexual predators or last seen with orphans. There was sweat and fear and for a while, I was hallucinating and insistent upon the fact that I'd murdered seventeen men up and down the east coast. Like kind gentlemen, after my total capitulation, they talked me out of it and got me to sign a statement saying I'd killed Auggie's father and Rural State's rapist football coach. On the question of accomplices, even while hallucinating, I kept my trap shut and never gave up the others. This makes me think I would have been a great tenured colleague; alas, even after all that has come to pass, I can't say my feelings of academic failure had completely faded.

During this time, I was kept in a private cell in a local jail near the courthouse. I'd see the crowds and the cameras when I was taken to court, but the rest of my time was quiet. One guard would tell me of gifts I was receiving, flowers and chocolates and money, which of course, I wasn't able to keep in my jail cell. The flowers then were donated to single mothers and churches across the region and the money was deposited in a savings account for me.

At the trial, there were no surprises. The fact that I had murdered twice did not work in my favor. Two murders to my name and despite the pattern of abuse, the guilt of my victims, I was ordered to serve twenty-five years in jail, reduced to fifteen for good behavior. The judge stated that we can never tolerate vigilante justice in a society organized by the rule of law. I heard "Amen" from more than one row behind me. I would be at least fifty-four when they set me free.

Life Lessons from Jonny November 21

Hey, listen up. I'm not done. I've got one last word on power. It's something Michael never learned even though he stuck his nose in a mountain of theory. Over a decade in philosophy, and he didn't learn squat.

Power is linear. It isn't complex. There's the fuckers and the fucked, and so on. There's no circulation through the system, intertwining discourses, competing ideologies, or any of that bull crap, cow plop, or however you want to gender all the shit that ain't.

Words are words, and a boot in the ass is a boot in the ass. I don't want to mix metaphors or mince words here. You got me? If your boot is in my ass, so deep it's kissing my liver, I feel pain. I don't debate the multiple perspectives, or discuss whether the shoe in question is leather or synthetic. Made in China or manufactured at home by a high-tech machine. No, it's far more simple than that. A thick steel-toed lodged deep in the dark place, and who gives a shit whether or not the weatherproofing is oppressive? I'm fucked. Is it subjugation? The alienation of labor? The postmodern condition?

Okay, you can throw syllables around if you want, but there's no complexity here. Operation Occupy Asshole is on, and that's all that matters. You got me? Rich and poor, black and white, and, yeah, I know in some cases black is the new rich, and Koreans are yesterday's Jews and all that. But largely speaking, power is power and you know if you got it, or if some whack-job holding onto it is making your life miserable because he has a lot more than you. It's just your warm, wet one shoved so far deep inside it's putting pressure on my scrotum from within. It's that simple. So don't start with any complicated baloney.

Chapter 19
Final Discourse

I'm stuck in the prison house of prison. This pokey isn't privatized, not yet, but it's worse than any critic could imagine. The bars are thick, black, and rusted. They remind me of the long, ugly sentences of the contemporary theorists, with their disregard of historical perspective and writing as a tool of communication. Alas, they had regard for the law and stayed within its confines. But that wasn't for me, and stuck in here, I now know it is an insult to jail anytime anyone ever alludes to it in metaphor. Or simile. Or image. Prison house of language, my ass. Do not be fooled by these clean, bare walls. Believe me, things are not as they appear. At night, they come out, creeping and crawling out of their cracks, slimy and black, their tiny appendages pinching and tickling and scarring my skin. They move along my legs and up upon my thinning, flabbing midsection and all over my face and into every orifice unless I protect myself. So I cover my ears and nostrils and mouth, and pray not they seek more Southern entry. But they creep and crawl and insist upon my inner person until finally meager daylight appears through my eight-by-nine inch window, high above even my outstretched arms. In the morning I can see clear sky and imagine the loftiest heights I could have attained.

I have no parents who know of my whereabouts. There's no one on the outside who cares about me. Man is born free and everywhere he is in chains, yes, and yet these chains do not always imply there are other human beings in a man's life. We grapple with rusted, flaking black steel alone; our manacles are not only self-inflicted but also self-preserving. For many of us, most, there is no "Other" keeping us down. No one did to me what had been done to Auggie. In the end, that's the only version of America I see and feel and hear breathe in my ear, in the darkness of my prison cell. It's solitary, as always, even if there are other men on either side of my cell. I could debate essentialism versus social constructivism as much as you'd love for me to do it, but in the end, in this life, in jail or in death, just like you, there is an "I," and I am alone. Which, now that you mention it, makes it all the more peculiar that the two of us would ever find each other and make it this far together. I suppose I should apologize if you found my plight less than entertaining and a rather harrowing affair.

Now that my essential solitude is laid on the table, I should apologize and revise. Writing as revision, no? Retell and revise until it comes out right? But wouldn't you prefer the real version, the rough-around-the-edges of my crimes? Whatever, okay. The truth is that before I began, I had no idea it would be this difficult to write an entire book, especially one in which I can't hide behind academic jargon. I know I've haven't provided only original sentences with a unique blend of words, but I'm doing the best I can.

At least I am allowed to use the library. This much is true; prisoners have their lending rights, and I take up to three books at a time back to my cell. They have a fine selection of philosophy—all the continental anyone could ever vomit over and enough analytical to give even the most poststructuralist prisoner a headache. So you see where this is headed, yes? The truth is that no Dame Philosophy comes to visit me in my cell— to teach and inspire as she did for my kindred spirit Boethius. In fact, the closest thing to this enchanting goddess was a visit from Melony. As if by magic, she came out of pity. Not to cry on the other side of the glass and tell me she would wait years, even decades, and that she forgave me for my crimes and poverty and homelessness. No.

"Like, Michael, I feel bad for you, but it's so icky here, I don't think I can come back."

"I understand."

"It's not like this at all in the movies. The beautiful woman shows up on the other side of the glass and says she'll wait forever.

But they never show you that she wants to wretch from the stench. It's like a combination of generic deodorant, industrial-strength sanitizer, and unflushed toilet water. It's gross in here!"

What else could I do but acknowledge the foul odor and bid her a great life without me?

As for philosophy? I try to dedicate myself to her reasons, but I fail. And, yes, I know this prison time is the perfect time to turn my dissertation into a first book, a bound volume full of knowledge to be passed on, what I'd avoided revising and improving for so many years. The truth smacks and it hurts though, and the truth is that when I'm not scrawling in crayon, all I can concentrate on are the novels and stories of Roberto Bolano. That melancholy backpacker, a Chilean-Spaniard, a failed Mexican if there ever was one, holds my attention with his images of murdered women and broken poets and transcontinental drifters ostracized by nations and laws and existence. His tears of anguish and madness have me hooked and who cares that some critics call him a middling rambler or popular craze? His tears alone speak to me.

For many he might be Bolano the Dove, but for me, he is more like a worm. In fact, he is not unlike Auggie now that I think of it. Auggie, yes, who at the beginning of this narrative slithered into my brain like a tropical insect, and yes, indeed, if he didn't murder the man, at least he led the man to murder. Bolano's literature, doused with tequila no doubt, leads me to any hallucination I'm lucky enough to achieve in my solitary hours. It is the prison library's Bolanos that provide my only relief. On the inside, there's no library copy of *The Feel Great Handbook* or any screenplay-writing guide.

But yes, forget about literature that infects the brain. Let me return to Melony. She'd heard about my trial on Philly internet news. In fact, as I said, she was kind enough to call and say goodbye and good luck in a friendly, matter of fact way, as if I were headed to promotion on the opposite coast as opposed to this barren cell I inhabit today. She said she would visit, and she did. I tell you now twice that she came only *once*. She came to my visiting hour and sat with me in a common room with all the obese wives and bawling children; she wore her pink bebe top and looked contrite, and for a moment I remembered the good times. The dinners at the diner and the barbecue sauce on her lettuce. And then she opened her mouth and said, "This is so depressing," and I knew she'd never return.

Melony never returned, but I do have one regular visitor yet.

Yes, it is so. It is Auggie who comes to me, Auggie regularly at least twice a month. Of course, we do not receive phone calls here, but I have the sense if telecommunication were available, he'd call regularly just to get my advice on his mad pursuits— the ongoing supermarket sagas concerning conquest of younger women. When he visits, he does all of the talking in his rapid, stream of consciousness way. Aye, it's a stream of complaint. He rehashes every detail, why his relationships failed and why our revenge succeeded, and he doesn't apologize for the results, his freedom and my captivity, but rather, he says, "Professor, I guess Jonny November was right about all of it. America's a scam. A Ponzi scheme just like he said. The fucked get fucked arbitrarily, and there's nothing the innocent among us can do about it because we're all too fuckin' fucked over, too."

That's it. In the end, Auggie learned to accept his innocence. Although the crime plan went awry, somehow through its enactment, perhaps even through my imprisonment, Auggie forgave himself for the childhood crimes committed against him.

But his newly won freedom didn't do me any good.

If I'm lucky my twenty-five gets reduced to fifteen because the prisons are crowded and I had no prior arrests.

Life Lessons from Jonny November 22

There was never any America. First to knock, first admitted? Fuck that, unless you mean first to pick the lock. Did you know the guy who wrote that entered as an illegal? Well, it was with his parents when he was a toddler, so it ain't his fault. What's the point? The point is that this country has always been bullshit and mirrors. Cut the crap about good jobs for the working man in the 1950s and cars and televisions and happy healthy cherry colas and cigarettes. Fuckin' A, America is all it was, is, or will be. Yeah, the '50s. Right. Tell me another one. Ten years of coaxing women back to the home, so some sad sap, a regular white guy, could drive his gas-guzzling sedan to and from a factory job that paid a living wage. One decade after we fed Hitler the high and holy one deep in his bunker, and we've got no blacks and Jews in the pool. You want to say America was an idealistic country founded on freedom with good will for all? Hah! You can believe whatever the hell you want, but fuck you, too. It's just a country full of capitalist pricks shoving their rough stuff deep in their children, the next generation, and god only knows the child cunts and cheaper orifices the commies and socialists wouldn't seek to invade and control. If you want escape, go to the movies.

Nah. I'm just fucking with you.

You're a good guy, and your country's okay.

But seriously, it's a shame what happened to the professor. Doesn't fit in with the PhD set, and he isn't quite up to snuff according to his dissertation committee. So he gets involved with the wrong crowd, grifters and orphans, guys to be stepped around and avoided. Yeah, the wrong criminals led him to the wrong crime, and now he's facing twenty-five in the slam while yours criminally remains a free man. There was cash from the safe, too, and I split it with Auggie and Melony. I like Michael, I do, but there wasn't enough to divide more than three ways, so we had to cut the professor loose. I'm trying to cash in on the story by writing the book you hold in your hands.

That's life in America.

First, you get screwed and are forced to work a shit job for shit wages. Then, someone comes and steals your story for journalism, Hollywood, or sociology lecture. The thief lives large off salary or royalty checks cut out of your asshole. (By the way, thanks for reading.)

Where am I living?

Wouldn't you like to know, but rest assured I ain't write this fucker from a trailer park in Camden, New Jersey. It's weird writing in his voice. I like to keep my philosophy crisp and clean, but Michael could get meditative and go on tangents. But he'll be the first to admit he's like that. Melony did the best she could to loosen him up, and I paid her accordingly for quality services rendered. No, I know your next question, and I'll say that her fling with Auggie was not my idea, and the little twat ignored me when I told her not to mix business with pleasure, even if the job offered a mix of each. I gotta admit that was Auggie, my star pupil since I did the best I could to raise him right, and he took the professor for quite a ride. Drove him to home base with the girl and got him to take the fall for all of us. But that's all Auggie knows. They say the abused learn more about how to abuse others than anything else from childhood tragedies they suffered. That's the heartbreak of the whole situation.

Chapter 20
Jonny Wrote Squat

The voices come and go and mingle and at times it is difficult to keep them separate and discrete. The stolen crayons I smuggled inside aid in a color coordination that helps me organize my thoughts, black for Jonny, pink for Melony, but the prison is frugal with its paper supplies so at times, my chapters are so scrunched together, it obfuscates and confuses my written speaking roles. Auggie bleeds into Jonny as Jonny's voice blurs with my own, and in the darkness it is difficult for me to keep the sections apart. Anyway, I resist my characters' non-static truths as best I can, and as I was saying, it is Auggie's *voice* that visits me here more than any other. First there was Auggie, and he has stayed until the end.

* * *

You think Jonny wrote this? Do you believe that crap? College of Convertible Securities? Dean of Retention? Performative U.? Emeritus of Easy-A Econ? Free Markets for Frat Chicks? Okay, maybe that last one, but no way Jonny knows anything about Nietzsche or Heraclitus or quotes Aristotle on his walk through the park. Jonny wrote squat. I'd like to hear him spell half the words in this book.

Jonny shits in a can. No, the voices must be Michael's. So Jonny got too angry and there's not enough Melony—Michael doesn't do his women right? Whad'ya expect? Yeah, she's gotta be more than BBQ and bebe—but Michael did the best he could to render us and make it funny. But serious, too, because at the end of the book you've gotta know these are our voices, and we count too. That's what the professor wanted, for you to know I count. That I matter, and everyone else fucked over well before pre-K, and I'm very grateful to Michael for that. Maybe Michael didn't write a perfect story, but our adjunct friend is the only one who could have written the book you hold in your hands.

Jonny organized our plot to put down my stepdad, but only Michael could have written this book. Yeah, Jonny and women. Jonny and philosophy. Tell me another one. Jonny's been around Collegetown a long time. When he's not stuffing his face with stolen Fritos and pinched potato chips, he reads the papers and keeps his eyes open. He knows a thing or two about rich and poor in urban academia. But Jonny and power? Jonny on tenured professors? That had to be Michael. Under my influence, no doubt, but these were his words. You think Jonny-Con-Game knows what "queer theory" is? Do you think he reads his Holocaust history when he's not out banging stay-at-home moms and swiping TVs? Yeah, right. Tell me another one. I'll sit back and listen.

* * *

Indeed, I alone can take responsibility for my murders and the book you hold in your hands. I didn't even know I had a book in me until I lied to Jacob at Rural State and told him my first would soon be coming out. As it turns out, that's this one, but, no, I didn't write him from jail in order to get it published. Aristotle wrote that truth is always rough around the edges, but that's the final word on authorship of this text. At times, I wish I'd written philosophy that could withstand a peer-review process, but at least I have this. I hope what I wrote went down okay with you.

I'm back at work, too. In here, they have me teaching. Not Hegel or Kant, but the GED. I'm helping men who fell off track pass the high school equivalency exam. Most of the "young bucks" snicker or glare when they pass the prison classroom, but the "old heads" are serious students. Facing long sentences for something foolish they did as young men, they have time on their hands, and they realize time will pass faster if they distract themselves with education. Indeed, they are often eager students. Years ago, too many were in the wrong place at the wrong time with the wrong complexion, drugs, parents, and peers. Behind bars, America's racism and classism is obvious, and at times it reminds me of other things I should regret. From encouraging Auggie's racist humor to not sharing a public-sink bath with a black man to refusing to offer my entire meal to the homeless seeking shelter from the rain.

Alas.

I do my best to ignore these wider concerns because if I don't, the pain grows too great. So I stick to routines, and remind myself to feel grateful for thin rays of sunlight that grace my cell walls for a few hours each day. A few hours of sun, a few more of sleep, a few pages of Bolano, and a few more for this book get me through my prison weeks. Teaching helps as well. In the end, jailed or not, that's all we need. A few distractions to save of us from all that makes the heart ache in this unforgiving place.

Acknowledgments

At the risk of leaving folks out, I'll attempt a long version here. These are people who've touched my writing in a positive way over the years. Thank you Chris Benson, Joe Berry, Dan Cafaro (Atticus Books), Patrice Carrer, Scott Chabala, Dan Fante, Thursday Cohen, Maryann Devine, Joseph A. Domino, Daniel Dragomirescu (CLH), Ana Maria Fores Tamayo, Jim Gladstone, Andy Glenn, Dan and Jennifer Gregory, Gordon Haber (Dutch Kills Press), Nathan Holic, Abeer Hoque, Hee Ja Kim, Muriel Kudera, Kate Ledger, Michael Leone, Iain Levison, Aharon Levy, Lavinia Ludlow, Andrew McCann, Hosho McCreesh (Mendicant Bookworks), John McNally, Karen Lentz Madison, Jamie and David Mandell, Joan Mellen, Merritt Moseley, Ian Mount, William Pannapacker, Matt Peters (Beating Windward Press), Philadelphia Area Disc Alliance (PADA), Don Riggs, Michael James Rizza, Jay Roberts, Mark SaFranko, Steve Sheldon, Elizabeth Stansell, Scott Stein, Isaac Sweeney, Ben Tanzer, Tim Sheard (Hard Ball Press), Eric Thurschwell, Benjy Usadi, Vanessa Vaille, Robert Anthony Watts, Steve Wilson, Cassendre Xavier, Marcia Zemans, Anthony Zielonka, and last but most, Xiaoli and Yiy.

About the Author

Alex Kudera's debut novel, *Fight for Your Long Day* (Atticus Books), was drafted in a walk-in closet during a summer in Seoul, South Korea, and it won the 2011 Independent Publishers Gold Medal for Best Fiction from the Mid-Atlantic Region. *Auggie's Revenge* is his second academic tragicomedy novel. His stories have been published as e-singles, "The Betrayal of Times of Peace and Prosperity" (Gone Dog Press), "Frade Killed Ellen" (Dutch Kills Press), and "Turquoise Truck" (Mendicant Bookworks), and been translated into both Spanish and Romanian.

A lifelong Philadelphian, Alex currently teaches writing and literature at Clemson University in South Carolina. When he's not writing or lecturing, Kudera frets, walks, reads, and helps raise a child.

CPSIA information can be obtained at www.ICGtesting.com
Printed in the USA
LVOW12s2251020316

477535LV00002B/2/P